Fatal Winds

Also by Roberta Summers

Pele's Realm
Into the West anthology

Fatal Winds

Roberta Summers

Printed in the U.S.A.

Fatal Winds

Written by Roberta Summers

Copyright © Roberta Summers 2019 All rights reserved
Cover Design DelSheree Gladden Bank Page Design Shop
Published by Roberta Summers

Printed in the U.S.A.
ISBN: 9781077058521

Dedication

My dear friend and first editor, Elizabeth Testa, passed away September 7, 2017 from a heart virus after a short illness. To honor her memory, I dedicate *Fatal Winds* to her.

Acknowledgments

I want to thank my editor, Elizabeth Testa, for her expertise and for coming up with the title, *Fatal Winds,* the San Juan Writers Critique Group, professors, Traci HalesVass, who did the final edit, and Vicki Holmsten, graduate student Caitlin Berve, the members of the San Juan College creative writing workshops, and author Lee Pierce, aka Ron McDonald, who sat with me and read the entire book out loud to ferret out slow spots, mistakes and ratchet up the action. Thanks also to DelSheree Gladden for the final read through, edit, formatting and cover design. Extra thanks to my late husband, Tom Miller who said over and over, "Aren't you finished with that book yet?" I also want to acknowledge my friends and family who put up with me, grieved and agonized along with me as I spent twelve years researching and writing *Fatal Winds*. Thanks to Bob Batley, who worked as a guard at Los Alamos, for the interview. Thanks to my sister-in-law, Pam Jorgensen, for loaning me the book her Aunt Zeena wrote on losing her seven-year-old son, Lonnie, to cancer caused by radioactive fallout. Young William in this story is based on him.

Although based on fact, certain characters and conversations attributed to real people have been altered for dramatic effect and to fictionalize the story. This story is based on research from declassified Atomic Energy Commission files, numerous interviews, field trips to museums, the Trinity Site, Los Alamos, etc. and personal family tragedies and experiences.

Contents

"We knew the world would not be the same. A few people laughed, a few people cried. Most people were silent. I remembered the line from the Hindu scripture, the Bhagavad-Gita; Vishnu is trying to persuade the Prince that he should do his duty, and to impress him, takes on his multi-armed form and says, 'Now I am become Death, the destroyer of worlds.' I suppose we all thought that, one way or another."

J. Robert Oppenheimer

This project funded in part by the Connie Gotsch Arts Foundation

Timeline

July 7, 1945–Trinity Test at White Sands – first atomic bomb test.
August 6, 1945–Little Boy, code name for bomb dropped on Hiroshima, Japan.
August 9, 1945–Fat Man, code name for bomb dropped on Nagasaki.
Pacific Proving Grounds–Atomic and hydrogen bomb tests
1946–1951–Enewetak Atoll, forty-three tests
*Note–First hydrogen bomb test done at Enewetak November 1, 1952
July 1, 1946–1958 – Bikini Atoll, twenty-three tests
1958–1972–Johnston Atoll & Johnston Island, nine tests
1960s–Christmas Island, twenty-five tests
January 27, 1951–First atomic bomb test at Nevada Test Site—total 1021 tests
1959–Santa Suzana, Simi Valley, CA nuclear accident, threatens Los Angeles area.
1957–Underground testing begins
1962–All atmospheric testing stopped
August 5, 1963–Partial Test Ban Treaty signed
1992–Testing ends at Nevada Test Site
        ...Ah, but has it?
December 7, 2012–Plutonium underground test the 27th in a series of tests since the nuclear ban in 1992
*Note—these 27 plutonium tests are not included in the 1021 tests mentioned above
September 10, 1996–Comprehensive Nuclear Test Ban Treaty banning all nuclear explosions was adopted by the United Nations General Assembly—not in force as eight nations have not ratified it including the United States.
1952–2009–There have been 99 nuclear power plant accidents, 56 in the United States according to Benjamin K Sovacool, Social Scientist and Energy Policy Expert.
March 11, 2011–Fukushima power plant disaster

*Authors Note—This timeline is as accurate as the information from which it was drawn. Some of these events haven't been included in the story, but are for the readers' information.

Chapter One
2004
Jimmy

"Katie." The frail man reached out a bony, yellowed hand.

She put her ear close to her husband's lips to hear his soft raspy voice.

"Take me home," he whispered, "I don't want to die here." The few words took all his strength. His hand fluttered down onto the white sheet like a dry autumn leaf.

The sky was black beyond the slats of the Venetian blind, the only adornment on the tall rectangular window. Raindrops glittered in the streetlights shining on the parking lot below. Roses on the bedside table perfumed the air, mingling with the smell of antiseptics and alcohol. Katie resisted the urge to cry out in protest and calmly said, "I will."

Her high heels clicked a soft staccato on the vinyl floor as she hurried from the room. She pushed her short brown hair behind her ears while waiting for the plump nurse seated in front of a computer at the nurses' station to acknowledge her.

"My husband wants to go home. How do I make arrangements for an ambulance to transport him?"

"I'll take care of it for you. First, I'll need doctor's orders." She smiled and picked up the phone.

On her way back to Jimmy's room, Katie saw her in-laws coming up the hall. "Reese, Julie, I'm taking Jimmy home."

"Is he in remission?" Reese leaned on his cane.

"No, he wants to go home. It won't be long now." Tears moistened Katie's eyes as she hugged her mother-in-law. "I've got to run. Jimmy will wonder where I am."

The older couple fell into step with Katie. "We came to see how he was doing. Come along Julie," Reese said as he took his wife's elbow. "We'll go with you."

Less than an hour later Reese and Katie followed a gurney rolling down the hall as a nurse wheeled Jimmy to the emergency exit. He grimaced when his body rocked back and forth as two uniformed male nurses collapsed the legs of the gurney and loaded him into an ambulance.

"Thanks," he murmured to them once the stretcher was secured. This would be his last ride. The sirens were silent, but the twirling red light reflected off the hospital walls as the ambulance pulled into traffic.

Jimmy had reached the last stage of cancer that was eating away his life, the stage of acceptance.

Five years of surgery, radiation and chemotherapy had drained his energy and sickened him. The image in the mirror told him he was nothing but a skeleton as he grieved for the tall robust man he once was. Glimmers of hope gave way to fear and despair. His blue eyes dulled from drugs and unrelenting pain.

Through the ambulance window, he saw red and green lights in the shape of trees perched on light poles, reminding Jim he'd be home for Christmas.

James Christensen didn't make it to Christmas. Surrounded by his wife, children and the parents who raised him, he died of cancer caused by radioactive fallout.

He was a Downwinder.

Chapter Two
1943
Reese

When Reese Mayfield heard the soft voice on the phone, he shoved the box of papers he'd been sorting off the chair and plopped down. It wasn't every day he got a call from J. Robert Oppenheimer, his former professor at the University of California at Berkeley—especially not a call with a job offer. He stared at the chipped paint on the door jamb of his tiny apartment as he listened.

Oppenheimer was insistent. "Your country needs you for the war effort."

Oh, that familiar charisma. Reese remembered it so well. But what drew him in were the words that the country needed him. *My country needs me, Reese, for the war effort?*

Oppenheimer pressed on, "It's a top-secret project. You'll be part of making history."

"But I start working on my Ph.D. next month." Reese had received his master's degree in theoretical physics just a week before. "What do you mean by a top-secret project?"

Oppenheimer bypassed the question. "How old are you, Reese? Twenty? You'll have plenty of time to get your doctorate after the war is over."

"I hate to put it on hold." Just last week, his advisor had encouraged Reese to continue on immediately, and although he lived off campus, he was close to Berkeley. If he left he'd be giving up his cozy apartment with its prime location.

"I understand," Oppenheimer sympathized. "But think of the experience. You will be able to call the shots to get your doctorate degree." He let that sink in, then into the silence, he added, "I want to have you working by my side, and you'll be doing your patriotic duty by serving your country."

3

Reese sighed inwardly. Oppenheimer was playing the cards he couldn't refuse. *Serve my country, top secret, help the war effort, my patriotic duty? And the promise of working by Oppenheimer's side?* Reese tried to absorb all he was hearing while he listened to instructions.

"Take the early train Monday morning. There'll be a ticket waiting for you. I'll arrange for a driver to pick you up at the station near Santa Fe. Don't be concerned that the ticket says Lamy. That's where the train to Santa Fe stops. When you get to 109 East Palace, ask for Dorothy. Dorothy McKibbin."

Reese ran his fingers through his wavy auburn hair as he mentally chewed on what Oppenheimer was saying. *Work with Oppenheimer—why wouldn't I go? What kind of scientist would I be, if I refused such an opportunity?*

"But I haven't said yes." Even to Reese, his protest sounded weak.

"Nonsense," Oppenheimer said. "Of course you have. My assistant will phone tomorrow with your itinerary."

Reese rationalized away his few remaining reservations. Surely practical experience would serve him better than continuing his university education right now, especially this kind of practical experience. "Monday morning?" He swallowed. "I'll be ready." *For crying out loud. How am I going to take care of everything in five days?*

"Good. Now, this is important," Oppenheimer continued. "Tell no one where you are going. Remember your assignment is top secret." Reese was to tell his family and friends only that he was going on a secret assignment for the government, and he didn't know when he'd return.

A tremor of excitement passed through him, or was it fear? *Mom will be beside herself.* But in truth, he was honored and flattered to have been chosen.

Reese's parents had recognized his genius when he was in elementary school. They enrolled him in an accelerated education program. He didn't disappoint them and graduated high school at fifteen. By the time he was twenty he'd finished his undergraduate and master's degrees at Berkeley.

A slight limp from a childhood bout with polio had rendered him 4F—unfit for military service. Most of his buddies were fighting the Axis forces in Europe or the Japanese in the Pacific. *Not even good enough to go to war.* Envy mixed with anger swept over Reese. It wasn't the first time he'd felt these emotions.

Caught in the patriotic fervor that swept the land after the bombing of Pearl Harbor, Reese, along with a dozen of his classmates, stood in line at the recruiting office eager to fight for their country. The rejection he felt was painful, but a relief for his parents. Now, finally, here was a chance to serve—a chance to do his part to help win the war.

That evening, he phoned his parents, asking them to meet him for dinner at the St. Francis in San Francisco. He arrived early. As he waited, he rehearsed a speech he hoped would convince them his decision was the right one. He thought the elegant restaurant with its formal ambiance might reinforce the seriousness of his intentions. He stood when he saw his parents and pulled out an upholstered chair for his mother. Sam and Donna Mayfield were university professors and looked the part—tall and slender, soft spoken and refined.

Once they'd been served drinks and ordered their meals, Reese told them about Oppenheimer's phone call.

"You've been asked to work on a top-secret project that will take you away from your studies for an indefinite period of time?" Donna seemed skeptical. "And you don't know where you're going?"

"I'm sworn to secrecy."

"Even with your family?" Donna narrowed her eyes. A remembered dread clutched at her throat. When he came down with polio, she feared he would be crippled for life, or die. That fear still lurked under the surface.

"Mom, I couldn't say no. This is my opportunity to help in some way." His tone was firm, but pleading. He looked up at the crystal chandelier as though it would provide moral support.

"Son, I can see how important this is to you, but I don't want you to forget about your education." Sam pushed his wire rimmed glasses up on his nose.

"I'll finish after the war, Dad."

"I'll hold you to that promise."

"I won't let you down," Reese assured him.

"You're much too young for a secret mission." Donna protested as she reached up and adjusted the tiny black pill box hat perched on her thick auburn hair. Reese's coloring resembled his mother's—same hair and sky-blue eyes.

"Mom, I won't be overseas." He offered this information like a bonbon, then wondered if he should have said that much.

"Your mind is made up?" The frown that had creased her brow relaxed in apparent surrender.

"You will be mindful of your health?"

"Yes, it is."

He squeezed his mother's hand. "I'll be careful."

Reese's eyes met his father's level gaze. "Dad, I promise to get my doctorate when I return from this assignment."

"All right, son. What can we do to help? Do you need money?" Sam reached for his wallet.

Reese waved the gesture off. "I have enough left in my college fund for travel and once I'm there, I won't need any. I'll be earning a salary."

"Ah, our little boy is producing revenue at the tender age of twenty." Sam smiled. "This can't be all bad." The tension of resisting his son's decision gone, he rested against the back of his chair and raised his glass to offer a toast. "Let's make this a celebration."

The clinking of their glasses heralded the arrival of the waiter with their dinners.

"You will write?" coaxed Donna.

"Yes, of course I will, Mother—every week."

* * *

On the drive home, Donna said, "I'm frightened for Reese. He isn't the strongest young man." She pulled off her hat and fluffed her hair.

"At least he's not at the front in the war—so many young men are dying." Sam shifted the car down into low to navigate one of San Francisco's steep hills, being careful to avoid an approaching trolley.

"I thought we were going to lose him when he got polio. Since then I've always worried about his health." There was a tremor in Donna's voice.

Sam reached over and patted her on the knee. "He's stronger than we give him credit for."

6

Chapter Three
The Atom Speaks

Well, he'd better be stronger than my radioactivity, but I am pleased that Oppie chose him. Genius like Reese's shouldn't be wasted. He'll do just fine freeing my vast energy. Of course, there are risks—more than you can ever imagine. You'll see. I have been lurking around, biding my time since my first encounter with Fermi when he challenged me, and I said, split me? I'm an atom. Go ahead, give it a try. Just tweak the process a little bit. What's the matter? Don't you know how to split an atom? I may be tiny, but I'm mighty. You have no idea of the destruction I'm capable of—sure you want to do this? You should see all the pretty colors, not to mention the god of all clouds I produce.

I know, I'm a show-off. Of course, you can't know yet how lethal I am, but what's the mutating of a few cells in your baby in light of the power I give?

So a million people die including Junior and Grandma, along with your favorite horse, the kitty who rubs against your leg and Fido. I haven't even tracked what radioactivity will do to the hawks, the eagles, the bees, or the trees and roses ready to bud.

Ah, there you are, Dr. Fermi. Now you've got it. Not only can I release neutrons, but those neutrons will go on to split more atoms which will release more neutrons—if we get enough atoms splitting neutrons, we have fission, then a chain reaction. Wow, what a blast.

Now let me see, what kind of havoc can I wreak in the oceans? Ah ha, how about the devastation of all marine life around Bikini Atoll? Of course, in a few decades when I fade to half-life, the fish will begin to come back— mutated, but alive. What's that? A lump next to your dorsal fin? Tsk, tsk. I didn't say you'd come back the same, did I?

7

Then there are the winds aloft. In only two weeks, my fallout can circumnavigate the globe. When it rains, children will be splashing around in radioactive puddles.

Downwind of my mushroom cloud, no one is safe.

* * *

Oblivious of the atom, Reese pressed his forehead against the train window to look down into Donner Pass. At the beginning, the new experience excited him as the train chugged uphill through wooden snow tunnels. When they left Reno to cross the flat lands of Nevada, telephone poles zipped by hypnotically, lulling him to sleep.

The train approached the Great Salt Lake near the afternoon of the second day of the four-day trip. It inched across the twelve-and-a-half-mile-long trestle that spanned part of the lake. Looking down, the train appeared to float on the glistening salt-saturated water. It picked up speed when they reached tracks built on land fill, then faster when they reached the shore and solid ground.

The brief stop in Salt Lake City was a welcome respite. *Pity there isn't time to look around the city and tour the famous Mormon Temple grounds.* Reese knew he had Utah relatives on his mother's side of the family, but he hadn't met any of them. Touring the temple might have given him some insight to their lives. He suspected they were Mormons from hearing his mother talk about them.

Refreshed by the break, Reese finished one of the books he'd brought along and started another. Although he'd changed clothes, the train provided no facilities for a shower. A shave and wiping down with a washcloth weren't very satisfying.

* * *

A nondescript man of medium height and build wearing a brown suit boarded the train in Salt Lake City. He grunted and nodded at the soldiers he passed and flopped into the first available seat. Pulling a pint of Jim Beam out of his suit pocket, he drew long and hard, smacking his lips and emitting a sigh. He settled in after shaking the folds out of a newspaper. Nobody paid any attention to him. From time to time he sipped his bourbon.

As evening approached, beer started flowing, and men in uniforms began to sing. Lured by the fun, Reese joined in. The more beer he drank, the more

8

he sang. As alcohol abated his shyness, he released his rich baritone voice. The singing got louder as more soldiers, sailors, and the two marines on board joined in singing *Anchors Aweigh*.

Everyone was in high spirits when the stranger pushed his way through the men. He approached Reese and poked his finger in Reese's chest saying, "Why aren't you in uniform? Are you a draft dodger? One of those conscientious objectors? You look fit enough." He slurred.

Crimson flushed Reese's cheeks.

The singing faded.

Embarrassed, Reese admitted, "I'm 4F."

"What d'ya mean you're 4F? You look healthy to me."

Reese tried to push past the man, but he blocked the narrow aisle and poked Reese in the chest again.

"Hey, mister," a soldier said, "Leave him alone." Most of the men had seen Reese's limp.

"You shut up. This is between Red and me. What's yer excuse? Huh? Too chicken to go to war?"

"Sir, I applied, but I wasn't accepted."

"That's bullshit."

The men closed in around Reese, cutting off the bully's attack.

"Hey, you guys on this draft dodger's side?"

"You bet we are, sir." The men held the bully back and made a clear path for Reese to escape. The man's jaw dropped when he saw Reese limp away.

"Jesus Christ, he is crippled. Hey, son, I'm sorry."

The words, *he is crippled*, stung Reese's ears and burned into his brain. He bit back his shame. Intellectually, he knew he shouldn't be ashamed, but he was. The pain of not being whole had plagued him since childhood.

Two soldiers marched the offender back to his seat and slapped his newspaper in his lap. "Dumb asshole," one mumbled as he walked away.

Reese retreated into a book, but his mind spun. *Will I be labeled a cripple when I'm on secret assignment?* Old fears slipped in to erode his self-confidence.

Reese had already felt conspicuous because he was one of the few travelers not in uniform. The raucous songs of the military men had kept him entertained and he was beginning to feel accepted. Now he was reluctant to go back to the car where the confrontational Mr. Brown Suit sat.

In Denver, a change of trains to take him south meant leaving his buddies to continue east. He hoped Brown Suit was headed east too.

Bored and weary of traveling, Reese stared out of the window, but all he could see was his own reflection in the glass in the darkness shrouding the landscape. Leaning back in his seat, he stretched out his long legs and wondered about the future until the gentle rocking and the steady clickety-clack of the wheels lulled him to sleep. The sun was high when he awoke to the conductor's call. "Next stop: Lamy, New Mexico. Santa Fe passengers get off here."

Reese stepped down from the train and shook off his stiffness. He looked around, wondering how he would recognize the driver who was to meet him.

A rail-thin man wearing Levi's and a Stetson walked toward him, the thump of his cowboy boots echoing off the wooden platform. "You Reese Mayfield?"

At Reese's nod the cowboy inclined his head toward a dusty green Chevy pickup. "Jes toss yer suitcase in back."

Reese had expected someone official, maybe a soldier.

"Come on, son, whatcha draggin' your heels fer? I gotta get you over to Miss Dorothy 'n get back to my cattle."

At the mention of her name, Reese hoisted his suitcase into the bed of the pickup and hopped into the cab.

Twenty minutes later, the driver pulled up in front of an unimposing, one-story tan adobe building with a wide portico supported by weathered wooden posts.

"Are you certain this is the right place?" Reese had expected something grander.

The cowboy snorted. "You can read it yerself on that small wooden sign. Jes' go yonder across that courtyard." He pointed a finger without lifting his hand off the steering wheel. "That's Dorothy's office."

With a quick thank you, Reese snatched up his suitcase and stepped across the courtyard. He contemplated the carved wooden scrollwork on the aged screen door for a moment before he squared his shoulders and pulled it open.

Chapter Four
Arrival

Ducking under the low jamb, Reese stepped into the cluttered office and approached one of two overflowing desks. A large gray poodle stood and sniffed him. "May I see Dorothy? I'm Reese Mayfield," he asked a smiling woman he judged to be in her 40s.

"Oh, yes. We're expecting you. Cloudy, *down*." She frowned in mock irritation at the dog, before standing to take Reese's hand. "I'm Dorothy." She pushed a mass of brown curls off her forehead. "Is this all your luggage?"

Reese nodded and stared at the stack of boxes and wrapped packages occupying half the floor of the small room.

"Oh, don't mind the mess. The ladies from the Hill leave their shopping packages here until a bus can deliver them." Dorothy reached under the desk and retrieved her handbag, fishing out a bundle of keys. "Come along. Sorry I couldn't meet your train. Did Hank have any trouble finding you? He lends me a hand when I'm stuck in the office. Cloudy, stay," she ordered the dog.

"No, ma'am. He seemed to know who I was."

"Oppie described you." She shooed Reese out and locked the door. "I told Hank to look for a lanky young man with red hair and here you are."

Reese followed her to a black 1939 Plymouth sedan and tossed his suitcase in the trunk before folding his frame onto the passenger seat. Dorothy pressed her foot on the starter and the engine chugged to life.

"Where are we going?" he asked.

"I have to pick up a family at the La Fonda Hotel and take them with us."

Reese winced as Dorothy ground the shift into first gear, but after a rough start, she proved to be a skilled driver through the narrow Santa Fe streets.

"I mean after that."

Dorothy checked the rear-view mirror and signaled a left turn. "How was the train? How long did it take? The people we're picking up came in last night from Chicago. They have a baby with them—I hope you don't mind." There wasn't time to answer her questions because they were already past the central plaza and at the multi-story adobe hotel.

Dorothy stepped out of the car and disappeared through the hotel's wooden doors, reappearing in a few minutes followed by a young family. Reese sprang into action to help.

"Reese, this is Ann and Joe Pope and baby Katherine. Ann, there are lots of young couples up on the Hill. You'll make friends quickly." Dorothy smiled her reassurance at the young mother as she opened the trunk for Reese and Joe to load their luggage.

Reese began to understand that the Hill was Dorothy's name for their destination. But what would that be, he wondered. A town? A lab? Dormitories? And how could it be kept so secret from the surrounding communities? His inquisitive soul—so valuable to a scientist—was anxious for answers. None were forthcoming, that was certain. He would have to wait.

Dorothy filled the silence with chatter about the scenery as they traveled north. She jabbed a finger toward a few squat adobe houses clustered by the roadside. "This little town is Pojoaque, named after the Pojoaque Indians. Their pueblo is off the road. You can see it back there on your right." She pointed to one adobe closer to the road. "Those red things hanging on that veranda are chile ristras. You'll learn all about chiles in New Mexico. I did."

"Do you cook with them?" Ann asked.

Dorothy laughed. "When I cook, I do."

She stuck her arm out to signal a left turn onto a dirt road that ran between two ancient cottonwood trees. The car kicked up puffs of dust as Dorothy maneuvered it over the ruts. "This is always tricky," she said, slowing the car as she aimed it at a one-lane bridge that spanned the flat, muddy Rio Grande River.

Reese pulled in his elbows, as if that would make the car narrower. The wood planks set up a discomforting racket as they clattered across. When they were off the bridge, he heard Joe exhale. Then the road widened to twist through sagebrush, scrubby juniper and countless piñon trees that dotted the peach-colored earth.

12

Joe asked, "Where are you from, Reese?"

"San Francisco. I was set to start working on my doctorate in theoretical physics when I was called for this job. And you?"

"I've been working at Argonne Labs just outside of Chicago. I graduated from Texas Tech a couple of years ago. Ann and I thought Downer's Grove would be our home forever, until I got the phone call to come here."

"This assignment changed our lives quickly, didn't it?" Reese wagged his head in empathy, but he wondered how Joe had avoided military service. He didn't want to ask, and he didn't want to say why he himself wasn't fighting overseas.

"You're awfully quiet, Ann. How do you feel about being whisked off to an unknown destination?" Reese smiled at the young mother.

"I'm not too sure, but if it's what makes Joe happy..." her voice trailed off.

"Maybe Joe was coaxed and charmed by Oppenheimer the way I was. It's amazing how effective the phrase 'your country needs you' is."

Joe nodded and laughed. "Especially when it seems as though all the male population is at the front."

Dorothy shifted down into second gear as the car labored up a dirt dugway carved out of the side of the mountain.

Ann tensed and held her baby closer. Joe, seeing her discomfort, put a protective arm around her.

The landscape fell off over a thousand feet on the right, and a sheer limestone cliff rose steeply on the left. In the narrowest places, a car coming from the other direction would have to give way to allow them to pass. Even to Reese, accustomed to the Sierras, this was rugged country. He leaned away from the door as if it would protect him should they go over the drop-off.

"Where are you taking us?" Joe took a turn asking.

After her earlier travelogue evasions, Reese was surprised when Dorothy actually answered.

"To Los Alamos," she said. "It's on the Pajarito Plateau in the Jemez Mountains. We'll be there soon—little over half an hour more." She peered at the clock on the dash. "With luck, we'll be there by two o'clock."

Well, at least that's one tidbit of information. Reese looked toward the distant blue mountains and squinted against the glare while Dorothy filled

13

them in about the Spanish influence and history of the area. As she twisted the car through a hairpin curve, she nodded her head to the left, indicating the mountains they'd left behind. "And those are the Sangre de Cristos."

A passing thought amused Reese. *No point asking her if she knew anything about the project ahead.* She wasn't giving away anything. Maybe top security started with Dorothy's example.

"It looks like we're headed for the top of the world," Joe said as the road steepened even more.

The last ten miles were slow going on a gravel road riddled with wash boarding and shallow dry *arroyos* cut by flood waters. The baby woke up and wailed at the jarring. Reese's own nerves began to feel frayed from excitement and lack of sleep. The high-pitched crying didn't help. Ann shifted Katherine to her shoulder to coo and pat the baby's back.

Finally, the car approached a security gate. Stepping from a white wooden shack that served as the guard house, two uniformed soldiers snapped to attention.

"I have everyone's passes," Dorothy said, handing them to the guard. Then she turned to the travelers. "I'll give them to you when he hands them back. From now on, you will use only these documents." She gave the men manila envelopes. "You'll notice each of you now has a driver's license and a birth certificate with just a number in place of your name. These will replace your originals for the duration of your assignment here." She smiled at Ann. "Your baby doesn't need them. From now on, your official residence will be P.O. Box 1663, Santa Fe, New Mexico."

The guard handed the documents back to Dorothy before saluting and waving her on.

Dorothy said, "These are temporary. You'll have to report to the Pass House for fingerprinting and regular passes right away. Use them every time you leave or return to Los Alamos. Don't lose them."

A frisson of anticipation ran through Reese as he scanned the documents. *My identity has just been usurped.* He denied the anxiety that crept over him as he faced the unknown and mentally grappled with the scope and power of the government.

Ann's face blanched as she looked at her papers.

"It'll be all right, honey," Joe said, patting her knee.

14

Joe's comforting tone bolstered Reese's courage. Despite his own apprehensions, he joined Joe in reassuring Ann. As his confidence grew, Reese's sense of adventure began to override his concerns, but he did wonder how tight security would be.

"Now to get you situated." Dorothy drove through thick Ponderosa pines, down a street she called "Bathtub Row," explaining that these particular houses had bathtubs—the only private residences in Los Alamos boasting that feature.

"Those houses are reserved for the highest-ranking scientists, officers and other officials." Dorothy continued driving through the maze of buildings. "The altitude here is over 7,300 feet so you may feel a little lightheaded or short of breath from the thin air, but you'll adjust in a couple of days."

Lightheaded doesn't begin to describe how this strange situation makes me feel. Reese eyed a phalanx of bulldozers clearing land. *This place is really primitive, for an outfit doing high level research.* He reflected back on the gleaming labs at UC Berkeley. *What have I gotten myself into?*

Dorothy pointed to a large log structure. "That's Fuller Lodge. It used to be a boys' school. You can get dinner there tonight at nineteen hundred hours." She grinned. "That's 7 p.m. to you newcomers."

Nodding her head toward the left, Dorothy said, "The green building over there is the Medical Center. Hopefully, you'll never need it."

Buildings in various stages of completion popped up everywhere. Dormitories and structures that weren't part of the original school had been expanded—hastily tacked onto, and looked it.

Glancing over his shoulder, Reese saw Ann's lower lip begin to quiver. She clamped her teeth down, regaining control.

Dorothy stopped the car at a bulky rectangular building resembling a dormitory. A row of outside doors opened onto small stoops. "Here we are," she said cheerfully as she jumped out.

Ann tentatively stepped out, covering her baby's face with a thin blanket to protect it from the dust flying around from a nearby construction site.

Noting Ann's discomfort, Dorothy said, "There isn't any grass or many deciduous trees like in Illinois." She pointed toward a playground about a block away where women pushed children in swings. "But there are a lot of young mothers like you."

15

Ann's shoulders relaxed a bit.

A petite brunette steered a baby carriage toward them. "Hi, honey," she chirped to Ann. "Welcome to the Hill. I'm Jill Hargrove. This seems like the end of the earth, but we're all in the same boat." Tiny laugh lines surrounded her sparkling green eyes. "Looks like we'll be neighbors. We live over there." She wiggled a finger toward the unit next door.

A smile of relief lit Ann's face. Shifting her baby, she reached out her hand.

Joe introduced himself over his shoulder as he yanked a suitcase out of the trunk.

"Let me know if you need anything," Jill said. "I've learned it all the hard way, but there's no need for you to. I'll share." She waved and pushed the baby carriage along.

"Your apartment is the one straight ahead." Dorothy picked up one of the lighter pieces of luggage and led the way. "It's small, but has everything you'll need." She unlocked the door and handed the key to Ann. "There's some information on the kitchen table to help you get oriented and settled." She patted the baby's back. "You be good, little Katherine. You'll be fine here." She clucked and cooed at the baby before saying, "I have to run. Good luck. I'm sure I'll be seeing you in Santa Fe when you come to town to shop."

Dorothy emerged and climbed back in the car next to Reese. "We'll get you over to the bachelors' quarters now," she said. Another trip through the labyrinth of Ponderosa pines brought them to rows of arced metal Quonset huts, with more under construction nearby. Bulldozers flattening the landscape kicked up clouds of dirt tainting the pine scented mountain air. The bleak, quasi-military tone of the place struck Reese. *Home? Oppie didn't prepare me for this part. I guess I really am serving my country.*

Dorothy pulled up in front of one of the Quonset huts with a large number 7 over the door. She handed him a key. "Your room is 4. You'll have no problem finding it. I really must rush. Cloudy will be missing me. Good luck. I'm easy to reach if you need anything. I'm sure I'll be seeing you in town." She reached for his hand and shook it before leaving.

Chapter Five
Los Alamos

Reese inspected his tiny quarters, a living room-bedroom combination, with no kitchen and a communal bathroom down the hall. *Hmmm—well, it's no worse than the dorms at the university. I survived there for two years before I found an apartment.* What he didn't expect was a roommate. Clothes were thrown on one of the beds and a stack of books lay piled next to the lone easy chair.

Dorothy had apologized for the meager accommodation. "This is the best we have to offer right now," she'd said. "But they are building new quarters as fast as possible, so it should improve."

Eager to have a shower, Reese unpacked and shoved the roommate's clothes aside in the inadequate closet to squeeze in his own sparse wardrobe. There was a small chest of drawers crammed full of his roommate's underwear and personal items. He snorted his displeasure and left the rest of his things in his suitcase which he laid on the floor with the lid propped open.

Linens and a blanket were folded on the extra bed, and a blue and white striped pillow lay at the head. Reese carefully made up the narrow bed, mitering the corners the way his dad had taught him. At last, armed with soap, towel, and fresh clothes, he headed for the much-needed shower.

Refreshed, he announced to the empty room, "I'm going for a walk," and pulled on a pair of oxfords. *I should have brought my hiking boots.* "Let's see what this 'Hill' place looks like."

Reese strolled away from the hubbub of construction toward the forested area. Soon he was alone with just the soughing of the breeze through the pines for company. Taking a deep breath, he filled his lungs with high altitude air. *Dorothy was right, I'm dizzy. But from what—the altitude, or excitement, anticipation, fear?*

Sizing up his surroundings, he decided hiking would be a good pastime. Would strict security allow him to roam as far as he wanted?

Back in his room, he scanned the bare walls and the single window. His roommate still hadn't put in an appearance. A knock on the door surprised him.

It was Oppenheimer. "Reese, good to see you, young man." He extended his hand for a hearty handshake. "Glad to have you on the team." He cast a disparaging look around. "Not very fancy, is it? We'll find something better for you when it becomes available, but the families come first, you understand?"

Reese shrugged. "It's okay. No worse than Berkeley's dorms."

Oppie laughed. "I haven't had the pleasure, but I'll take your word. Mind if I smoke?" He pulled out a pack of Lucky Strikes, tapped one out, flipped open his Zippo and lit it. He offered the pack to Reese.

"Haven't acquired that habit yet," Reese slouched in an attempt to minimize their difference in height. Oppie was several inches shorter, small boned, and slender.

Exhaling a cloud of white smoke, Oppenheimer said, "Tomorrow morning, go over to the lodge about 6:30. A bus will take you and some of your colleagues to the labs. The first event of the day will be orientation. Afterward, you'll receive your assignment."

"Thank you, sir."

"Oh, by the way, my wife Kitty and I are having a little cocktail gathering Saturday evening to introduce some of the newcomers. Drop by around six, and tell your roommate Ward when you see him. My house is on the corner of Bathtub Row and Peach Street. I'm sure you drove right by it."

With a slap on the back and another handshake, Oppie left, leaving the lingering smell of cigarette smoke behind.

Reese was flattered by the visit and the personal touch.

Moments later, the door seemed to fly open of its own accord, and in walked a tall man with a wry grin. "Ah, you're here. I'm Ward Porter, old chap, actually Edward, but everyone calls me Ward." He extended a hand in greeting. "I wondered when I'd get a roommate."

Charmed by Ward's upper crust British accent, Reese smiled and introduced himself. "How long have you been here?"

18

"About six weeks. I just dropped by for a shower and a change of clothes." He winked. "Got an engagement." He brushed an unruly lock of sandy hair away from his eyes before collecting shaving gear and pulling clothes from the closet. Catching sight of Reese's open suitcase, still full, he said, "What's this, then? Looks like I've bloody well taken up all the drawer space. I'll move some of it tomorrow."

"No hurry. By the way, Oppie dropped by and wanted me to tell you you're invited for cocktails at his house at six on Saturday."

"Good show."

Cleaned up and ready for his date, with a breezy, "Toodle-loo," Ward was off.

Ward must have gotten lucky. Reese didn't see him again until the next morning as he stood waiting in front of Fuller Lodge for the transport.

"Hi, old chap. Ready for your first day in the labs, eh?"

Reese nodded and swung up on the bus.

If Ward noticed Reese's limp, he didn't comment. Reese began to appreciate his growing sense of the Hill's camaraderie. They were all here for a common purpose.

* * *

Ah yes, a common purpose: me. That's what I want to hear. Look at all this testosterone driven brain power. This is promising. Now after millennia of being ambient radioactivity I have a chance to shine, or perhaps I should say glow. It won't be too long before these young scientists will be aglow. Ignorance is bliss—has to be, or none of them would be here.

* * *

Twelve hours later, the bus door opened, spilling out its load of scientists in front of Fuller Lodge just in time for dinner. Afterwards, sated and excited, a weary Reese walked the few blocks back to his quarters. His mind was full as he savored the cool evening air. Fragments of what he'd learned in orientation crowded his thoughts. Manhattan Project…Project Y, nicknamed the Gadget…don't talk to anyone but the other scientists…don't talk about the Gadget to military personnel…don't make friends with people in the nearby villages…building a bomb that will end the war…. At last he felt a part of the war effort. Yet, he wondered how his former professor, the man who had chosen him, was selected to build an atomic bomb.

19

However indeed?

* * *

Major Leslie Groves turned down the job of overseeing the Manhattan Project. When told about building an atomic bomb, he said, "Oh, that thing." Groves wanted nothing to do with temperamental scientists and said they were all a bunch of prima donnas. Groves had just spent the past three years overseeing the building of Oak Ridge Laboratory in Tennessee. He wanted action, to see military service. He wanted an opportunity to earn the rank of general fighting with men at the front. When Groves was promised an immediate promotion to general if he agreed to head up the Manhattan Project, he caved. Now he had to find a scientist, a capable physicist whom he could get along with—one who could locate, hire and manage a team of the most brilliant and talented scientists in the country. He didn't like any of the several theoretical physicists, except the charming J. Robert Oppenheimer.

Groves was overheard saying, "Now, there's a scientist I can get along with."

* * *

As Reese neared the door to his quarters, he bumped into Ward coming out of the door.

"Orientation day for you? Did mine a few weeks ago. Got a date. See you around, old sport." Ward flashed a quick smile as he strode away.

Taken aback by Ward's rapid-fire chatter and haste, Reese speculated Ward's date must have been something amazing.

* * *

Reese settled into life at Los Alamos. He took his meals in the mess hall at the Lodge with soldiers and ladies of the Women's Army Corps, nicknamed with the acronym WACS. Single people, lodged in dorms like his, lined up in the cafeteria with him. From time to time, some of the married couples joined them.

Gossip was inevitable in this most secret of small towns. Even the formidable Dorothy McKibbin was fair game. As their lifeline to Santa Fe and shopping, she was an object of curiosity. People speculated that she was under security surveillance. Of course, they would agree, everyone was. Phones were tapped, homes were bugged by the FBI, and anyone working on the Gadget was closely watched—even Oppenheimer. From time to time, Reese picked

20

up on whispers about Oppie's communist friends, and he wondered whether this was a problem for the lead scientist's top-secret status.

Reese felt honored to be working with Oppenheimer and other equally extraordinary minds, like Enrico Fermi and Edward Teller, the imported British scientists, and numerous young physicists like himself. But all the secrecy made life at Los Alamos intensely isolating.

He often heard the young wives talk about how much they missed their friends and families. There was constant conversation about rationing, and not just of food, but gas, tires, sugar, and shoes. Shoes were a favorite topic among the women, shoes and nylon stockings.

He overheard Ann Pope reminiscing with Jill Hargrove about buying pretty shoes. When they noticed his interest, they laughed and confessed to hoarding ration stamps to save up for a pair, showing off the coveted new ones with their slippery leather soles.

Unlike the ladies, Reese hadn't used any of his ration stamps. He had enough saved to buy a pair of hiking boots on a rare trip into Santa Fe.

Rationing wasn't the only culprit. Almost everything had to be brought from Santa Fe or Albuquerque, hours away.

They had to make their own fun, too, which meant parties on Friday and Saturday nights at each other's homes, frequent and popular potlucks and dances at Fuller Lodge.

Reese found himself sneaking glances at the pretty WACS—even at the not so pretty ones. There were so few available women that his more aggressive colleagues and servicemen kept the ladies occupied. To stave off his need for feminine companionship, he took up hiking in the summer and skiing in the winter, going out with groups of friends from the labs. During these times, he got the opportunity to chat with some of the women.

One Sunday afternoon, Reese had some free time at last. He headed out toward the edge of the mesa. He'd seen a stream below and wanted to search for a trail that might lead him to it. Lost in his thoughts, he didn't hear the approaching car. When a warning beep-beep sounded, he dashed across the road to get out of the way. Turning, he saw a custom-made Packard Clipper. It appeared to have been cut in half to make room for two extra rows of seats that were installed in the middle. Oppie waved as he drove by, transporting several men, probably new arrivals he'd picked up at the train station. Reese thought they must be important to have the boss giving them special attention.

It didn't matter to a lot of the scientists that they couldn't discuss their work in the labs. They were hungry for news of the outside world. They'd discuss the plays showing on Broadway, the books they'd just read, art, music and especially, the latest news on the war.

Reese ached to talk about his work with people outside of the labs, but was guarded in social conversations with army personnel. He felt awkward forcing himself to share their talk about day to day life outside the Hill. He perked up when Ward or Joe stopped by his lab for a visit and to compare notes on what they were doing.

Quiet by nature, Reese spent most of his time engrossed in the physics of fission and how much uranium and plutonium it would take to make significant explosions. One of his lab partners, Julius Franz, often interrupted him and the other physicists, peppering them with questions. Some of his colleagues were happy to share what they were doing and how it worked, but Reese was more reserved. He'd heard rumors that there may be spies among the staff and kept a rein on his tongue. Franz had arrived at Los Alamos from England with other British theoretical physicists.

Franz was visiting Reese in his lab when Ward dropped by. Ignoring Ward, Franz asked Reese probing questions. Ward pulled a stool up next to the worktable in between Reese and Franz and interrupted the interrogation by changing the subject. "Reese, how about taking the bus to Santa Fe with me this afternoon?"

Franz frowned, turned on his heel and left slamming the door behind him.

"Bloody good. There's something about that bloke. He's too nosy. I don't trust him."

"You think there are spies among us?"

"I don't know, old chap, but as a Brit, I think there's something off about him."

"He is multi-national. Not only a Brit."

"Don't give him any info. Mark my word, he's a bad apple."

"Have you told Oppie?"

"Not yet. I've no proof, but I bloody well will when the opportunity presents itself." He pushed off the stool and clapped Reese on the shoulder. "Oh, there isn't a bus going to Santa Fe." He ambled off.

Reese wondered how this would work. Oppie wanted the scientists to share what they were working on, thinking it would speed up building the bomb—many minds working together creating synergy. How could anything be kept secret?

One afternoon, both Ward and Joe dropped by his work station.

"We're trying to figure out an implosion assembly method," Ward told Reese.

"Really, that's a unique approach," Joe interjected. "We're working on an explosion device."

"Sounds like you are ahead of us here," Reese said. "We're still working on which Uranium atoms will provide sufficient critical mass to create enough fission to detonate the bomb."

After kicking around a few ideas, they separated and returned to their respective labs.

Most evenings, Reese skipped the socializing and instead collapsed into bed after dinner, exhausted from the intense, long days in the lab trying to make the uranium 235 on hand stretch further than appeared to be possible.

Ward rarely put in an appearance at their quarters. Reese didn't mind—it meant he had the place to himself. On occasion, though, he thought it would be nice to have someone to talk to in the evening. Although he was in a different lab than Ward, they would have been able to discuss their work.

Chapter Six
Rumors

The scuttlebutt going around among the scientists alleged that, for some time, the Brits had been working on fission, the process of splitting the atomic nucleus to release large amounts of energy, long before the Manhattan Project was birthed. Scientists at Argonne Labs in Chicago were also working on nuclear energy, and Enrico Fermi himself had led the Chicago team that had demonstrated the first artificial self-sustaining nuclear chain reaction.

Another noted mind on the Hill, Edward Teller, expanded on Enrico Fermi's work. Teller wanted to proceed toward developing a super bomb—a thermonuclear bomb—bypassing the fission atomic bomb. Disappointed by having to work with the other scientists, the arrogant, temperamental Teller was downright hostile if he was asked to work on a theory.

"Any student can work on equations," Reese had heard him sneer.

Teller had difficulty with relationships, and his volatile disposition caused people to avoid him. Finally, Teller told Oppie he would quit if he couldn't work independently on his super bomb. Reese caught the story as it made the rounds, bringing somewhat rueful laughter among the scientists.

Apparently, Oppie had said, "What will you do if I say no?"

Teller said, "I'll resign and go where I can work on it."

"And what will you do if I say yes?"

"I'll stay, but only if I can work alone."

For security reasons Oppie knew he couldn't allow Teller to leave before they had completed their work. "Then, I'll say yes," he said.

Supposedly, for once, the stormy Hungarian had grinned.

Oppie hated the loss of Teller's expertise in the lab. He needed everyone he could get, but Teller's personality kept people on edge, which wasn't productive. Maybe it was better if Teller didn't have the opportunity to interact with the others after all. Everyone worked long hours and at breakneck speed—they didn't need personality conflicts thrown in the mix. Oppie brooded over the shipments of enriched uranium and plutonium not arriving in time to keep pace with other progress.

Oppie was leaning against the outside of the lab building, taking a break, when his younger brother Frank came through the doors and approached him. "What's going on? I heard the A-bomb test is being moved to Nevada."

As a particle physicist, Frank had worked at Oak Ridge, Tennessee on uranium enrichment and was brought to Los Alamos to continue that work.

"Where did you hear that?" Oppie tamped some tobacco into his pipe.

"I overheard some of the army guys talking about it when I was having drinks last night. They were huddled together and I didn't get any details. Do you know anything about it?" Frank lit a cigarette then leaned against the building next to his brother.

Oppie struck a match and, with a few pulls on his pipe, the smoke rose languidly in the thin high desert air.

"Frank, there are always rumors flying around here. I never pay attention to them."

"Well, do you think the test will be moved from Alamagordo to Nevada?"

"If Groves does that, I'm sure I'll hear about it." Oppie was privileged to most information, but he didn't know anything about a move. Changing the subject, he asked, "Where are we with the enriched uranium? Do we have enough to proceed?"

"We're almost there. I'd better get back to work on it." He snuffed out his cigarette with the heel of his shoe and went back into the lab.

Getting sufficient enriched uranium limited their progress. So far, they had enough to build one bomb which would be used for the test. Scientists had been working at the Hanford plant in Washington State and at Oak Ridge, Tennessee hoping to make sufficient enriched plutonium for two more bombs.

When shipments did come from Hanford and Oak Ridge, Reese, along with Oppie and the other scientists, worried there wouldn't be enough. Over time, they amassed enough for one uranium and two plutonium bombs. The pressure was on to produce enough to end the war in Japan. If they were right in their calculations, if these bombs were as powerful as they believed, they wouldn't need many. And if they were lucky, the first test would be successful and they could ship the other two to Tinian Island in the Marianas for an air strike.

If. If. If.

Reese sometimes lay awake at night, the refrain of "if" playing through his tired brain.

Chapter Seven
Tickling the Tail of the Dragon

Walking back to the labs after dinner on a hot evening in August, Reese and Ward chatted about the about the implosion technique for detonating the bomb. "I wish Joe were here to give us the information he's gleaned from his work on neutrons," Reese said.

"If I had a pretty wife like Joe's and a wee one at home, I wouldn't be coming back to work." Ward pointed toward a lighted window. "Looks like someone's working late in Omega Lab,"

Reese swiveled his head to follow Ward's finger. " It's probably that Canadian scientist, Thornton."

"That bloody bloke works all the time. He'll probably have the detonation device figured out ahead of the rest of us."

A sudden flash of blue startled them. "Holy crap. That's not good. I wonder how many rentogens that produced." The instinct to help caused Reese to run toward the door.

Ward grabbed his arm. "No," he yelled. "You'll be fried if you go in there. Give it a few minutes to diffuse, then we'll see if we can help." Before Ward could finish his sentence, the door opened and Thornton staggered out.

"What happened?" Reese dashed to steady the scientist.

"The screwdriver slipped." Thornton leaned on Reese.

"We need to get you over to the Medical Center." The two men helped Thornton to a nearby jeep.

"Thanks guys. I'm burning up…I think I'm going to vomit."

Reese had learned those symptoms were signs of extreme radiation exposure.

Thornton took a deep breath and swallowed hard. "Maybe I got a lethal dose."

27

"Don't even think that, mate." Ward jammed his foot on the gas. "We'll have you right as rain in no time."

Reese knew Ward's words were empty reassurance. Another scientist had lost his life to radiation exposure only a month ago. "What were you trying to do?"

"I was testing the core of the plutonium bomb. As I moved the top half of the sphere closer to the stationary lower portion, the screwdriver slipped. I thought I was being careful. Apparently not careful enough." A half-hearted laugh turned into coughing. "The halves of the sphere touched and the plutonium went supercritical."

"Jeez, man, is that what the blue flash was?" Reese asked as Ward sped toward the hospital.

"Yeah, a chain reaction. The gamma and neutron radiation caused an instant ionization of the lab's air particles. I knocked the sphere halves apart, but it was too late." Thornton gasped for air. "The Geiger counter went bonkers...needle jumped all the way over...got too much radiation." He was quiet for a moment. "I think I'm a gonner."

"Nah, the medics will get you fixed up. Keep your chin up." The tires of the Jeep spit gravel into the moonlit night as Ward sped over the rough road. It was a short distance, but seemed like it took forever before he jammed on the brakes in front of the Medical Center.

Reese ran through the door yelling, "Emergency. Get a doctor."

A nurse ran for a wheelchair while another phoned for a doctor. Reese and Ward helped the scientist into the wheelchair. The nurse grabbed the handles of the wheelchair and sprinted through the double doors into Emergency.

Ward and Reese stood stunned and helpless, staring as the doors swung shut. "He tickled the tail of the dragon and awakened the Demon Core," Ward said. "It could have been one of us."

* * *

And the atom said, "Don't you know there's an ever-present possibility of being roasted by dragon fire. Take care not to awaken my Demon Core."

Nine days later, Thornton died.

* * *

As completion of the test bomb neared and the site of White Sands, not far from Alamogordo, New Mexico, was being prepared, General Groves, pulled Oppenheimer aside. "Walk with me, Oppie." He headed for the door into the cool morning air. "We have a change of plans. Instead of testing the bomb at Alamagordo Test Range, we're moving the test to Jackass Flats, Nevada."

Oppie stopped mid-stride and stared at Groves. After a long silence, Oppie said, "That's a long way to transport enriched uranium, the detonating device, and staff."

"I know, but there's been a security leak and we can't risk staying with our original plan."

"Too bad. We've put a lot of work into that site, built the tower, and right now they're working on the bunkers."

"Can't be helped. We'll just have to rebuild those things in Nevada."

"Where's Jackass Flats? Is that a real name?"

"Yep, it's just northwest of Las Vegas."

"That change is going to slow things down. Logistically, it's going to be a nightmare." Oppie fished a cigarette out of a pack and offered one to Groves.

"Yeah, we'll have to push to be ready in time." Groves lit his cigarette and gave Oppie a light.

"Our July fourth date was optimistic at best. We're still having trouble with the detonation device. This change of location will delay us further even if the bomb is ready."

"Well, you can tell your team they'll have a little more time because of the change in test sites." Groves blew three perfect smoke rings.

"If there are spies in our midst, wouldn't we have the same risk if I tell my team?"

Groves narrowed his eyes. He had painted himself into a corner. What he'd said didn't make sense. In order to make this ruse work, he'd have to take Oppenheimer into his confidence. "Look Oppie, this is for your ears only." Groves glanced around to make certain nobody was within earshot. "We aren't changing the test site. It will still be at White Sands, but we want the team and everyone else to think we are moving the test to Nevada. You mustn't tell anyone, not Kitty, not your brother. No one is to be taken into your confidence."

29

Chapter Eight
1945
Rosa

Eager to get out in the cool mountain air, Reese tied his new hiking boots outfitted with custom orthotics to accommodate his limp. At six o'clock on a Sunday morning, he thought he'd have the mesa to himself. He wanted to climb down to the stream below and stroll among the cottonwoods wearing their summer green. Peering up at the clear blue sky, he felt a swelling in his chest. He'd come to love the high desert. The skies had to be the most beautiful asset of New Mexico. Looking past the chain link fence topped with razor wire, he saw the cascade of radioactive waste that had been dumped over the edge of the mesa. "We'll probably live to regret polluting the desert like that," he thought as he headed for the gate so he could hike outside the fenced area. His newly purchased hand-carved walking stick dug into the dirt on the slope as he eased himself sideways down the steep incline.

Despite his love of the area, he was relieved to hear the time had come to do an actual test on the Gadget. A successful test may bring his time in Los Alamos to an end.

Reese had been chosen to be part of the team to travel south to Alamogordo Army Air Base to prepare for Trinity, the first atomic bomb explosion. Although facing a long road trip, he welcomed the chance to get away. His jeep would be caravanning in a convoy carrying equipment to Alamogordo, across the White Sands desert, then onto the bomb site. Curious residents stared as Jeeps and trucks lumbered through Albuquerque. As the jeep Reese was traveling in left the outskirts of the city, Oppenheimer's customized Packard Clipper limousine tooted its horn and zipped by carrying General Groves and other high-ranking military officers.

After a short stay at the Army base, Reese would transfer to base camp near the test site with over a hundred others to prepare for the blast.

* * *

It was pure freedom to be at the Army base after Los Alamos. His first Saturday night there, Reese's colleagues persuaded him to join them for a regular feature at the base—the USO dance in the mess hall.

Reese was astonished at the crowd. A group of local women showed up dressed in their party best, carrying plates of cookies and wearing big smiles. Entertaining the men was their contribution to the war effort. Tommy Dorsey's big band music blared from a phonograph. Couples lit up the dance floor dancing the current rage, the Jitterbug.

As Reese watched from the sidelines, the music changed and Glen Miller's *In the Mood* poured out of the speakers.

A petite, vivacious girl grabbed his hand and pulled him toward the dance floor.

"But I don't—" Reese began.

The girl flicked her dark brown hair over her shoulder and gave him a wide smile. "I'll teach you," she said.

She planted his hand firmly on the small of her back. "Now just follow me."

He tried his best, while she spun and twirled and laughed when he stepped on her foot. Halfway through the dance, she gave up.

"I'm thirsty," she said. "Let's get some punch." They wound through the dancers to a table with pitchers of red Kool-Aid and plates of cookies.

"We'll try again on a slow dance," she said, handing him a cup of punch.

Reese's skin pinked from his collar to his hairline. As he followed her to a line of chairs along the wall, he tried to keep his eyes off her derriere, which filled her slim skirt to great advantage. He shook his head to still the thrumming in his ears. He'd have followed her to the moon.

"I suppose I ought to know your name, Miss…er…" he said.

"Call me Rosa," she said. "Rosa Castillo." The very slight Spanish inflection was pleasant to his ear—melodic. He wondered fleetingly if she was from one of the Spanish families who had settled New Mexico hundreds of years before.

There was barely enough time to exchange introductions before the next song came on, Bing Crosby's mellow voice crooning *I'll Be Seeing You.*

"Oh, I just love this song. It's so romantic." Her tongue caressed the r. "Come on." She stood and placed her cup on the chair to claim it later. Reese gulped down the rest of his drink and followed her to the dance floor.

"Now, this one is easy." Again, she placed one of his hands on her back, taking the other in hers. "Just sway back and forth to the music."

Reese saw the way the other couples danced and drew her close.

She snuggled her head against his chest and turned her soft, coffee brown eyes up to gaze into his. "I can hear your heartbeat," she murmured.

Reese's cheeks burned. The bare hall and loud tinny music were suddenly transformed into an elegant ballroom with a twenty-piece orchestra. His cheeks stretched into a grin.

At the end of the evening, he offered to see Rosa home.

"Oh, I can't. My papa will be waiting for me outside in his truck. We live on a ranch about twenty miles from here."

He followed her out of the building onto the wooden steps. She went to the pickup waiting at the curb and tapped on the driver's side glass. Her father had been snoozing. Roused, he said, "Ready, *mi niña?*"

"Papa, I want you to meet my friend. This is Reese Mayfield. He's stationed here as a civilian employee for the military."

Senor Castillo reached his hand out of the truck and shook Reese's. "*Mucho Gusto.*"

"Good evening, sir." Reese looked down at Rosa. "May I phone you?" he asked.

"Papa?"

Señor Castillo sat up straighter and sized up the young man. Reese met his level gaze.

"Papa?" Rosa's voice had a slight edge.

Señor Castillo chuckled. "For eighteen years," he said to Reese, man-to-man. "I have known from that look she would get her way, so…" He tweaked Rosa lightly on the chin. "So why fight it now?" He dug out a pencil from the glove compartment and tore a corner off a receipt. "*Si, chica.* Let this nice young man have our phone number." He held up a warning finger. "But I am telling you—"

Reese broke in. "Yes, sir. I understand."

As Reese walked to his quarters, whistling and fingering the scrap of paper in his pocket, he couldn't feel the earth under his feet. He would gladly break the rules to spend time with Rosa, but he would have to be careful about what he told her.

The next morning, Reese woke in high spirits. He resisted phoning Rosa too early, but when his watch showed ten a.m., he found a phone in the mess hall and called. His heart leapt when she answered.

"When can I see you again? I'm free today, but tomorrow I have to leave." Although rain had delayed the test and given him the day off, his orders instructed him to go to base camp near ground zero early the next morning. Of course, he couldn't tell her that.

"I'll be in Tularosa today. Can you meet me there? Meet me at one o'clock at the St. Francis de Paula church. It's easy to find."

Reese hesitated—could he locate a car? If not, he'd hitchhike. "I'll be there."

In a borrowed Jeep, he drove the twenty miles to Tularosa. He arrived early and had no trouble locating the church. He scanned the outside. *Either she isn't here yet, or she's inside.*

Reese had never been inside a Catholic Church and was uneasy, but he pushed the heavy wooden door open. It took a moment for his eyes to adjust to the dim interior. Rosa was lighting a candle at the right of the altar. He walked down the aisle and touched her lightly on the shoulder. When she turned, there were tears glistening on her cheeks.

"For my big brother, Armando. He was killed during the Normandy invasion."

Reese lightly brushed away her tears, aching to take her in his arms and comfort her. He didn't know a family that hadn't lost someone in the war. Heartache upon heartache, but the nation was united in its purpose.

Drying her face with the backs of her hands, Rosa shook off her momentary grief and brightened. "Let's go to the drugstore and get a coke," she said. "Have you had lunch? They make good egg salad sandwiches." She grasped his hand and led him out of the church.

Rosa's bubbly personality brought Reese out of his shell. She soon had him chatting about his childhood, school, and family. When the moment came

33

for them to say goodbye, he explained that he'd be gone for a while, but would phone her as soon as he could. She reached up to kiss him on the cheek. On impulse, he wrapped his arms around her and kissed her long and hard. When he released her, she caught her breath and said, "I'll wait for that call."

Chapter Nine
Trinity

The next morning, and three days before the test, Reese left with Ward, Joe Pope and a dozen others to travel from Alamogordo to the Trinity base camp, ten miles from ground zero.

In the pre-dawn darkness the three buddies and several other scientists boarded an olive-colored bus. Although a light rain fell, the sun rose between the clouds casting a pink glow on the white sand. On his left, the desert looked like a rolling white ocean. On his right, scrubby shrubs covered the landscape. Early rising deer chomping on grass near the road ran from the approaching bus. Admiring the glistening gypsum sands, Reese listened to the voices buzzing around him.

"I wonder if those bloody bunkers will be stout enough to protect us," Ward said.

"Sure. They're more than five miles from ground zero."

"I'll bet twenty bucks it'll be a dud."

"I'll take you up on that." Ward was always up for a challenge.

A new voice joined the fray. "I'll bet it'll start a chain reaction and destroy the world." His tone was joking.

Nervous laughter answered him.

"Nah, it'll ignite the atmosphere and we'll all be toasted, so I'm not betting," chimed in yet another voice. "How about you, Reese?"

"Count me out," he said. Then he added what they all didn't want to admit: "It's an unknown."

"Will the test go ahead in this rain or will this be just one more delay?" asked Joe.

"It's been raining for almost two weeks. It's got to quit sometime."

"Yeah, it never rains in New Mexico." Again, laughter followed that comment.

"The weather report said today would be clear and sunny. Besides, I don't think they would bus us out here if the test isn't a go."

The bus stopped at base camp and the men grabbed their duffle bags and cases of equipment and disembarked.

After dropping off their personal belongings, Reese and the other members of his team continued on to the old McDonald ranch house where the master bedroom had been converted into a clean room to serve as a lab. His team was responsible for assembling the nuclear capsule.

Finally, after more than two years of preparation, the day arrived. Project Y—the atomic bomb they called "Fat Man" was ready to be tested.

* * *

It was still dark the next morning when a jeep transported Reese to the North Shelter. Ward and Joe were assigned other locations. Tension was high inside the bunker. Oppenheimer paced and chain-smoked, while Fermi appeared relaxed and cool.

Weather conditions weren't favorable, again delaying the test.

Oppenheimer sat on a concrete bench next to Reese. "Well, young man, are we going to succeed? That is, if this damn rain ever stops?"

"We've done everything we can. All of us are concerned, I know. But I'm going for the positive, sir. It'll work."

Without another word Oppenheimer stubbed out a cigarette, fished out another, lit it and resumed his pacing.

At last, the rain stopped and the countdown started. Following instructions to turn away from the tower holding the bomb, Reese and his colleagues covered their faces with their hands.

At 5:29.21 a.m., a blinding flash illuminated the sky and the inside of the bunker. Even through his hands Reese saw the brilliant light—so bright he saw the bones in his fingers. A moment later, a deafening roar. The earth shuddered, reminding him of earthquakes in San Francisco. When the light subsided, he looked through the slit in the bunker and watched as a huge red ball dispersed in stringers of purple and gold. A massive cloud billowed upward and spread outward for what seemed like miles. The sight was at once glorious, beautiful, yet unnatural and terrible. A metallic smell permeated the dust filled air.

Reese was both elated and awed. They had done it. But never in those two long years at Los Alamos, even in the furthest reaches of his imagination, had he envisioned something of this magnitude. The depth of emotion took his breath away.

Cheers of triumph erupted. "It worked," said one and was repeated by others. Scientists and soldiers slapped each other on the back in congratulation. Reese heard one say, "I won the bet. Fork over twenty bucks."

America had developed a super weapon that could end the war in the Pacific. *Perhaps*, Reese thought, *it could end the threat of any war in the future.* Almost everyone was jubilant.

It was Oppenheimer who was quiet. He stood for some moments staring at the dissipating cloud. Then Reese overheard him whisper a phrase he recognized from the Bhagavad Gita: "I am become Death, the destroyer of worlds."

* * *

That same morning at five-thirty, Rosa and her father were enjoying a pleasant ride to check on their cattle, chatting about ranch matters as they ambled along through the scrub. Rosa was thinking about gathering some yellow chamisa flowers. In fact, she was about to mention it to her papa, when the entire world—sky, cows, sage brush, sandy ground—lit up in a flash of otherworldly brilliance, more blinding than any imaginable lightning, shocking Rosa and her papa into an abrupt halt. There was a moment of silence, a heartbeat of a second for Rosa to marvel at the light. As she turned, bedazzled, to her father, a deafening boom engulfed them, making the very earth unreliable beneath their horses' feet. Rosa's mount gathered up his powerful muscles under her, then with all his might, the confused and terrified animal tore straight into the wall of wind blasting at them from the explosion. She was helpless to turn him.

Her father urged his horse to a gallop. To Rosa, it seemed like miles before he caught up and snatched a rein. The horse slowed and finally stopped, its sides heaving. Breathless, Rosa dismounted and hugged her papa's leg, sobbing as she gasped, *"Gracias, gracias, mi Papa."*

37

The wind passed, leaving them to wonder about the sparkling ash that fell on them and covered the ground.

Chapter Ten
Love and War

The nineteen-kiloton explosion vaporized the hundred-foot tower that had held the bomb. The blast left a crater one-thousand feet in diameter and ten-feet deep. Heat melted the sand on the desert floor, coating the crater bed with a new atomic mineral that looked like green glass. Scientists named it Trinitite.

Reports started coming in. Because of the top-secret nature of the test, ranchers hadn't been contacted—even those living a mere fifteen miles from the blast site. Windows shattered, the ground rolled and shook underfoot, frightened animals ran wildly trying to escape. Believing they were under attack, people panicked.

For three days after the blast, Reese collected samples to take to Los Alamos for examination—samples of Trinitite. Most of it was green, but he also found some pieces that were reddish and black. Some were teardrop shaped, having cooled as they fell back to earth, but most were flat. He collected sand and dirt from areas close and far away from ground zero as well as water from rain puddles which he sealed in test tubes. It was essential to measure the radioactivity.

Eager to see Rosa again, he rushed through his tasks with the thought he might be able to spend a day with her in Tularosa before returning to Los Alamos.

Reese lucked out. The same driver who had brought him from Los Alamos was to drive him back to the Alamogordo base. "Any chance I can borrow your Jeep again? There's a girl I want to see." Every time he thought of Rosa, he felt giddy.

The driver grinned, pursed his lips and made a couple of kissing noises. "Ah, young love. I'll see what I can do."

Reese blushed.

As they travelled through Alamogordo, Reese asked the driver to stop. He wanted to pick up a paper to catch up on the news. He snorted when he read that an ammunition magazine at Alamogordo Army Air Base had exploded. Reese figured the FBI had done its job—any report of the blast would be cleansed or kept out of the news altogether.

When Reese reached his barracks at the Army base, he spotted a discarded copy of the *El Paso Herald Post*. The headlines shouted news about a massive explosion. The article was purported to be an eye-witness account. The reporter made it clear the blast came from something larger than an ammunitions supply depot. *Apparently, the FBI didn't get to the* Post *in time,* Reese thought, and wondered how long that reporter would hold his job.

But Reese shrugged off the other cover-ups. It was war time. It was the government's job to keep people calm—and safe from invasion. It was simple patriotism to accept that.

Although Germany had surrendered, war raged on in the Pacific. Soldiers in Europe who'd hoped to go home were sent to islands they had never heard of: Luzon, Iwo Jima, and Okinawa. Thousands would never make it home. A few with injuries sustained in combat against the Germans would be hospitalized state side and avoid being sent into action against the Japanese. Some considered themselves lucky, others hated not to be part of the battle.

Reese hurried to a phone and called Rosa. "May I see you? I only have today and tonight before I have to leave again. If it's okay, I'll come to your ranch. Tell me how to get there."

"You'll never find it. Tell you what. I'll meet you in Tularosa at the church. Just look for papa's pickup. You can follow me to the ranch. It's only about ten miles from there. About an hour from now?"

Reese wanted to find a gift for Rosa and one for her mother. He looked up the driver whose jeep he was borrowing, sought a little counsel about where to shop, and took off. Armed with a bottle of good whiskey for her papa, chocolates for her mama and a shawl for Rosa, he sped to meet her.

As he followed Rosa down a dirt road, he realized the ranch must be downwind of the test. Was the dust being kicked up radioactive? Just how far had the explosion and wind carried the dangerous ash?

Señora Castillo was as bubbly as Rosa. She welcomed Reese and made a big fuss over the chocolates, admired the shawl and good naturedly scolded him for the whiskey. "Papa will get drunk," she said.

Señor Castillo laughed as he said, "We always need something in the house for snakebite."

During a dinner of tamales, carne asada, ensalada, and Mexican beer, Señor Castillo and Rosa told Reese about the morning of the explosion. Did he know about it? He couldn't deny it. Did he know what the strange sparkling ash was? Still sworn to secrecy, he said he didn't, but inwardly, he worried how much radioactivity they'd been exposed to.

Reese and Rosa excused themselves to go sit in a swing on the wide veranda to watch the sunset. The colors waned and the warm summer night sky started organizing itself into its familiar pattern of stars. Rosa nestled her head against him when he put his arm around her. It was after midnight when he said he needed to leave—promising to phone.

On the drive back he wondered if she would marry him. *What am I thinking? I hardly know the girl.* But his heart told him she was the one he'd always hoped for.

* * *

Since the Trinity test had been successful, it was full speed ahead to build more bombs.

There was controversy among the scientists at Los Alamos about the humanity of dropping the bombs on Japan. Some sent letters to Washington, urging not to use them. Some argued, too, that Russia seemed about to enter the Pacific Theater against the Japanese, which would create a solid chance of ending the war.

The government countered with the projected loss of American soldiers—hundreds of thousands, possibly half a million. In light of the expected deaths from traditional warfare, President Truman issued formal orders to go ahead with the bombings.

The Enola Gay took off with its payload and dropped "Little Boy" on Hiroshima. Three days later, "Fat Man" devastated Nagasaki.

Collectively, Los Alamosa scientists heaved a sigh of relief. Their work had paid off. The bombs preformed exactly as expected. The will of the

Japanese people had been broken. All ears were tuned to the radio when the words of Japan's surrender were announced. The war came to an abrupt close.

Despite mixed emotions about the humanity of using the atomic bombs, there was a big party up on the Hill. President Truman thanked the scientists at Los Alamos on behalf of a grateful nation.

* * *

As news began to filter in from Japan, a niggling thought was born in Reese's mind. Had the military really needed to drop both those bombs? He could accept the first one—with reservations—but Nagasaki? Had Japan really hesitated to surrender? Did it have something to do with the money the government had invested, reported to be somewhere near ten million? Or did the bigwigs in D.C. see the bombs as giving the U.S. an edge on the postwar world stage?

Soon, film footage became available and, along with his fellow scientists, Reese saw visible proof of the devastation—the flattened cities, the empty schoolhouses and hospitals, the radiation burns on children, the elderly and anyone who wasn't immediately incinerated by the blast. Reese was staggered by the massive destruction and loss of human life—80,000 in Hiroshima alone, another 40,000 in Nagasaki. It made him physically ill, sick to his stomach. What had they done?

In the small Los Alamos movie theater, some in the audience were ecstatic and cheering. Others were quiet, like Reese, introspective. He wondered if they, too, were having doubts about what they had created. Slowly, Reese recognized a new feeling—not one that sat easily on him. After two years of intense labor on a project, which he had up until this moment viewed as absolutely necessary, absolutely in the best interests of his nation, he was beginning to feel remorse. The targets had been cities with civilian populations, not military bases.

In the darkened theater, one scientist asked aloud, "We had to do it, didn't we?" To Reese, the question sounded like a plea for validation.

Oppie, in the first row, turned in his seat to reply. "I think," he said, "we have blood on our hands."

Reese was forced to agree. *We don't know what we've unleashed.*

He thought of Rosa, becoming so dear to him, of the marriage he was beginning to hope for, the children they might have. *What kind of world will it be for them, now that our government has this power?*

Chapter Eleven
End of WWII

With the war over, joyous celebrations rang out in cities and towns all across America. Girls cheered from the sidewalks as cars drove down main streets honking their horns. Confetti floated down from buildings in Times Square as sailors grabbed girls to kiss them. Families reunited and factories retooled to make peacetime machines. Grateful to be home, war weary fighting men held tight to loved ones and started rebuilding their lives.

Cyrus Brenner had been back from Europe for three months. Right before V-E day he'd been hit in the legs with multiple pieces of shrapnel. His injuries weren't life threatening and required less than a month to heal. Unlike others, he wasn't sent on to fight in the Pacific. After a stay in Walter Reed Army Hospital in Washington, he was awarded the Purple Heart, mustered out and sent home to his ranch near Cedar City, Utah.

Cyrus was in the prime of his life, over six feet tall and stocky. Still, he panted as he reached the top of a rise that looked down over the land he owned with his younger brother, Luke. When their parents retired, they passed the ranch on to their sons and moved into town.

Cyrus's wife, Verna, his dad and a couple of hands kept the ranch running while he spent four years fighting the Germans.

A fullness swelled his chest bringing tears to his eyes. How he'd missed the ranch. He loved the country his Mormon pioneer ancestors had settled in the mid-1800s. He was the fourth generation to farm and keep livestock on the 1500 acres he surveyed. A breeze ruffled his sandy blonde hair as he inhaled deeply and turned 360 degrees, taking in the panorama. In the distance, blue mountains had lost their winter snow caps from the summer heat. With the onset of autumn, a mantle of snow would soon blanket the peaks again.

A pickup truck kicking up dust caught his attention. It was his dad's old green Ford speeding up the dirt road toward Cyrus and Verna's ranch house. A man and a woman stood in back leaning against the cab waving their arms. He squinted to see who it was.

"Luke!" Cyrus waved back, arms flailing over his head as he raced down the hill and across the field.

Luke had joined the Army the day after he graduated from high school. He would have gone into the service sooner if his dad had allowed it. "Son, you have to get your diploma," his dad Ike said with such vehemence that Luke didn't think to argue. His mother Lily stood by him, nodding her agreement and said. "Your dad's right. You need to finish high school."

Steering with one hand Ike waved back at Cyrus as they pulled up in front of the house. "Look at that boy run," Ike said to Lily seated beside him.

"For his size, he's fast," she said while opening the door to step out.

Luke jumped from the bed of the pickup and lifted down Sherry, his high school sweetheart.

Panting from his dash Cyrus pulled Luke into a bear hug. "Good to have you home safe and sound, little brother." He released him, but not before he ran his hand over Luke's blonde crew cut. "Looks like they took your hair."

"It'll grow back. I had too much anyway."

When Luke pulled himself free, he grabbed Sherry's hand. "We're getting married. I asked her today."

"Congratulations. He's been hanging around you since tenth grade. Glad to hear you're putting him out of his misery." Cyrus pumped his little brother's hand with a hearty handshake.

Sherry laughed. "I'm just hoping he'll give me time to shop for a wedding dress."

"What's this I hear?" Cyrus's wife Verna pushed open the screen door. "There's gonna be a weddin'?"

"As soon as we can arrange for the Church," Luke said as he dashed around the pickup to open the door for his mother.

Verna frowned. "You're not gonna have a Temple weddin'?" It was customary for LDS couples to wed in the Temple if they were in good standing with the church.

45

Luke looked down as if studying his boots. When he turned his gray eyes up to meet Verna's, he said. "We can be sealed in the temple later. Right now, we want to get on with our lives and start a family."

A special ritual in the Mormon Temple bonds couples, seals them together not just in this life, but for time and all eternity.

"What do you think about that Ike?" Verna rested her hands on her hips.

Ike followed Lily onto the porch. "If it's what they want. Any man who's spent two years in a war ought to do what he wants. I'm just glad to have him home." He leaned back against a post supporting the roof that covered the porch and bowed his head. Sentiment and gratitude overcame him. A single teardrop fell and left a round wet spot on the wooden porch before he took a deep breath and collected himself. So many families had lost sons in the war.

"And you Lily? Verna pressed.

"I agree with Ike," Lily said.

"Well, Cyrus and I were married in the Temple." Verna pursed her lips. "But then, that was before the war. Land sakes, people are in such a hurry these days."

To lighten the mood, Cyrus interrupted. "Hey, great tan Luke. Is that what being stationed on an island in the Pacific does for you?"

"Yeah, sun always shines there. The Philippines are beautiful, but not as nice as home." Luke draped his arm around Sherry's shoulder and pulled her near.

"C'mon Lily. Help me fix some lemonade to cool off this bunch." Verna held the screen door open for her mother-in-law.

Cyrus and Verna's children came running. "Uncle Luke," they shouted.

The four-year-old boy held back. He didn't remember his Uncle Luke, but the two older children did. Small replicas of their parents they were blue-eyed, rosy cheeked blondes. Luke squatted down and held out his hand to his nephew. "Put it there my man." He shook hands with the boy before gathering his niece into his arms for a hug. "How would you like to be a flower girl at my wedding?"

"I don't think she knows what that means." Sherry knelt to be on eye level with the child. "It means you get to scatter flower petals in front of the bride. I think you'd like it."

"Maybe I'd like it." The girl cast her glance toward her feet and tugged on one of her long braids.

"Sure, you would," Cyrus said.

Luke sat on the steps and pulled Sherry down beside him. Looking up at Cyrus, he said, "Dad has given us the old log house down by the crick."

"That's only fair," said Cyrus. "When the folks moved into town they gave Verna and me this one. Half this spread belongs to you including half the livestock." In addition to the sheep, there were thirty head of cattle, half a dozen pigs and numerous chickens. "As soon as you're settled, I'll send half a dozen laying hens and a rooster down to the old chicken coop near the cabin."

Verna and Lily brought glasses and two pitchers of lemonade out to the porch and poured the pale liquid, handing everyone a glass.

"This is about the last of the ice in the ice house. This bein' a special occasion, we went ahead and used it." After pouring lemonade, Verna fanned herself. "It's a hot day for September."

"That it is. Won't be long before we'll be taking the sheep to winter pasture on Bald Mountain." Cyrus sipped his drink.

During the winter months when snow covered the scarce browse on the hillsides near Cedar City, the Brenners moved their herd to Nevada for the warmer climate. Tender grasses, black sage and nutritious forbs—a low broadleafed plant—provided plenty of forage for the sheep.

"Better hustle with wedding plans so Luke can go with me to the winter range." Cyrus said.

"I'll bet my mother is already working on it. It's been all of three hours since we told her. She's probably phoned every lady in our Church Ward by now." Sherry said.

Luke stood and said, "Dad, can Sherry and I take the pickup down to check out the house?"

"Sure, son." Ike was beyond happy to have both his sons home. Happy and relieved, he had prayed every day for the Lord to spare them and bring them home to him. He'd paid his ten percent tithe and volunteered on the church farms. He'd maintained the ranch so Cyrus and Luke would have a livelihood when they came back. Now that his sons were home, he would do everything in his power to support and further their happiness.

* * *

Donna ran a well-manicured finger under the flap of an ivory envelope. It was a wedding invitation. "Sam, we've been invited to a wedding in Cedar City. It's short notice—just a week from now. I haven't seen anyone from that branch of my family in years. Can we go?"

"I don't see why not. Do you need to RSVP?" Sam asked.

"Doesn't look like it. I need to go shopping for a gift—wonder what the happy couple needs. I'm going to phone the bride's mother. She's my second cousin. She'll advise me, and I'll let her know we're attending. I wish Reese were here to go with us. He needs to know his relatives. I miss him. I wonder if he'll be home soon, now that the war is over."

"I hope so. I miss him too."

The rest went unsaid. Thoughts such as, I wonder if he's changed? What has he been doing? Will he talk about his work and where he had been? All they knew was that his letters came from Santa Fe.

* * *

Donna arrived home after picking up Sam's navy-blue suit from the cleaners. She had just hung the phone up when it rang. "Hello."

"Mom? It's Reese." Donna collapsed into the chair next to the phone table. Covering the mouthpiece with her hand, she called, "Sam, come quick. It's Reese."

"Where are you calling from, dear?"

"I'm in Santa Fe right now. The project I've been working on may allow me to come home. I'm going to ask to be released from my position."

"That's such good news. Is there any way you could come to a wedding in Cedar City this week?"

"Who's getting married?"

"Your cousin Sherry."

"I don't think I remember her."

"Maybe you wouldn't. She's younger than you. Your dad and I are leaving in a couple of days to drive to Utah."

"Mom, you have more Utah relatives than I can keep track of."

"Well, that happens if you are raised LDS in Salt Lake City." Donna had married outside the Church. As a result, she drifted away and wasn't a practicing Mormon, but most of her relatives were.

48

"I won't be able to leave on such short notice, but I should be home within a month."

Sam had hurried into the room and stood awaiting the news.

"He's coming home." Donna's voice broke with emotion. "Here, talk to him." Tears shone in her eyes.

* * *

Sherry and Luke were married in the Cedar City Second Ward Church on October tenth, 1945. Almost half the town attended bringing wedding gifts that would keep them in sheets, towels, and dishes for years. Donna and Sam gave the bride and groom a set of crystal glasses.

The reception became a family reunion, and a reunion of men who'd survived the war, though some would carry wounds the rest of their lives. The event was only saddened by the absence of one of Luke's classmates who had enlisted in the Army with him. He lost his life on Okinawa just months before the Japanese surrendered.

Luke and Sherry skipped a honeymoon and instead spent that time fixing up their home. Lily and Verna helped Sherry sew curtains. The ladies in the church Relief Society made quilts for the newlyweds and stocked their cellar with canned fruits, vegetables, and jams.

Ike had run electricity to the log house several years ago. It had running water, but lacked an indoor bathroom. Men from the church got together and put one in with Ike paying the bill.

Luke used what was left of his mustering out pay for a down payment on a pre-war pickup. Now that Detroit was building cars again, people were eager to part with their old vehicles.

Halloween signaled the time to move the herd to the winter pasture. Luke didn't want to leave Sherry for the winter and, although she said she'd be fine, he knew she didn't want him to go.

* * *

Cyrus rode his horse down the two-track road that led to Luke's house. He stopped at the front porch and looped his horse's reins over the porch railing. Sherry saw him coming and opened the door before he knocked.

"I have good news for you," Cyrus said.

"What is it?" Luke pulled out a chair for Cyrus.

"Dad and I have been talking. It's only been three weeks since your wedding. You've still got a lot of work to get this place in shape. We'll take the sheep to Bald Mountain. You and Sherry can come in the pickup in a couple of weeks. Dad's arranged for old Joe Heath and Saul Johnson to tend the herd over Christmas. They don't have family and are glad for the extra money. That way you won't be apart so long and I'll be back for the kid's Christmas. It'll be the first Christmas in four years that I'll be home. I don't want to miss it."

"That's wonderful." Sherry made cocoa and put a cup in front of each of the men.

"We're pretty well set financially from selling off some of the cattle, so we can afford the men's salaries for the two weeks we'll be home over the holidays." Cyrus leaned back and hooked his thumbs in his suspenders.

* * *

Sherry hoped to have a baby right away, but it wasn't happening. Each month, Sherry was puzzled. All her friends seemed to get pregnant on their honeymoon. "Why don't I?" she asked her mother.

"All in God's time," her mother replied.

The holidays came and went. Luke and Cyrus went back to the winter range. They wouldn't be home again until lambing season in April.

Sherry made baby quilts and knitted booties in pink, blue and yellow. She went to Church all day on Sunday and again on Tuesday evenings. She attended Relief Society meetings and volunteered for everything. She thought that should be enough, but it wasn't. She was bored and further saddened when she learned Verna was expecting again.

In wintertime there wasn't that much for her to do on the ranch, so she went to see her Uncle Ted at the bank to inquire about work. The only job Sherry had held before was at the local Dairy Queen. Since she was an excellent typist and a whiz at math, Uncle Ted gave her a ninety-day trial period job.

When Luke came home, she'd been working at the bank for six weeks. He was glad to see her keeping busy so she wouldn't brood about not being pregnant.

Another year passed before an elated Sherry learned she was going to have a baby. William Brenner was born September 25, 1947.

50

Sherry phoned her cousin, Phyllis Christensen, in Redfield to announce her good news.

"I'm so happy for you. And I have an announcement of my own. I'm expecting." Phyllis was already raising two sons and yearned for a daughter. "I'd love to have a little girl to sew pretty clothes for, one to curl her hair and put ribbons in it."

"I'll pray for a little girl for you," Sherry said.

Chapter Twelve
Rosa

Now that the war was over, research at Los Alamos felt less pressing. Eager to finish his education, Reese made an appointment with Oppenheimer.

"Sir, I would like to be released from my work here. I want to go on to work on my doctorate degree.

"Of course. I interrupted that, didn't I?" Oppie smiled. "And I'm grateful you let me. But it's time, and I understand."

"Thank you, sir," Reese said.

"I think some of your research here can be credited toward your Ph. D. It may shorten your doctoral work. I'll write a letter to the university—it's still Berkeley, isn't it?" Reese nodded. "If you need further verification, let me know." Oppie stood to shake Reese's hand. "Good luck, young man, and thank you."

A week later, Reese packed his suitcase as Ward stood by and watched. "I'll miss you, old chap. We had some good times. I'll never forget when we almost ended up in the brig in Santa Fe—never drank so much in my life."

"Me neither," agreed Reese as he folded a shirt.

"And the pretty little birds almost drank us under the table."

"Those gals could really put it away. Good Lord, what a hangover I had. There wasn't enough tomato juice and aspirin in the world to cure it."

Reese snapped the latches on his suitcase and scanned the room. "Well our promised better living quarters never materialized, did they?"

"At last, I'll be able to spread out in our palatial quarters," Ward joked as he followed Reese out to the street. "Keep in touch."

"I will," promised Reese.

On the way to catch his transport to Santa Fe, Reese stopped by Ann and Joe Pope's to say goodbye. Little Katherine was toddling around now.

From Santa Fe, Reese thumbed a ride to Albuquerque. A bus schedule let him know he'd have time to go shopping. It took him little time to find what he sought—a jewelry store.

Inspecting the sparkling gems, he nervously wondered if Rosa would say yes. After an hour of listening to words such as clarity, cut, and carat, he chose a ring.

When the bus arrived in Tularosa, he phoned Rosa. Once again, Reese waited for her in the church. When Rosa opened the door, a shaft of light broke his reverie. He turned to see her dip her fingers in holy water and cross herself. He stood and met her halfway down the aisle. They sat in a pew with heads together, hugging and quietly talking. Reese took Rosa's small hand and begged, "Please wait for me to finish my studies." He produced a small, royal blue velvet box and opened it. "Marry me? It will be about two years."

The eighteen-year-old tearfully nodded. As Reese slid the diamond solitaire onto her finger, she said, "Papa wants me to wait until I'm twenty to marry anyhow, but yes, yes, I'll marry you." As she wept, she covered his face with kisses.

* * *

They wrote long letters, the fragile air mail paper overflowing with the minutiae that made Reese and Rosa real to each other. Reese found in her an acute intelligence that allowed her to understand at least the fundamentals of his studies. His loneliness evaporated. At last, he had found the life companion he had hungered for. The months passed.

Then the letters stopped coming so frequently, and when they did come, Rosa mentioned fewer details. Reese phoned and learned she was gravely ill. Señor Castillo told him she had cancer.

Reese remembered her comments about the explosion, the "sparkling ash." Then he considered the reports he'd heard about the people in Japan who'd been exposed to the bomb's radioactivity. Reports of cancer were increasing there.

He flew to Albuquerque where Señor Castillo met him. Rosa's beloved papa had aged far more than the time should have allowed. "Rosa is very sick." Senor Castillo said as they drove to the ranch. "Prepare yourself."

"What happened?"

"Only God knows."

The fragment of a human who greeted him from her pillows bore little resemblance to his vibrant fiancée. Reese resisted showing his shock.

He held her frail body and stroked what was left of her long dark hair. All afternoon and evening, they talked when she had strength, were quiet when she couldn't speak. She showed him that her fingers had grown so thin she had wound tape around the engagement ring to keep it from sliding off.

"I won't let them take it away," she said, her voice barely louder than a whisper. "It reminds me to try to grow well again."

She can't die. I won't let her.

"We're together now, sweetheart. I'll take leave from school and stay here to help you get well."

She smiled as he continued. "As soon as you're better, we'll get married in the church in Tularosa. You'll be beautiful..." he swallowed hard, "beautiful, in a white wedding gown. There'll be a big fiesta here at the ranch." Reese's voice trailed away when her hand went limp in his, and she drifted to sleep.

Rosa didn't wake up. She died early the next morning.

The grief that filled the family's home was palpable, and the funeral was almost unbearable. Reese forced himself to walk to the casket. She looked even thinner and more wasted against the pink satin lining. He touched her cheek and walked out of the church.

I never should have left her. If I'd been here, maybe I could have saved her. I should have taken her to San Francisco, to the finest doctors there.

Filled with sorrow and guilt, Reese found a bar and got very drunk.

Señor Castillo worried about the young man and went to find him. He found him walking toward the ranch in the early morning. "Getting drunk won't bring her back," he said. "It doesn't honor her memory."

Reese crept into bed and wept, stifling his sobs with the pillow. All the could-haves and should-haves couldn't save Rosa now. It was too late.

* * *

Reese was numb as he waited to board the plane. He moved robotically through the line and handed his ticket to the attendant. His thoughts were a jumble. Was it radioactive fallout that caused her cancer? Why didn't Rosa's parents get sick? She was too young to die, and in so much pain. Was it

54

connected to the Trinity test? Underneath the questions lurked a far more terrible one: *Am I responsible for killing her?*

He found his place and fastened the seat belt. Picking up the airline magazine, he thumbed through it, blind to anything on the pages. Was there any way he could absolve himself of the guilt?

His highly abstract doctoral work seemed useless now. *What's so grand,* he wondered, *about theoretical physics?* What could he do that was more concrete? Exhausted, he fell into a deep sleep lulled by the steady thrum of plane's engines.

The Atom offers its condolences

Gee, Reese I'm sorry about Rosa. She was the first to die from the Trinity test, but she may be one of the lucky ones—a quick kill—better than a long agonizing death. As I see it, a lot of people downwind had no idea they were in harm's way. Even I didn't know how toxic my radioactivity was, a few genetic mutations here and there. It was just a small bomb. I didn't think it would hurt anyone—much. Oh well, a little miscalculation here and there is to be expected, but someone really should have warned the ranchers in the area. Of course, how could you have known? It's new to me, so how could naïve scientists know? Of course, would it have mattered? Wouldn't you have gone ahead anyhow? The object was to end the war as quickly as possible. Collateral damage? Ah, such a useful phrase.

* * *

When Reese wakened, his first thought struck with stunning clarity. With so little known about the effects of radiation on humans, surely there would be a need for medical research in the field. He would finish his doctorate and go on to medical school.

* * *

Reese heard his mother's muffled gasp when he told his mother over the phone that his fiancée had died. When he deplaned at the San Francisco airport, they were there to pick him up.

Donna hugged him tightly. "I'm so sorry, Reese." Knowing she wasn't given to emotion, Reese was surprised to see tears in her eyes, but yielded to her embrace.

The moment was broken when his dad put an arm around his shoulders. "Sorry, son."

While they waited at baggage claim, Reese blurted out, "Dad, Mom, I've made a decision. I am going to attend medical school after I finish my doctorate. I want to do research on the effects of nuclear fallout on people. I think Rosa died from exposure to radioactivity from the bomb test."

"Son, have you thought this through? Is this a knee-jerk reaction to what happened to her?" his dad asked.

"Possibly, but what if it is?"

Donna gasped at the hard edge of Reese's voice.

He shrugged. It didn't matter. They wouldn't dissuade him. They couldn't possibly understand the demons that haunted him now, but he softened his tone and took a tack he knew would help them understand. "It's a new field," he said, "and I think it will soon be one of the most important."

* * *

Like a man possessed, Reese completed his doctorate in record time, then spent the next four years in medical school, followed by his residency at L.A. County Hospital.

One night during his residency, after many drinks at a local bar, his colleague Lisa Menninger propositioned him, making it clear that she had no interest in marriage, children or the whole housewife scene. Perhaps it was the alcohol, perhaps it was that he hadn't even dated since Rosa's death. Reese didn't stop to analyze it.

Lisa's dark good looks, perky nose, and brown eyes reminded him of Rosa, but that was where the resemblance ended. She was worldly, travelled, and educated. Earthy, outgoing, and sure of herself, Lisa boosted Reese's spirits and his confidence. She had a voluptuous body that she used skillfully and without a hint of shyness.

It wasn't a love affair. In fact, he still loved Rosa, even though she had been dead for some time, but he would have married Lisa if she had wanted to—after all it was the right thing to do if you'd slept with a woman. In truth, what they'd had was sex, pure and simple. He enjoyed it and Lisa jokingly

56

referred to it as research. Neither looked back with regret when the affair ended at the conclusion of Lisa's residency.

* * *

At the time Reese finished his training, he discovered that Enrico Fermi was doing research using radioactive isotopes in medicine. Fascinated at the prospect of working on Fermi's project at Oak Ridge Laboratories, Reese applied for a position there. After he received his security clearance, he was notified that he'd been accepted. He packed his bag and flew via Army plane to Tennessee and his new job.

The laboratories were scattered, built between rolling hills, intended to protect them from each other in the event of a nuclear accident.

"No more nuclear weapons development," he vowed.

Oak Ridge still bore signs left over from WWII—signs that warned about secrecy, such as, "Loose Lips Sink Ships," and "Loose Talk Helps Our Enemy." Chain link fences surrounded the area. Everyone had to come and go via seven gates, and personnel needed a security clearance to enter.

After orientation, Reese was given a film badge to detect exposure to radioactivity. *Too bad we didn't have these at Los Alamos. It may have saved scientists' lives.* In the labs at Los Alamos, they were naïve to the dangers of handling materials like uranium and plutonium.

Content to hide out behind closed doors in his laboratory, Reese searched for the link between radioactive fallout and cancer, and hoped he was taking a first step to finding a cure. He spent countless hours with his eye pressed to a microscope, searching, always searching for answers. Answers to why Rosa died so young. Was it the fallout? He believed it was and still thought it was his fault that her life had been cut short because he helped build the bomb.

Chapter Thirteen
1950
Washington DC
The Oval Office at the Whitehouse

President Harry Truman looked up from the papers he'd been reading and closed the file. Checking the time, he punched the button on the intercom. "Send the gentlemen in." *Not bad, I'm only five minutes behind schedule.*

As the door opened, Truman stood, walked around his desk, and greeted three men dressed in dark suits and conservative ties. He shook their hands as they filed in and sat in the ornate velvet chairs. He was meeting with the head of the Atomic Energy Commission, David Landon; the Secretary of Defense, Bill Jackson; and the Secretary of State, George Hampton.

Returning to his desk, Truman said, "I've read the reports on the proposed nuclear testing, and I have some questions. Why the Nevada Desert?" he asked. "I thought we were planning the test at the Pacific Proving Ground in the Marshall Islands. What is the name of that atoll? Enewetok?"

"Yes," Jackson responded. "We want to scrap the Enewetok plan. Since we're in a war in Korea, we think it's unwise to test in the Pacific. As for testing in Nevada, there isn't much out there—very little population—mostly snakes, coyotes, some Indians and a few Mormons. The test sites near Area 51 will be set up to blow the radioactive fallout away from the West Coast with its larger population."

"I've heard the stuff from that mushroom cloud can be deadly. Maybe we can get rid of a few of those polygamists." A deep chuckle rumbled up from Hampton's ample stomach.

Landon averted his face and stifled a look of disgust. He held little regard for the obese politician. "The prevailing winds will carry most of the radioactive fallout across the lower half of Utah, maybe as far north as Sevier County. Since the Mormon population is probably among the healthiest in the country, it will make an interesting study in the effects of exposure to low level radioactivity."

"Do we need that?" the president asked. "I thought Hiroshima and Nagasaki provided us with enough information." He reached across his desk and picked up a fancy wooden box. Opening it, he said, "Cigar anyone?"

"We don't have any studies on the downwind effects of the fallout from those bombs, and we don't know how our relationship with the Japanese will be in years to come. It's better to have studies here in the good old U. S. of A.," Jackson said as he selected a cigar.

Landon backed him up, adding, "It would be better if we had our own research to draw from. We know about radiation burns and what has happened to the Japanese who were injured from the bomb, but we may never know the long-term effect of radioactivity from the Japanese. However, we've set the safety limit at 3.9 rads of radioactive exposure. That isn't enough to harm anyone." Landon leaned forward as he spoke, to add emphasis to his words. "The Mormons don't drink or smoke. Most of them don't even drink coffee or Coke—bound to be the healthiest people in America. They can withstand a little fallout if they are exposed."

President Truman pulled hard on his Cuban cigar and waved away the cloud of blue smoke as he exhaled. "I know how important these tests are for the security of our country, but I need to think about this. I don't want to use our people as human guinea pigs. When do you propose testing the bombs?"

"We'll be ready within two or three weeks of getting the go ahead," said Landon.

"Thanks gentlemen. I'll get back to you with my decision."

While Truman pondered, the atom was busy whispering in his ear.

* * *

Think of the power. That's what politicians want, isn't it? The United States will be the most powerful nation on earth once you've fully developed my finest assets—nuclear submarines and warheads on missiles, things you've never dreamed of. Together we can control the planet. Think of industry. There'll be a money boom with all the weapons developed, and labs devising new ways to create weapons of mass destruction. You'll be ultra-popular with the boost to the economy. Don't forget, the Russians have the technology also. Their "First Lightning" test was successful—about the same size as the Trinity test. Have you considered that you may need bombs to end the war in North Korea? Go for it, Harry. Sign that bill. We'll have a blast.

* * *

In early January of 1951, President Truman approved Operation Ranger, the first series of atomic bomb tests in Nevada.

* * *

Haunted by the massive human deaths in Japan and his role in building the atomic bomb, Oppenheimer pleaded with the Atomic Energy Commission not to test more bombs. "But now that that the world is at peace, we don't need the bombs anymore," he said. He was on the advisory board to the Atomic Energy Commission. He met with David Landon, head of the AEC. "It was my understanding that once we ended WWII, we wouldn't pursue anymore bomb testing." Oppie pulled his pipe from his pocket and said, "May I smoke?"

Landon nodded his consent. "Ah, my friend," Landon said as he bent forward and rested his elbows on the oversized mahogany desk, "Things change. You aren't taking into account the Cold War with Russia. We are in a race with them to develop even more nuclear weapons. These weapons are our power. It will keep the Communists at bay—perhaps neutralize the threat from them completely." He reached for a cigarette and lit it.

Oppie tamped tobacco into the bowl of his pipe as he searched the face of the man across the desk. "I understand, however, we've seen what radiation did to the Japanese. It's just too dangerous to test in Nevada. The prevailing winds will go right across Southern Utah. The population will be at risk, like so many people in Japan that weren't even in the areas of Hiroshima and Nagasaki." Oppenheimer stood and paced as he took deep puffs on his pipe. He'd been having this argument since he'd seen the films of the horrors the Japanese people endured. His conscience burned with guilt for being the one who was most responsible. He'd been trying to stop further development of nuclear weapons since then.

"Suppose, for a moment, that the Russians developed a bomb with the capacity to reach the United States and our citizens were the victims." Landon steepled his hands in front of his face and raised his eyebrows in inquiry. "Do

60

you think the Russians will have the same compassion for our people that you have for the Japanese?"

Oppenheimer didn't answer right away. He stopped pacing and took a couple more pulls on his pipe while he weighed his response. "There is so much to consider. The enriching of plutonium at the Hanford Plant is polluting the Columbia River." Another puff. "We know Teller's hydrogen bomb totally destroyed Elugelab Island. That test and the ones we've done on Bikini Atoll made the ocean radioactive for miles. We don't know if the sea life will ever recover in those areas. Moreover, we don't know what to do with nuclear waste."

"That's why General Eisenhower has agreed to use Area 51, which includes Yucca Flats and Frenchmen's Flats in Nevada. This is the old Groom Lake lakebed. There's nothing for 50 miles in either direction." Landon stubbed out his cigarette in a crystal ashtray.

"Two hundred miles would be better, but even that distance won't stop the wind from carrying radioactive fallout for hundreds of miles in a northeasterly direction. We aren't sure how far, and it doesn't end at building and testing the bombs. There's so much that hasn't been considered." Oppie snuffed out his pipe and shoved it in his pocket. "Science hasn't caught up with the impact of the use of nuclear."

The atom speaks to Oppenheimer

Why are you so against me? This is a losing battle for you. The warriors always win—the warriors and the money. Reason and common sense don't prevail when fear and greed enter the picture. As Hermann Goering said, "Keep the people in fear and then tell them you'll protect them and they'll do your bidding." Isn't that what's at play here? My buddies Edward Teller and Stanislaw Ulam are hard at work building bigger and more powerful hydrogen bombs. You won't be able to stop them. My power is limitless. The bombs will need testing. Never mind that they decimated an entire Pacific Island and wiped out the fish and sea creatures. As long as there's money in it and the warriors are in power, which may be forever, you won't have a chance of stopping the development of nuclear weapons.

Landon's voice interrupted Oppie's thoughts. "You do realize I can't do anything now that the president has signed the order to go ahead with the testing?" he said. "If the Russky's hadn't tested a nuclear bomb, things may have played out differently. But now, I don't see that he will rescind the order."

"You have his ear," Oppie pleaded. "Please talk to him and tell him it will endanger the population not just of Utah, but parts of Nevada and Arizona, even Idaho may be at risk." Oppenheimer worried that his worst fears would be realized if both Russia and the United States attacked each other with nuclear weapons. It would mean the annihilation of life on planet Earth. "Try to persuade him to give us time to do impact research before any more testing begins."

Landon said, "I'll see what I can do."

But he didn't. The bomb testing proceeded as planned.

* * *

Oppie, Oppie, will you never learn?

The warriors will defend their weapons, even if it means they kill themselves along with their enemies. Everyone has underestimated me, just as you did. Sadly, I must move on, so I'm saying goodbye. As advisory head of the Atomic Energy Commission, you've been able to suppress the proliferation of atomic weapons, but the winds of change have gone against you. Now, I'll be Edward Teller's buddy. You lost in your attempt to thwart Teller building his super bomb, but he got the go ahead from President Truman. When you said that the hydrogen bomb was evil, you were called on that comment. Your response was, "And you think it's loveable?" Well, I happen to think I'm loveable.

It's been a good time, but you've been opposing me for years. Oh, I'm not ungrateful—you did give me my debut at White Sands. I even impressed myself, but now I must bid you adieu. You turned against me. Darn, how that hurt my feelings, but now I'm back on top and, with luck, more popular than ever.

Chapter Fourteen

They [nations] feel moreover compelled to prepare the most abominable means, in order not to be left behind in the general armaments race. Such procedure leads inevitable[y] to war, which, in turn, under today's conditions, spells universal destruction. (Excerpt from Albert Einstein's writing: On my participation in the Atomic Bomb Project)

President Harry S. Truman raised his head in response to a knock on the door of the oval office and called, "Come in."

His secretary opened the door and walked across the blue eagle crest rug. "David Landon to see you, sir." He turned to admit the head of the Atomic Energy Commission.

Truman rose and walked around his desk with hand extended. "David, good to see you."

"Mr. President."

A warm handshake then a pat on the shoulder intended to put Landon at ease. "I summoned you to talk about Oppenheimer. He's been sending a lot of letters with documentation detailing the hazards to our people from radioactive fallout. As head of the Atomic Energy Commission, I thought you'd be the best man to shed some light on this matter." Truman motioned toward a chair. "Oppenheimer's report also details unusual human experiments." Truman returned to his chair behind the desk. "What can you tell me about this?"

Landon's neck and ears reddened, but he crossed his legs and leaned back in his chair. "Oppenheimer has become increasingly vocal about stopping the atom bomb tests because of the effects of radioactive fallout and experimentation using nuclear materials. Frankly, he has become a thorn in my side."

"Does his position have validity? Is our population in danger? According to his report, we're conducting nuclear experimentation on people who aren't capable of giving consent. He further states we have fed school boys oatmeal containing radioactive substances. That, I can't condone." Truman leaned toward Landon, peering over his wire rimmed glasses as if by examining the man's eyes he might detect whether he was telling the truth.

Landon shifted uncomfortably in his chair. "There have been such experiments done. We felt it was crucial to the national security to know exactly the effects of strontium 90 and cesium."

"Oppenheimer's report claims that pregnant women have been injected with radioactive mixtures. Are you confirming this?"

"You are aware that Oppenheimer is under investigation by the McCarthy Committee for un-American Activities and his security clearance is in jeopardy." Landon grasped at a straw to discredit Oppenheimer's report. "We can't trust what he says. He's opposed to ongoing atom bomb testing. He thinks it's too great a risk for the safety of our people. We on the Commission feel we need all the power available to win the Cold War with Russia. Ongoing testing and experimentation are in the interest of our National Security."

Truman banged his fist on his desk. "National security be damned. If Oppenheimer's report is factual, I want all experimentation on humans stopped immediately or I'll be the thorn in your side."

From the look on Truman's face, Landon determined there was no room for debate or justification. He simply replied, "Yes, Mr. President. I'll take care of it right away."

"Before you go, there's one other thing. There's a young man named Reese Mayfield doing research at Oak Ridge. I hear he worked at Los Alamos and has a PhD in Theoretical Physics and is an MD. I want to meet him. Arrange for him to come to Washington. I want his opinions on the health issues surrounding radiation."

Chapter Fifteen
1953

Arriving home after visiting his parents in San Francisco over the Christmas holidays, Reese heard his phone jangling as he unlocked his apartment door. Rushing in, he kicked aside his suitcase and grabbed the receiver.

"Reese Mayfield? Gordon Dean here."

Reese knew who he was, the new head of the Atomic Energy Commission who replaced Langdon.

"We need you in Nevada."

"Yes, I have your letters," Reese said. "As I wrote to you twice, I must respectfully decline. I'm happy here at Oak Ridge."

The following week, he received a phone call from the White House.

"Invited" by the President himself—how could one refuse? *I should have expected this after my visit with Truman at the White House. Wonder what would happen if I turned down the President.*

Reese promised to give the offer his full consideration. He was still chewing on it a couple of weeks later when a letter arrived with a written offer of a salary he'd only dreamed of. Reluctant to give up his research, Reese didn't respond.

Four days later, Dean phoned wanting to know if he'd received the letter.

"Yes," he assured Dean and told him he had given it his full consideration. Reese breathed a heavy sigh. *The pressure's on.* He rationalized, as long as they were continuing atomic bomb testing where people and animals might be subjected to radiation exposure, he might be instrumental in keeping them safe.

The next day, during another phone call from the White House, he agreed to take the position at Yucca Flats Testing Labs on the condition he could finish the project he was working on.

Somewhat to his chagrin, he discovered he was one of the few in the U.S. who held doctoral degrees in Theoretical Physics and the new specialty, Nuclear Medicine. This made him—however unfortunate for his free will—a valuable asset for the U.S. government.

* * *

On March 1, 1953, Reese boarded a plane and flew to Las Vegas. When his plane touched down at McCarran Airport, he searched the crowd before almost running over an army corporal with a buzz cut holding up a cardboard sign with "Dr. Mayfield" scrawled in large cursive writing on it.

"Sir, I'm your driver," the young soldier said. "I'm Corporal Russell Cooper, I'll take you to Mercury."

After collecting Reese's luggage from baggage claim, they left the terminal. Corporal Cooper led the way to an olive drab military sedan. He opened the back door for his passenger. "I prefer to ride up front with you, if you don't mind."

"Of course, Dr. Mayfield."

His driver drove him toward the sun sinking in the west, coloring the barren landscape coral and pink. It was more than an hour later when they pulled up in front of a neat white house trailer without a smidge of landscaping.

"These are the temporary quarters assigned to you, Dr. Mayfield. With all the building going on, permanent housing may be available soon." He opened the door with a key, then dangled it over Reese's hand and dropped it.

Same old story, Reese thought.

Mercury was a hastily constructed community still in a building frenzy reminiscent of Los Alamos. The place was similarly isolated—it sat sixty-five miles northwest of Las Vegas, on the fringe of the Nevada Test Site, in an area once known as Jackass Flats. The secret Area 51 lay beyond that on Groom Lake, an ancient inland sea, now dry.

What am I doing in this godforsaken place? A pang of regret stabbed Reese. The rolling green hills of Tennessee and the Clinch River were a far cry from the desert that stretched endlessly before him.

Although the sun was down, construction hadn't slowed for the day. Bulldozers stirred up dirt in the clear, dry desert air in preparation for erecting housing and administrative buildings that would replace temporary quarters. In another area, concrete foundations promised permanent buildings.

66

Currently, civilian and administrative personnel lived in mobile structures like the one assigned to Reese.

Reese thought he'd put makeshift living behind him when he left Los Alamos. Sure, his position and credentials afforded him quarters with a private bath and he didn't have a roommate, but it couldn't begin to match his neat little one-bedroom apartment in Tennessee. *Well, it is what it is.*

The corporal put Reese's bags in the small living room. "Is there anything more I can do for you, sir?"

Yeah. You can zap me back to New Year's and not let me be persuaded to take this job. But, he said, "No," and thanked the driver.

"I'll be here at 0700 tomorrow to pick you up and take you to the laboratory." He stepped back and saluted.

Reese offered his hand and Cooper shook it. "Thanks for the ride. See you in the morning."

Reese glanced at the brown sofa and matching overstuffed chair before peering into the fully-equipped kitchen with a tiny yellow Formica-topped chrome table and matching chairs. He opened the fridge to see if there was any food. Nothing. "Good thing I ate on the plane." He picked up his suitcase and strolled into the bedroom. Dropping the bag, he sat on the bed and gave it a bounce. He wrinkled his nose at a wisp of dust spiraling up. Sheets and blankets were piled at the foot of the thin mattress. "I'll give that a good shake before I make it up."

* * *

The next morning, Reese stepped into the building that housed the laboratory. A desk, typewriter, telephone, filing cabinets, a water cooler—the usual things one would expect, filled the outer office. It even came with a secretary who was in the middle of dropping papers into a file. "Good morning," he said

The uniformed WAC turned toward him and said, "Good morning, you must be Dr. Mayfield." She crossed the linoleum space between them in three strides holding out her hand. "I'm Sergeant Angela Pope."

In her regulation two-inch high oxfords, she stood eye to eye with Reese. Thin and wiry, she wore starched khaki slacks and a short-sleeved shirt bearing three stripes. A firm handshake and the level gaze of her hazel eyes made him think, *This is a no-nonsense lady.*

67

"Welcome. Since you arrived last night, I thought you wouldn't have a bite to eat in your new home so I stopped by the PX and got donuts. There's coffee, too," Angela said as she reached for a coffee mug and filled it.

"You must be a mind reader. I'm starving." Reese snagged a donut.

"They're all for you. I ate at the base before I came. Cream and sugar?"

"Thank you. I take it black."

"As soon as you inspect the lab and settle in, I'll take you on a tour of the Test Site." Angela led the way. "I think you'll find everything you need here." Sunlight streaming through one of the two windows that flanked the entry door highlighted streaks of chestnut in her dark hair.

Reese grabbed another donut on the way.

Reese studied his new lab. *Nice, with the latest equipment.* "Sergeant Pope, are you also a lab assistant?" He wolfed down the second pastry.

"Yes. We'll be working closely, so please call me Angela. May I call you Reese? Or do you prefer Dr. Mayfield."

"Reese is fine." He was glad to have that out of the way.

"Let me know when you are ready to tour the site. We should go soon. Even in early spring, the sun can get hot."

"Give me a few minutes to put away my equipment and we can go."

Ten minutes later, Angela escorted him to a shelter housing a jeep. She tossed a briefcase in the back and got into the driver's side and started the engine. There was no question she was an in-charge lady. Reese scurried around to the passenger side. He was barely seated when she sped off leaving puffs of powdery dirt in her wake.

"They are preparing for another test in a couple of weeks if conditions are right. I think you'll be surprised at what's out there. It'll take us about half an hour before we see the first buildings."

"Buildings?"

"They've built a mock city we call Doomtown. I'll show you around when we get there."

Reese propped his foot on the side of the jeep to steady himself against the bumps in the dirt road. "Pope isn't a common name. I was at Los Alamos with a family named Pope, Joseph and Ann Pope."

"Joe's my cousin."

"We arrived at Los Alamos at the same time. We met in Santa Fe and rode up to the Hill together. I haven't seen them since I left. Katherine was just a toddler then."

"She's nine now. I see them about once a year when I go to Chicago to visit family."

"He's back with Argonne Labs?"

"Yes," Angela said before pointing to the artificial village. "Here are the first outbuildings of Doomtown. We won't stop here. We'll go on to the ones that are closer to the blast site and tour them."

Reese looked beyond the buildings at the dry lake bed pock marked with craters from prior tests. Beyond that, the desert was denuded of vegetation from the bomb blasts and fierce winds that accompanied them. In the distance, an endless panorama with spots of sagebrush, Yucca plants, and mesquite rose and intermingled with pale shades of green on the hillsides before fading into distant blue mountains.

"They've been doing a lot of testing at this site? How hot is the dirt here?" Reese wasn't sure he wanted to spend a lot of time tramping around in radioactive dirt.

"Not as bad as one would expect. They've been testing in areas 5 and 11 located in Frenchmen's Flat while they've been building Doomtown and other structures. There's a Geiger counter in back if you want to take a reading."

Should I or shouldn't I? Maybe ignorance is bliss. "Yes, I think I will. I'll want the readings for my research."

"I thought you might. I brought along something to record them."

Lucky for me, she's efficient to a fault.

Buildings loomed around them as Angela pulled up in front of what appeared to be a house. "Here we are." She reached for a steno pad and pencil from her briefcase.

"This is a good place to take a reading." She nodded toward the Geiger counter. "When things cool off enough after the test, you can come back to this same location and take another reading. That is if you can recognize the place. There probably won't be anything left standing. Of course, that depends on the kilotons of the bomb. I haven't been given that information yet."

As Reese listened to the clicking of the Geiger counter, he cocked his head. He heard hammering and looked around to see where it was coming from.

"Looks like they're still building." Angela pointed out a partially constructed two-story structure. "They seem to have a lot of work ahead of them."

Reese recited the readings from several places for Angela to record. Some were much higher than others—hot spots—to be expected after so much testing in the area. He glanced at the carpenters hammering nails.

"Angela, I'd like to be able to examine those men to see if they are getting too much radioactivity. Will you make those arrangements?"

Reese stood in front of a small house with a fully clothed manikin posed on his knees in newly laid sod with a gardening tool in hand as though he was going to weed a bed of petunias. He noted that someone had gone to the trouble to plant a petunia bed. *I'll be curious to see how the petunias fare.* Angela led the way inside where the mother manikin sat in a chair with her three doll-like children on the floor playing with toys.

"This is to see how an ordinary house and its occupants will withstand an A-bomb explosion a mile away. Doomtown is built with different construction materials from wood and metal to concrete to see which will better protect people inside."

As Reese and Angela walked through the streets of Doomtown, they passed manikins as pedestrians and the usual people one would see on the streets of any downtown USA. They passed two-story buildings and mock places of business—a barber shop, a drugstore.

"Eerie, isn't it."

Reese nodded, again wondering what he was thinking when he accepted this position. Then he recalled the pressure from the White House and shrugged away his regrets.

Angela turned back toward the jeep. "Next is something that is hard for me to see." She drove closer to the tower that housed the bomb. Chained to stakes in the ground were dogs, Beagles. They had food and water, but their fate was certain. Some had wooden doghouses, some had shelter for shade, but neither of those offered much protection.

"This *is* hard to see." Even though, in medical school, he'd dissected animals and even had his own cadaver, Reese thought of that as necessary. It hadn't prepared him for the deliberate destruction of helpless animals. He recalled the films of Hiroshima and Nagasaki he'd seen after the end of WWII. It wasn't just the people, but their pets and livestock that were incinerated, or worse, suffered horrible burns. He couldn't see this as necessary—not in such volumes. *Why so many?*

"They shouldn't have been brought here so soon," Angela said. "Even with food and water, this place is beyond bleak. They were better off at the kennels where they were raised." She didn't stop the jeep, but drove by the Beagles which set up an awful racket barking and howling. "It isn't just the dogs, there will be pigs, goats, sheep, cattle, horses, rats, birds—all at varying distances from ground zero. Most of them haven't been brought in yet, but they will be. There will also be some animals that call this part of the desert home. Hopefully they'll head up the hill, but since the test is in the early morning when it is cool, coyotes may be curious and come to look. There are wild donkeys around, too, and it's also the time when the birds start waking up. They may fly over the test site."

At the end of Doomtown, she made a U-turn. "This isn't even the worst of it. For this test they'll be positioning soldiers in trenches—some two miles away, some three miles away and more four miles from the blast."

Reese drew his eyebrows together.

The worried expression didn't go unnoticed by Angela. "Oh, and there will be a lot of press and some dignitaries from D.C. I think I've shown you enough. Maybe I've said too much."

"No, not at all, I need to know what I'm dealing with." Reese thought she would be on thin ice with someone who was more militant. "You've been candid. Do you disapprove of the testing?"

"I question whether we need so many. Do you want to take more readings?"

"One more here, then I'll be ready to go."

"It'll be noon when we get back. We'll grab some lunch at the mess hall at Base Camp Mercury. I've arranged for you to have a jeep. We need to go over to the motor pool at Nellis Air Force Base to pick it up. It's just over sixty

71

miles from here, so it will take us a couple of hours, plus the time to do the paperwork."

Reese was relieved to know he'd have the freedom of a personal vehicle.

* * *

The next day, Angela handed him files to study as part of his orientation. He had been well aware of Able, code name for the bomb tested at Bikini Atoll in 1946, and subsequent tests in the Pacific. What he hadn't kept up with was the Ranger series of five tests—bombs dropped from airplanes over Nevada's Frenchman Flat in 1951.

Then his eyes widened. There were even more: Greenhouse, five tests; Buster-Jangle, seven tests, all in 1951. In 1952, Tumbler-Snapper, eight tests, and then Ivy, two tests including "Mike," the first multi-megaton thermonuclear weapon.

A low whistle emitted from Reese's lips. *I'm surprised everyone here isn't glowing in the dark.* Looks like Edward Teller finally got his way.

Fifty miles east of San Francisco, Teller and Earnest Lawrence founded a branch of the University of California Radiation Laboratory for the sole purpose of developing bigger and more destructive bombs. Teller, Lawrence and their team worked in competition with Los Alamos scientists. The detonation of the thermonuclear bomb, Mike, earned Teller the label, "father of the hydrogen bomb."

His bomb is as explosive and volatile and he is, Reese thought. *Scary? Scary isn't a strong enough word, perhaps terrifying, apocalyptic.*

* * *

Three days later, Reese was still reading the files Angela had given him. In one of them labeled Tumbler-Snapper 1952, he came across some letters with the United States Army letterhead at the top. Attached were two reports on each of the letters. He wondered why these were in the files. As he perused the reports, he noticed that two separate reports were stamped with the same file number, only one was dated a day later. He compared the reports. One gave the number of roentgens of test Shot Charlie and the amount of radioactive ash that fell on St. George and areas farther north in Utah. The second report said the number of roentgens at St. George was negligible and there was no measurable ash. There were also two reports on Shot Dog with the same discrepancies and identical file numbers. A wave of anger washed over Reese. *The original reports have been cleansed.*

It dawned on Reese that he wasn't supposed to see these files. *The AEC is hiding the dangers, covering up.* A copy of another letter was tucked in between other documents. It was a letter from the Nevada Test Site manager to the head of the AEC in Washington. It read: "Please be advised that the reports from Charlie have been altered per your instructions."

Further into the files, Reese found a letter stamped Top Secret. His eyes widened when he read instructions not to inform communities downwind of the tests of the dangers of radioactive fallout. The public wasn't to know they were getting any more radiation than they get from sunshine. Reese's gut turned sour. He left his lab and walked into the outer office where his assistant was busy typing, "Angela, have you seen these?" He handed her the papers.

Angela's eyes widened when as she read them. "Where did you get these?"

"They were in some of the files you left for me to read."

"These must have been misfiled by someone. We aren't supposed to have them."

"What will we do?"

"Let me think about it for a while." She started to put the papers in a drawer in her desk.

"Here, let me have them. I'll put them back where I found them."

Reese had no intention of putting them back in the files. Instead he put them in his briefcase. He wanted to hang onto them—for what he didn't know—yet.

Chapter Sixteen
Duck and Cover

Reese watched a convoy of trucks through binoculars from his vantage point on Nob Hill, the designated viewing area for dignitaries and reporters. A TV cameraman jostled his elbow, distorting his view of a convoy of army trucks transporting soldiers toward ground zero. Adjusting his binoculars again, he watched where the trucks deposited the men. *What the hell are they thinking? Why is the AEC allowing those men so close? All of them will be subject to radioactive poisoning from fallout. The military either isn't properly informed about the risk, or they think the men are expendable.* Reese shook his head to clear away that horrible thought.

Lowering his binoculars, he elbowed through the growing crowd as he made his way down the hill. Political representatives jockeyed for positions on bleachers vying for the best view of the first bomb test of 1953, code named Annie. Reese stepped onto the lower tier of the bleachers and looked through his binoculars again to see soldiers spill out of trucks and grab shovels. He spotted a landmark to guide him to their location. Reese wanted to see what the military was up to.

On the way to his jeep, he snagged a cup of coffee from the Civil Defense volunteers who had set up tables to distribute beverages and blankets to help ward off the chill in the cool pre-dawn March morning. Hopping into the vehicle, he sped off in the direction of the convoy.

* * *

Two hundred men of B Company stationed at Dugway Proving Ground in Utah had been trucked to Yucca Flats, Nevada. They had been chosen to watch an atomic bomb explosion up close. Most considered it an honor. Starting six miles from the blast site, they dug the first trench. Fifty yards behind that, they dug another trench. Back another fifty yards, a third trench.

"Dig those trenches at least six feet deep," a sergeant bellowed. "You men'll wanna hunker down when that bomb goes off."

Reese pulled his jeep up next to the sergeant. "Why are you stationing men this close to the bomb site?"

"Those are my orders."

"This isn't a safe distance."

"Mister. I take orders. I don't make them." The sergeant stomped off to another trench.

"Damn the stupidity." Reese hit the gas pedal hard, spun out and headed back to the safety of the observation tower.

This current series of tests, code named Upshot-Knothole, designed to test weapons delivery systems, was projected to measure blast and radiation exposure. The nuclear bomb would be shot from cannons seven miles from the target—expected detonation altitude approximately five-hundred feet, if all went as planned.

Interest in the tests wasn't only expressed by the scientific community, the ever-involved military had a huge presence. Members of Civil Defense also wanted to experience an explosion first-hand and scrutinize data from the test.

Impotent to stop what had been set in motion, Reese determined to do his job and help as many of those affected as possible. He was sure the soldiers in the closest trenches would be sick. Animals staked out nearest the blast site would be vaporized instantly.

Damn, I didn't know what I was getting into. I should have held my ground and stayed at Oak Ridge. This is a disaster. His thoughts raced, grappling with possible outcomes.

* * *

The Atom Watches

Another bomb test—this one bigger and better. It won't make any difference how deep they make those trenches. They'll get the benefit of my finest dose of radioactive fallout. Hey, you in the uniforms. Your efforts are fruitless. Nothing will protect you from my blast.

* * *

The men were oblivious to the Atom. Despite the cool desert night, sweat dripped off their faces. In a frenzy of effort, shovels full of dirt flew over the tops of the trenches. The sergeant marched from trench to trench, holding one arm high and the other one low, indicating that he wanted the trenches deeper. The men had been digging all night and were eager to finish. The test was scheduled for sunrise.

* * *

Keep digging boys – but you can dig half way to China and you won't be protected from my radiation. I see the glitter of anticipation in your eyes. Happy to be a part of this history making explosion? Be warned, there will be a price.

* * *

"I can't wait to see that mushroom cloud," Private Pat Conklin said to his buddy Bob Culpepper.

"Okay, men. All of you, into the trenches," barked the Sergeant. "She's ready to go in about three minutes."

Men scrambled to find safe positions. Conklin and Culpepper were in the last trench.

"Wish we'd been assigned to the first trench," Conklin said putting on the dark glasses they'd been issued.

"Not me." Culpepper crouched down as deep into the dugout channel as he could and curled his arms over his GI helmet.

Soldiers sank down to sit in the bottom of the six-foot-deep trenches. As the moment approached, they covered their eyes with dark sunglasses and donned their helmets. When the countdown started, they turned their backs toward the blast site wrapping their arms over their heads.

Countdown—3, 2, 1. A blinding flash. The earth shuddered. A deafening blast.

Conklin braced his arms on the edge of the trench and hiked himself up for a better view. He looked into the heart of the cloud before a wall of rushing air knocked him back.

The bomb's signature mushroom-shaped cloud blossomed in the early morning sky. And the colors, brilliant—red, orange, blue, green, black—every color—expanding, growing, rising, fading, followed by ash—sparkling ash peppered down on the men—deadly ash.

"Unbelievable," Conklin whispered. "That oughta stop them commies," he said to Culpepper, who still covered his head with his arms.

"Let me know when it's safe to look," Culpepper muttered.

The cloud grew higher and wider. It was a calm day and the explosion formed a perfect stem with a puffy white cap.

Sparkling fallout turned to white ash. "I think it's okay to look now," Conklin said.

"What the hell is this stuff all over my arms?" Culpepper shook the ash off and glanced up. "Holy shit. I'm glad I didn't look sooner." The cap of the mushroom expanded. He stared up into the red and yellow heart of the cloud. "It looks like doomsday. Are we going to survive this?"

"Hey, man, we already did."

Conklin looked up when he heard the roar of airplane engines. A "V" formation of aircraft headed toward the cloud. "They're flying right into it," he shouted.

Culpepper wagged his head back and forth in disbelief. "Crazy bastards. You wouldn't catch me doing that."

A breeze picked up and pulled the cloud apart and carried it along leaving red stringers behind. Rising higher into the atmosphere, winds aloft carried the radioactive cloud over Utah and continued in a northeasterly direction, strewing ash in its path.

"Hey, Conklin. Looks like you got singed." Culpepper pointed at red spots on his friend's face.

"That's what I get for being nosy - should have kept my head down." Conklin touched his face gingerly. "Ouch. How bad does it look?"

"Pretty nasty, you'd better check with a medic."

Six hours after the blast, Conklin stood second in a line of a dozen soldiers. He clasped his arms around his body to still the shivering. Beads of sweat trickled over his red and blistered forehead. A nurse handed him an emesis basin when he said, "I'm going to throw up."

"Here, sit down." She pointed to a chair as she shook down a thermometer to take his temperature.

When Reese turned his attention to Conklin, the nurse said, "He has a fever of 103.1 and is nauseated." At that moment, he vomited. When Conklin's nausea passed, Reese examined the blisters formed from radiation burns. "That must be painful," he said. "We are going to put you in sick bay until your fever and vomiting subside." Conklin's eyes rolled back and he slid off the chair, unconscious.

* * *

Ah, my finest and most powerful show to date, bragged the Atom. Tsk, tsk. He didn't observe the rule of "duck and cover"—not that it will do most of these men any good. One of the side effects of my fallout is cancer, if not soon, then later. He does have quite a sunburn, or should I say a blast burn.

* * *

The Atomic Energy Commission set an arbitrary "no closer than seven miles," however, the Department of Defense wanted more realism to duplicate wartime conditions. They negotiated a distance of 3.7 miles for subsequent tests despite Reese's, other scientists and doctor's warnings about the health hazards of being near ground zero.

In its zeal to simulate a realistic military situation, the Department of Defense had troops moved to as near as 1.5 miles during some of the tests. Then, after the blast, advance even closer into intense heat and heavy fallout. Some were in trenches, some were not and they didn't wear protective clothing.

To convince the public of the safety of atomic bombs, and as a deterrent to prolonged wars, maximum news coverage was given these troop maneuvers.

Soldiers who started vomiting within an hour of exposure were immediately confined to the infirmary. Most with burned faces were treated and released.

Reese asked several soldiers, "Weren't you instructed to stay down?"

The reply was always a version of, "Yes, but I couldn't resist looking. How many times does one see such a sight?"

Looking into the heart of a nuclear cloud bore great costs. Not being able to resist seeing such a sight might result in cataracts, severe radiation burns, possibly enough inhalation of gamma rays to cause cancer, and a myriad of other dangers. He feared the soldiers' commanding officers weren't sufficiently briefed to warn their men of the downside of chancing a *look*.

No point in berating the men. It was much too late for that; however, he would talk to their commanding officers.

Ten years later, Private Pat Conklin succumbed to cancer so wide spread that the doctors didn't know how or where to treat. He died at twenty-nine.

78

Chapter Seventeen
The Mines

Early the morning after the Annie bomb test, Reese headed off to a tungsten mine on the slopes of Bald Mountain. Bride's Mine was only forty miles from the blast. He wanted to check on the people who owned and worked the mine.

On his way to the mine, he passed Papoose Lake. A large bird swooped right in front of Reese's jeep, a vulture. *Wonder what he's after.* Reese slowed, then stopped. He picked up his ever-present binoculars and followed the flight of the vulture. The lake came into focus as the bird landed. *There's a carcass down there.* Reese pressed on the gas, veered off the road, bumping over rocks, sagebrush and uneven ground to get near. The vulture eyed him, but didn't take flight. He was busy tearing at the hide of a gray-brown burro. Other small creatures lay dead around the banks of the pond, birds, rodents. A faint odor of decay wafted on the morning air.

There's something wrong with the water. That vulture might not live too long after feeding on the burro's flesh.

Reese returned to his jeep to get his camera and lab supplies. He wanted samples of the lake's water, some dirt from the shore and, if he could get past the determined vulture, a bit of meat from the dead burro.

The vulture didn't want to abandon his meal and flapped his wings to scare Reese off and protect his breakfast, but gave up and flew several feet away to watch and worry. Far enough away for Reese to carve off a sample of flesh and to take a photo of the unfortunate burro.

As soon as Reese walked away, the vulture flew back and resumed eating.

I'll bet this water is radioactive. Reese pulled on rubber gloves and gathered his sample bag from the jeep. He added a dead bird and a field mouse to his samples and stashed the bag in the jeep before picking up his Geiger counter. Disturbing the feasting vulture again, he ran the Geiger counter over the burro. The needle jumped past the highest setting.

This must be a regular watering hole for the area wildlife. I wonder how much water an animal the size of a burro would have to drink to kill it. Did it die from the last blast, or is it cumulative?

Reese wondered if the lab tests would answer that question as he started the jeep to continue on to his destination.

As the jeep chugged up the sage dotted mountainside, Reese became aware of how much he missed the green rolling hills of Tennessee, his home for the past five years, and didn't think he could ever appreciate Nevada's desert landscapes, but they started to grow on him. First, it was the skies that went on forever. Almost always a bright cerulean blue with occasional clouds, then it was the subtle nuances of color. It reminded him of New Mexico with its bluer than blue skies and panoramas where he could see for miles—so unlike the mist and fog of his native San Francisco.

Reese shifted the WWII surplus jeep down into second gear as it labored up Bald Mountain. He pulled over, stopped, and stepped out to look back over Area 51 and beyond at craters made by various atomic bomb tests, some dropped from airplanes, and some that had been mounted on hundred-foot tall towers. There were even some detonated that had been suspended from balloons tethered to towers. He hated the devastation created by the bombs. Even in this desolate area, it seemed to violate nature's beauty.

Spring showers encouraged wild flowers and fresh shoots of grass to blanket the mountainsides. He drew in a deep breath of clean morning air. Then he frowned. He didn't want to play a role in developing and testing bombs. He remembered rationalizing his reasons for becoming part of the Nevada Test Site team.

Erroneous thinking. He chastised himself. *But, on the other hand, maybe I can help the people. That's why I'm here.* That bit of thinking resolved, he climbed back into the Jeep and continued on his way. The old Jeep complained until it crested the steep rise of the foothill. Reese shifted into high gear when the road flattened and straightened. Still, he didn't speed up, the drive was too pretty. He relaxed and leaned back. He thought about what he could say to the Stevens at Bride's Mine, his destination today, to convince them to leave the mine until the bomb tests concluded.

Reese was jerked out of his thoughts when he saw a dead antelope and farther up a big horn sheep with its head hanging over a rocky outcrop. It caused him to worry more about the miners.

When he arrived, the owners of the mine seemed to be all right. Their good fortune was they had been inside during the previous day's blast, which occurred before dawn at 5 a.m.

Don Stevens invited him into their cabin.

"Hot cocoa?" Mrs. Stevens offered.

The offer surprised Reese. He hadn't had cocoa since he was a child. "Yes, thank you."

"I made biscuits this morning and there's homemade apricot jam."

"This is an unexpected treat," Reese said and helped himself to a biscuit.

Mrs. Stevens passed the butter and jam. She was a good cook and, from the looks of her broad smile, one of her joys in life was feeding the men around her.

Reese quizzed the Stevens about the usual symptoms of radiation sickness, headache, nausea and vomiting.

"May I check your horses?" he asked the mine owner after looking the humans over.

Stevens took him to the corral. The horses were skittish.

"They've been nervous these past coupla years since the bomb tests started."

Reese loved horses and reached out to stroke the mare's cheek. She shied away. "Shh, girl," he cooed to her. Figuring he might be around horses at the mine, he'd made certain to put a few sugar lumps in his pocket. He held one near her muzzle and made a friend. One more and she was calm enough that he could run his hands along her sides. He frowned. There were burns on the horse's back. He moved from her to another horse that had even more burns. "When did this happen?"

"I noticed them this morning."

Reese sucked air through his teeth. *Beta burns.* "Is there any way you can keep these horses under a shelter when the explosions go off?"

"So far we haven't known when that would be. We could put them in the mine until we can build a shed."

81

"I'll make sure someone notifies you so you'll know when to get them under cover. And for your own safety, stay indoors with your family, especially in the early mornings. The blasts are usually before seven."

When Reese got back to the lab, he phoned the head of the AEC and told him about the dead burro and wildlife and the burns on the horses at the mine.

"I recommend relocating the residents of Bride Mine and Lincoln Mine until the testing is over," Reese said.

"If we did that, the possible risks of the tests may become public. Then we'd end up having to answer a lot of questions, maybe cause a panic," Dean said. "We can't call negative attention our work. It may slow down our progress in the arms race.

"If the horses are at risk, so are the people," Reese pressed.

"Send me a report of your findings and recommendations and I'll discuss it with my staff." Reese wondered if Dean was truly aware of the horrendous effects of radioactive fallout, the beta burns, and cancer, but he questioned if he could change the AEC's position—never admit to a problem.

Reese hung up the phone, believing he'd made some headway toward warning people about the dangers and possibly relocating them, perhaps even stopping the bomb tests until further research had been done.

Far from it. From that day on, representatives from the Atomic Energy Commission visited Bride's Mine and Lincoln Mine before each test. The charming and personable AEC men continually reassured Stevens and his men that the burns on the horses were harmless, just a little hot ash from the blasts. They said the roentgens, or rads for short, which were measurements of gamma rays, were well within the limits for humans and animals—3.9.

Reese knew from experience, burns like that didn't happen unless the rads were significantly higher. The AEC didn't respond to his report, and no further action was taken. When he tried to find out what had happened to his report, he got stonewalled.

I wonder why they brought me to Nevada if it wasn't to protect the people. Why aren't they paying attention to my phone calls and reports. I feel like I'm treading water and not making any progress. How do I get through to them?

Reese started visiting the miners frequently to check on them. He'd been told that Mrs. Stevens hadn't been feeling well. His thoughts turned to hot biscuits, homemade jam, and cocoa. He wondered if she was up to treating him today.

On the way to the mine, he drove through sheep country—he'd barely given a thought to the animals grazing in the open meadows within range of the blasts. His stomach did a flip flop when he thought of how dangerous it could be for them to forage on sage and grass with radioactive ash on it. *Had the sheep herders been warned?*

Chapter Eighteen
Harry

The day for testing Harry, the next bomb in the Upshot-Knothole series, arrived blustery and stormy. Dignitaries, reporters, and cameramen, a crowd of some 600, maneuvered for a good spot, atop Nob Hill. Volunteers passed out coffee and donuts and blankets to ward off the pre-dawn wind. The sun hadn't begun to lighten the skies to take the chill off the desert.

"Is this shot going to come off? The weather doesn't look promising," a shivering senator queried one of the newsmen.

"It's still early—could clear up," he offered, a note of hope in his voice. "I don't want to spend another day in this miserable place," he muttered.

"I certainly hope so. I've got to get back to D.C. I think I'll get one of those blankets." He shuffled off to find the volunteer handing them out.

A ripple of disappointed voices washed over the gathering when the announcement came that the test had been delayed until the next day. The next morning, the usual audience gathered again. Once more, volunteers served coffee and donuts and passed out blankets. The crowd mumbled and complained about the weather. "Looks like there may be another delay," one of the newsmen commented. When the announcement came, the crowd slithered away grousing about their misfortune, giving up on their hope to see an atomic bomb test up close and personal.

* * *

Humph. Sorry you won't be around for the test. My Harry is going to be a showstopper, loaded with toxic plutonium. I hate the waiting, too, but in the broad scheme of things, what's another day considering the billions of years I've been waiting around to show what I can do?

* * *

The third morning arrived with only the most stalwart dignitaries, reporters and cameramen on Nob Hill. "Looks like there may be another delay. The wind is too high," grumbled a congressman. Half his colleagues had already abandoned him to fly back to Washington.

Reese had been among the group for two days. Now on the third day, with weather conditions less than optimum, he decided his time would be better spent going to St. George to meet with AEC monitor, Chuck Bickman, to check out radioactivity readings. Because fallout was inconsistent, creating cool and hot spots, Reese didn't trust the information he was given and wanted to do his own tests—not that he didn't trust Bickman, he didn't trust the fallout to be equally distributed.

Reese enjoyed working with Bickman. He was a cheerful sort with a ready smile and an easy laugh. He had the look of most of the Utah people Reese had met, sandy hair, blue eyes and ruddy cheeks—didn't drink or smoke, but looked well fed judging from his ample belly.

Reese hadn't been on the road half an hour when the sky lit up. *Oh shit, I can't believe it. They went ahead with the test. This isn't good. I'd better hustle.* He punched his foot down on the gas pedal. He mentally thanked his assistant, Angela for making sure he had a Jeep enclosed with a canvas cover.

* * *

Whoopie. Here we go again. Even with warnings of high northeasterly winds, they detonated my dear Harry—thirty-one kilotons of raw energy. Fools! Don't you know Utah, then Idaho, will be covered in radioactive ash. Wonder how far the ash will travel in the winds aloft. Could reach New York. Hum, someone must have miscalculated something more than the weather. My cloud is picking up loads of dirt. They'll probably nickname this test Dirty Harry. Thirty-one kilotons was ambitious, three times the size of the bomb dropped on Hiroshima. Now with the wind and all the radioactive material, there will be lethal consequences. I wonder how those Washington Warriors will cover this up and discount my power. No more radiation than humans get from the sun—piffle, what a bunch of rot. The powers that be don't deserve the patriotism and trust of unsuspecting citizens. There I go getting sentimental again. But then I didn't make the bomb, and a bomb has no conscience. It doesn't know or care who it hurts.

* * *

Each time Reese drove the hundred plus miles from Las Vegas to St. George he was reminded of his ride from Santa Fe to Los Alamos. That trip was his first glimpse of peach and rose-colored earth. St. George's red-rock mesas were more intense, warm and inviting, deep terracotta reds and vermilions sharply contrasting with cerulean blue skies and the green trees that lined the banks of the Virgin River. Unlike the high country of New Mexico, St. George was hot in the summer and pleasant in the winter. An early morning spring rain had deepened and intensified the colors. He yearned to drive with all the windows down and inhale fresh air, but he knew the air would be laced with radioactivity.

Reese knew that the Mormon Temple, built in the late 1800s, was central to the farming and ranching community of less than 5,000. During the winter months, St. George's population grew when the well-to-do from Salt Lake City and other communities up north escaped the snow to bask in the temperate climate.

When Reese found Bickman at their designated meeting spot, the man was in a dither. "This is bad. The Geiger counter doesn't register high enough to get an accurate reading. It's way over the highest number."

Reese grabbed his instrument and slung its strap over his shoulder. As he was taking readings, he noticed children out playing in the school yard in the next block. "Didn't anyone notify the schools to keep the kids indoors?"

Bickman jerked his head toward the school. "Dang. I'll run over there and tell the teacher to get them inside immediately." He sprinted off, covering the distance in seconds, his speed belying his girth.

A quiver of fear crept up Reese's spine. *It's probably too late.* He followed Bickman to take readings at the school. In his heart, he knew these children had received too many roentgens. *Dammit, why didn't the school administrators keep the students inside?*

* * *

The Atom answers: Well, Reese, children can't be confined too long or they tend to explode. You may not understand because you don't have children, but I do, and my little neutrons and protons are very active, radioactive, that is. My electron is the worst. I can't keep it inside. It zips around outside all the time. The children were kept inside for two days while the test was delayed. With the weather being nasty today, the teachers figured the test would be delayed again. But, no, Harry, my dirtiest bomb yet carried dirt laden fallout right into the schoolyard. Oh, some of them will be very sick and some won't be too ill, but there will be a few who won't make it to adulthood. Sigh. The cost of being top dog in the nuclear cold war.

* * *

A scientist at heart, Reese took several readings, the clicks indicating high levels of radioactivity. With each reading, his brow furrowed deeper. *I can't be in my right mind. What am I doing out here? My job? I could let Bickman do this measuring while I stayed indoors in my lab. This place is hottern' the hubs of hell.* Saliva collected in his mouth as he fought nausea, one of the first signs of radioactive poisoning.

Reese called to Bickman. "We need to get in our cars. We're getting too much exposure."

"Yeah, I'm beginning to feel a bit feverish." He sprinted toward his pickup. "I'll phone my report to you tomorrow morning."

"Go home and take a shower," Reese yelled after him, then chided himself for not following his own advice. He stopped at a gas station and found the men's room. "This will have to do until I get back to Mercury," he spoke to his image in the mirror as he splashed water on all of his exposed skin and rinsed his hair, drying it with paper towels.

Still patting his mop of hair with paper towels, Reese got into his jeep and headed for St. George Hospital. He wanted to see if there were any new cancer patients. If there were, he hoped to interview them as part of his research. He loved the children, which made it harder each time. On the way, he stopped by the local drugstore to buy penny candy hoping to make the lives of the little cancer sufferers a bit better.

He searched around for a pay phone to call Angela. He wanted to know why they went ahead with the test.

"This was a nasty one," she told him. "I didn't think they'd go ahead, so fortunately, I was inside here at the office. Where are you?"

"St. George. It doesn't look as though anyone was warned to stay indoors. I'm worried."

"With just cause," she agreed. "Maybe you need to stay indoors, too."

"Too late. I've been with Bickman taking readings. Now I'm headed to the hospital."

"Be careful out there." A dial tone signified she'd hung up.

"Careful? How can anyone be careful with death raining down on them?" There was nobody listening to his comment.

* * *

Ah Reese, the atom chided, don't be so negative. The species will adapt and survive. After all, look at Bikini Atoll—everything dead as a door nail. Now sea life is beginning to come back and it's only been seven years. I wouldn't advise eating the fish unless you want to glow in the dark, but they are adapting and so will humans—eventually.

By the way, you know those fancy little radium dials on watches? That's not such a good idea, especially for the people applying the radioactive material to the hands and numbers. Just thought I'd give you a head's up.

* * *

During his hospital visit, Reese met William, a seven-year-old boy who had been admitted just an hour earlier. The child put on a tough face and thanked Reese as he accepted a piece of penny candy. He opened the treat and popped the hard candy into his mouth. "Orange, my favorite flavor," the boy said. "Thank you."

"What are his symptoms?" Reese asked William's doctor and ground his teeth as he recognized them as radiation sickness. It was too soon to tell if they would diminish or worsen. Reese followed the doctor into the hall. "He may have radiation sickness. Has anyone else come in with the same symptoms?"

"Not yet. William is the first. Do you think fallout is causing his illness?"

Reese said, "I saw children playing outside in the schoolyard and worried that they hadn't been kept inside." He didn't want to unnecessarily alarm the doctor, but wanted him to know there may be more sick kids. He hoped William would have a full recovery.

After visiting cancer patients, Reese glanced into the ward and saw the lad vomit into a basin. His brow furrowed and his heart went out to the child.

* * *

On the way back to Mercury, Reese encountered a road block. "What's going on?" he asked a policeman.

"We need you to go to that service station," he gestured toward a cluster of vehicles across the road. "They'll wash your vehicle, and then you can get back on the road."

"But I came from St. George," Reese protested.

"Doesn't matter—orders." The cop swept his arm toward the service station.

Reese had been driving north when Harry detonated. "Can't hurt" He'd wash the jeep himself to save time. *I can't be anymore radioactive than I already am. Someone at the AEC must be very nervous to issue an order like this. And they ought to be.*"

An image of William emerged in his mind. *That child could die.* Reese swiped his hand across his face in an effort to erase that thought.

Chapter Nineteen
1953
On the Slopes of Bald Mountain in Nevada

Cyrus Brenner snuggled down into the camp quilts and drifted off to sleep, listening to the soft clanging of sheep's bells and blessing his stars that he had such a reliable younger brother. If the sheep wandered off too far, Luke, on the early watch, would ride out and herd them back closer to camp.

Their winter grazing land in southern Nevada was a hard twenty-day trail drive from their ranch in Cedar City, Utah. The trip was worth it, though—the plentiful grass and sage kept the 2000 head fit and healthy. The Brenners' compact sheep wagon was home for the few months they were out on the range. Cyrus would sleep for five hours, then relieve Luke for the rest of the night watch.

Cyrus awakened at two a.m. to the aroma of coffee, rich in the crisp night air. Luke had climbed into the wagon, stoked the tiny camp stove and put on a fresh pot. Cyrus yanked on his trousers before rolling his ample form out of the high bunk, then he pulled on his Mackinaw coat, plopped a battered felt hat over his thick shock of unruly hair, and went outside.

"Coffee will be ready in a couple of minutes," Luke said. The glow from a kerosene lantern lit his handsome face as he lifted the saddle off the palomino and laid it on the grass next to the wagon.

"I'm ready," Cyrus said and wandered off into the darkness to take a leak. When he returned, Luke handed him a tin cup filled with coffee, sweetened with honey and made light with canned milk.

"Ahh, just the way I like it—blonde and sweet." Coffee was Cyrus's only vice. Otherwise, he closely followed the Word of Wisdom of the Mormon Church.

"The sheep are pretty quiet tonight—stayin' close to camp. I just rode out and checked on them," Luke said. "I'm going to get some shut-eye." He heaved himself up into the wagon and tucked himself into the rumpled bed that his brother had left.

Cyrus saddled his horse to be ready, poured a second cup of coffee, and hunkered down on the flat rock Luke had just vacated. The sliver of new moon provided little light, and he squinted into the darkness, looking in the direction of the herd. He cocked his head, putting his better ear to work listening for sheep bells. Satisfied, he leaned back to rest his head on Luke's saddle. Staring up at the brilliant night sky, he picked out the Big and Little Dippers and wondered, as he had since childhood, whether anyone could count the millions of stars.

A dim clang alerted him to wandering sheep. He swung up into his saddle and urged his Appaloosa toward the herd. Two Australian sheepdogs walked next to him. Cyrus prized the dogs and said each one of them was worth three hired hands. He spoke softly to his horse, stopping every so often to listen for bells. Finding half a dozen sheep farther up the slope, he signaled the dogs and made quick work of rounding up the strays and herding them back to the rest of the flock. Cyrus returned to camp and resumed his stargazing as dawn approached. He was on his fourth cup of coffee when a blinding flash lit up the sky. A moment later, the ground shook and a deafening boom caused his horse to rear and tug on his halter. The gelding picketed nearby, uttered a worried whinny. The clamoring bells let Cyrus know that the sheep were running. He sighed and tossed the rest of his coffee into a bush. He was reaching for his gloves when Luke appeared in the wagon opening and yelled, "Was that another damn explosion?"

"Yep, got the sheep all stirred up again. I'm off to round 'em up." Cyrus quieted the horse and mounted. He galloped off with the dogs dashing ahead. *God only knows how far the sheep will go. Sixty miles from the test site and it still shook us up. Those bombs seemed to be getting bigger and bigger. Or closer and closer.* Or maybe he was just tired of them.

Luke saddled his mare as fast as he could and rode out after Cyrus. As he shortened up the reins to keep her focused, he wondered if the horse would ever get used to that peculiar wind that followed every blast. Then he wondered if he would. That, along with the predictable rain of ash, made him more uncomfortable than the explosions themselves—at least he could explain the blasts.

The herd had scattered everywhere and it would be an hour or so before first light when they could make a thorough search. So far, the dogs had done a good job, but a quarter of the frightened sheep were still out there.

* * *

Two days later Cyrus walked up the hillside onto a meadow near camp to check on the sheep. He frowned at the sight of a dead ewe, then he noticed another. He knelt to examine the first and found sores on her mouth. Then something about her coat struck him as odd. With a gloved hand, he pulled at the patchy wool on her back. It came out in a clump.

"What in the devil is happening to our sheep?" His booming voice drew mild attention from a ewe and an early lamb nearby. The rest kept eating. He stood and continued on to the other carcass. Same problems—skin sores, hair falling out. *These sheep seemed to be all right a few days ago. But what kind of disease?* He had never seen anything like this.

He checked the rest of the herd, which grazed placidly. Fine gray ash puffed up from the grass with each step he took. He stopped, looked down at his ash-covered boots, then at the ground next to his feet. Every blade of grass had some gray residue. *This has to be from the bomb. The sheep are eating it. I've got to get this herd out of here. Twenty days drive or not, best to take them back to the feedlots at the ranch and give them hay and grain. It'll be better than losing them.*

Cyrus, Luke and the dogs rounded up the sheep, then hitched Cyrus's horse and the gelding to the sheep wagon. Cyrus drove the wagon, trailing the herd. Mounted on his horse, Luke, with the help of the dogs kept the sheep together and moving forward.

Generally, they would cover five miles a day. This time they were taking almost twice that time. It was excruciating. Ewes lagged, clearly exhausted. Most of them were carrying lambs, which took extra strength. Even the dogs nipping at their legs didn't motivate them to hurry. Some simply dropped and died.

Cyrus and Luke pushed the animals on—there was no alternative while they were still on the remote range. Finally, near Ash Springs, Cyrus sent Luke into town to hire a flatbed truck with racks and driver, so they could pick up

92

sheep too weak to walk. Cyrus had no idea how many had lagged behind and didn't make it. At least now, they could pick up the dead ones, instead of leaving the carcasses to rot.

They struggled on, the drive made only a little easier with the truck. Ewes prematurely gave birth on the roadside or on the truck. A lot of lambs came out pink-skinned, without wool, many of them without legs, some pot-bellied or deformed in other ways. Even the normal ones were undersized. Seeing a fully formed, healthy lamb became a rarity.

* * *

Reese drove along a back road on his way to check on the people at the mines when he came across a dead ewe. Then another, and another. He detoured to follow the trail of dead carcasses until he caught up with the Brenner herd just beyond Ash Springs. He saw Cyrus Brenner pick up a ewe and lay her on the truck.

Reese introduced himself and asked, "What's going on here?"

"Just tryin' to get this herd back to Cedar City. Somethin's killin' 'em," Cyrus said.

"I'm with the testing lab at Yucca Flats." Reese hesitated a moment, then said, "If it's all right with you, I'd like to take a couple of those dead sheep back to the lab and see what's wrong."

"Boy, would you do that?" Cyrus pushed his hat back off his forehead to give Reese a level gaze. "I'd sure like to know. I was goin' to get my vet out to the ranch to look 'em over when we got home. We're sure losin' em fast. And the lambs." He pointed to a couple of tiny carcasses. "A lot of 'em comin' out like that." He peered at Reese. "Reckon it's the bombs?"

"Can't tell from just looking at them." Reese knew he was being evasive. Of course it was the bombs. And he guessed that the ranchers would figure it out before long, too. Or maybe they had and didn't want to flat out say something that would sound so unpatriotic. It made his burden greater. *How can I keep these people and their livestock safe?* He shook his head to erase the thought. It would bring up too much anger and he'd lose perspective and that, for sure, wouldn't help.

Luke arrived back from another trip to town accompanied by a trail hand he'd hired to help drive the sheep.

93

"Luke, help me get Doc Mayfield a coupla those dead sheep into the back of his Jeep." Cyrus tipped his head toward the pile of ewes heaped on the truck bed. "He's gonna autopsy them."

"Before I do that, I want to feed those orphans." Luke gestured toward the sound of bleating lambs peeking their heads over the boards of the sheep camp wagon. "I bought some canned milk and nipples and rustled up some old soda pop and beer bottles."

Luke and the new hand busied themselves filling the bottles, snapping on black rubber nipples. They picked up the lambs and fed them. "It ain't mother's milk, but it'll have to do."

"I can help," Reese offered and Luke handed him a bottle and a lamb.

Cyrus cocked his head listening to the plaintive sound of a newborn. He turned his head to see the lamb trying to suckle from its dead mother. In a dozen long strides he picked up the baby and brought him back to Reese. "Here's another one for you to feed. You may have to put a squirt of milk on your finger and put it in his mouth so he gets the idea."

Reese blinked back tears. *What a way to come into the world. So tiny, so helpless.*

The orphaned lambs fed and put back into the wagon, Reese said, "I'll get some of the soldiers out to bury the dead ones along the trail." *For sure the AEC will want to downplay this.* Leaving dead sheep out in the open would not be part of the Commission's game plan. He would play his part, too, and not say anything to the Brenners until he had indisputable evidence from his lab. *But once I have proof, what do I do then? And I will have proof. I know it.*

"Thanks," Cyrus shook Reese's hand. "Sure do 'preciate it." The rancher waved Reese off and resumed trudging down the road with the sheep, his mouth set in a hard, thin line.

"What are we going to do if we lose this entire herd?" Luke asked.

"I don't know, brother, but we'll be in trouble. Somehow we have to save as many as we can. Hopefully enough of the lambs will make it to replenish the herd. It doesn't look like we'll be able to send many to market and I don't know how much wool we'll get from shearing the way it's coming out in clumps."

Cyrus stared after Reese's jeep. "Hum, Mayfield, doesn't Sherry have relatives named Mayfield?" he asked Luke.

94

"Yes, they came to the wedding. Donna and Sam Mayfield. Do you think they're related to this Doc Mayfield?"

"Why don't you ask Sherry when we get home?"

* * *

Doc Connor, the Brenner's veterinarian, came out to the ranch to examine the living sheep.

"During the drive we musta lost 200, give or take," Cyrus said. "That Doc Mayfield from the test site labs didn't admit anything," he told the vet. "But he for sure knew it had something to do with the bombs. Otherwise, why did he take 'em to autopsy?"

"Let's see what the report says." Connor took off his gloves after examining a dead lamb. "Did he say when he'd get it?"

"Nope, just said he'd be in touch."

"I think I'll take this dead lamb back to my lab and see if I can find something out." *I'm going to scan this animal with my Geiger counter as soon as I'm out of their sight.* Connor carried the animal to his pickup.

* * *

When Reese autopsied one of the sheep, the roentgens of radioactive iodine known as I-131 were over 400 in the animal's thyroid—100 times the safe limit. He shipped the other one to a colleague at Oak Ridge. He wanted his findings confirmed by someone else.

When the phone rang, Reese laid down the Geiger counter he'd been holding over a water sample. "Yucca Flat Testing Lab, Reese Mayfield speaking."

"Doctor Mayfield, this is Larry Connor. I'm Cyrus and Luke Brenner's veterinarian. Do you have a report on what killed their sheep?"

Reese bit his lip. It galled him that his top secret security clearance prohibited him from revealing the truth to civilians. "Yes. Although the sheep did register radioactivity, the cause of death is inconclusive." He hoped he'd have truer news for them soon and again pressed for action from the AEC.

Brenner, Brenner. Why does that name sound familiar?

That night Reese phoned his mother. "Mom do we have relatives in Utah named Brenner?"

"Why, yes son. Your cousin Sherry married a Brenner, Luke Brenner. Why do you ask?"

"Just wondering. I came across them herding sheep from Nevada to Cedar City and I wondered why the name seemed familiar."

"If you are in Cedar City you might drop in on them and get to know them."

"I'll keep that in mind."

After the usual how's Dad, how is work going, and other chit chat, Reese said goodbye.

So the Brenners are family. How can I warn them without jeopardizing my position?

Reese had hoped there would be more time after Dirty Harry but, six days later, Grable was fired from an atomic cannon, and then nine days after that explosion, an air drop test named Climax, the last of the Upshot-Knothole series of tests. Reese feared the atmospheric tests most because of the greater risk of the winds aloft scattering the fallout to God only knew where and how far. *Geeze, where are they getting all the uranium, plutonium, and other components for all these bombs. I can't imagine the cost—must be in the billions. Maybe we'll get a break now—some quiet time.*

The next series of tests, code named Castle, scheduled to be done in the South Pacific meant there wouldn't be any more tests at the Nevada Test Site until early in 1955. Reese hoped it would be never, but he couldn't count on that.

* * *

It was two weeks after the Climax test before Reese found time to get away. "Angela, I'm have some business in Cedar City. I'll be gone all day, but I should be back tomorrow morning.

He wanted to locate the Brenners and advise them to find other grazing land. When he arrived in Cedar City, Reese stopped at the Sinclair service station and borrowed the phone book to look up the Brenner's number. While he turned the pages, he happened to glance up and spotted Cyrus pulling into the station. Reese dropped the book on the counter and waited for Cyrus to get out of his pickup. Approaching the man as he pumped gas, he said, "Mr. Brenner, I'd like to talk to you."

"Doc Mayfield, what brings you to town?"

"Actually to see you."

96

"Is there somewhere we can talk privately? Your brother Luke might want to be in on this too."

"Sure, soon's I finish here, I'm headed for the ranch. You can follow me there. Ain't no place more private."

After a ten-mile drive on a gravel road, they arrived at the Brenner spread. Two fields of alfalfa lined the road behind barbed wire fences. Two barking sheepdogs dashed down the road toward Cyrus's pickup. He stopped and they leaped into the bed, eyes bright and tongues lolling out.

After they came to a stop and the dogs greeted their master, Cyrus said, "Luke will be down at the sheep yards." He gestured for Reese to follow him.

Reese had to hustle to match Cyrus's long strides down a lane, past the hay yard and through a wooden gate. Spring freshened the air and the soft bleats from new life sounded from lambs just born. Toward the north, streaks of snow still snuggled into the shaded areas of the mountains.

Having found Luke, the three men hunkered down near the lambing sheds. Because of the weakened muscles in his leg, hunkering down wasn't the easiest position for Reese, but he did it anyhow. "I've just learned we are related. Sherry is a second cousin to my mother." After comparing familial notes, Reese said, "I came here to try to protect you and your livestock." He had their full attention. "You can't go back to the Nevada winter pasture. It's too close to the bomb site. That's why you're losing your sheep. I can't go into details or it will cost me my security clearance and my position."

"We figured as much." Cyrus picked up a piece of straw and chewed on one end.

"Is there anywhere else you can find winter pasture?" Reese asked.

"Maybe Kanab Creek or even farther east. We'd have to apply for a Federal Grazing Permit." Luke said.

"I suggest you take action right away. Keep in mind that the winds from the test site are northeasterly. Try to find a place more southeast from here. Is that possible?"

"Bald Mountain has been our winter pasture since before I was born," Luke said.

"Looks like it's time for a change, whether we like it or not." Cyrus flicked away the straw he'd been chewing on.

"It doesn't appear that there will be any tests scheduled soon, so you have some time. Make sure you know when the tests are and keep you and your family indoors for a few hours, all day if possible. Keep your livestock under cover. We don't fully understand the effects of radioactive fallout yet, but assume the worst and protect yourself. Children seem to be most vulnerable." Reese knew he was sticking his neck out. What else could he do in all good conscience?

"So you think fallout is killing the sheep?" Luke asked.

"It isn't proven or official, but let's assume it is and take precautions. If you can quietly let the rest of the ranchers know without telling them I told you, I'd appreciate it." Reese looked the two men in the eye and decided they wouldn't expose him. "If you see a lot of ash on the grass, bring the sheep in to the corrals and feed them hay and grain until the ash either blows away or it rains and it gets washed away. Let's not take chances on losing more livestock."

"I'm going to drive back to Cedar City to see if we can get a grazing permit. Can you handle things here, little brother?" Cyrus stood, ready to go as Luke nodded a yes. "Thanks Doc." He extended his hand.

"We're family. Call me Reese. I'll do what I can to help." He pulled out his business cards and handed one to each of the men. "Call me if I can do anything." Reese shook hands with Luke, asked him to give his best to Sherry and followed Cyrus back to the vehicles. *I need to get to know these people.*

Chapter Twenty
1953
Redfield, Utah

Phyllis Christensen didn't get the little girl she'd hoped for. She had another son and named him James. She let his light brown hair grow long. It fell into springy ringlets Phyllis delighted in twirling around her fingers. On his fifth birthday, a sister-in-law offered her a silver dollar if she would cut it, saying, "You can't turn him into a girl. Let him be the boy he is." Phyllis sighed and took little Jimmy to the barber and had the hair cut off. She saved the treasured locks in a box she hid on the top shelf of a closet.

* * *

Miss White's class of second graders squirmed around in their wooden desks, awaiting the appearance of a special guest. Some of them stared out of the windows at the overcast pink sky. Since the children couldn't go outside to play at recess today because of *cloudshine* from that morning's A-bomb test, the day seemed to drag.

Engrossed in reading, Katie Hatch was unaware that one of her long braids, tied with pale blue ribbons, lay on the desk behind her—on Jimmy's desk. The temptation was too great for the restless seven-year-old. Gently tugging on the bow, Jimmy untied it and stretched the satin ribbon out. Holding his tongue between his teeth at the side of his mouth, he spread his fingers to hold the ribbon down and proceeded to print his name on it with a stubby pencil.

"Jimmy! What are you doing?" Miss White's eyes widened when she saw him writing on the ribbon.

"Nothing."

Katie leaned forward and felt the tug on her hair. She reached back and yanked her braid free, leaving the ribbon behind on Jimmy's desk.

Miss White marched toward them and snatched up the ribbon. She handed it to Katie. "I hope it isn't ruined." Lips pursed and wearing a deep frown, she faced Jimmy. "When are you ever going to…"

She was interrupted when the classroom door opened. All the children turned to look at an impressive uniformed figure striding into the room with firm long steps. He was followed by the school principal, Mr. Larsen, and Reese.

Miss White's face lit up as she hurried to the front of the classroom. "Children, we have the great honor of having General William Blotchett here to speak to us on matters of National Security." Principal Larsen put his hands together and clapped. Miss White signaled the class and they joined in the applause. "And, Dr. Reese Mayfield with the Atomic Energy Commission." Another round of applause, albeit less enthusiastic.

Jimmy's sky-blue eyes widened at the array of medals on the big man's uniform. He put his pencil down and fastened his attention on the general, who held a military hat tightly under one arm.

Blotchett flashed a smile at Miss White. "May I put my hat on your desk?" he asked.

Her cheeks crimsoned. "Of course, sir."

The general turned to face the class. "You know, kids, we're in a Cold War with the Russians. I came to talk to you about what you can do to serve your country, and help out the president and the Armed Forces." One of the general's hazel eyes squinted as he scrunched his brows together.

"I see that your teacher, Miss White?" He looked to her for reassurance that he had remembered her name correctly. "Miss White has hung Civil Defense posters around the room. Do you all know where your fallout shelter is if we are under attack?"

Some students waved their hands in the air and General Blotchett pointed at Billy Crane.

"We're 'sposed to go the city offices under the libarry," Billy said.

"That's right. Hear that class. You all know where to go."

"Now, I want you all to be a part of something called Sky Watch." The general leaned forward and searched the faces of the children.

Half a dozen hands shot up.

The general stopped them. "Now hold on, I'll explain it all to you. We want you to watch for Russian airplanes and let your parents know if you see any planes that don't look like ours. We call it Sky Watch." His face became more serious and he lowered his voice. "You all know about the atomic bomb tests that are going on in Nevada, don't you?"

Several of the children nodded.

"These tests are necessary to keep our citizens safe. You all know what a citizen is, right?" Solemn nods answered. "That includes you. What else can you do to help? When your teacher or your parents tell you to stay indoors, obey them."

Waving his hand in the air, Jimmy interrupted without being called on. "I know. I know. You can tell when it happens because the clouds are pink. You shouldn't play out-of-doors until after it blows away. Then it's okay to go out."

"That's right, young man." The general started passing out the brochures he'd been holding in his hand. "I want you to take these brochures home to your folks and ask them to read them. You'll be helping your country. Remember, our president is counting on you."

Reese had remained silent, but his mind protested Blotchett's soliciting the children's participation in Sky Watch. *What the hell? Asking these kids to look for enemy airplanes?* Reese felt appalled by the general's speech, but bit his tongue. He was grateful that the general warned the children to stay inside, but to enlist their help to spot enemy airplanes?

Jimmy shoved the brochure in his pocket and hurried home. He wanted to finish building the ham radio station he was working on. The men were coming next week to put up the transmission tower at the back of the house. Now, he had something really important to broadcast to other ham radio operators. Maybe he would help save America. His sweaty hand crumpled the precious paper as he sprinted toward home.

* * *

Much as Phyllis had wanted a daughter, she was proud of her bright son. So much so, she had his IQ tested. He was well above genius level. When it came to science, she indulged him, spending beyond their means. Her husband, Arden, had given in to every request and had just ordered a forty-foot metal transmission tower. Everyone in the small town of 1,600 knew Jimmy wanted

101

to be a scientist. Skeptics came to see the young genius working on his ham radio, and they had left, convinced.

Jimmy bounced up the front steps. "Mom, mom! I'm home."

"I can hear you," Phyllis called from the kitchen. "You don't have to shout. Go wash your hands. I've made oatmeal cookies."

Jimmy's brown leather oxfords clattered on the oak floor as he dashed into his mother's immaculate kitchen.

"Mom!" he said breathlessly, "A general came and talked to us. The president needs our help. He said to give this to you." Jimmy yanked the crumpled brochure out of his pocket.

Phyllis took the pamphlet and laid it on the table. "Go clean up and then you can tell me all about it."

* * *

Jimmy's idea of cleaning up was to splash a little water on his face and rinse his hands. The dirt ended up on his mother's white towels. Evaporation would have to take care of the tiny droplets that clung to his blond eyelashes. He was too excited to dry off thoroughly before telling his mom about the general's visit.

Jimmy slid into the chrome chair at the kitchen table where his mother had set out two cookies on a small plate and a large glass of milk. The best milk around came from her sister Elva's four cows. Too bad, Phyllis thought, they weren't giving as much milk as usual right now.

* * *

The atom perked an ear, always wanting any news about its accomplishments. Hum, diminished milk production. Could it be that cows don't like their grass seasoned with sparkling ash?

* * *

"Mama, do we have binoculars? The general said the president wants us to watch for Russian planes."

"Yes, Jimmy. I'll let you use them if you're very careful. The president is going to be on the television talking to the nation tonight. Do you want to watch? I'll let you stay up past bedtime if you want to."

"Wow! That's great, Mom!" His chest swelled with pride at this special dispensation.

Phyllis and Arden Christensen were one of the first families in Redfield to have a television. Family and friends were always dropping over to watch. Jimmy had been fascinated by the installation of the thirty-foot aerial antenna on the roof with all the guy wires and the cross bars that were necessary to pick up the signal from Salt Lake City, 150 miles north.

After supper, Jimmy plopped down on the flowered carpet with his nose practically touching the screen. The ending of *I Love Lucy* was followed by a commercial for Colgate toothpaste. Then, the big moment arrived. At the end of the commercial, Edward R. Murrow introduced the president. The camera zoomed in on the face of Dwight D. Eisenhower, former military hero.

A rush of patriotism flooded Jimmy's young body. Smart as he was, he didn't understand most of the speech, but the president needed him and he felt special being included with the grown-ups.

The next morning, Jimmy marched into the classroom, conscious of his important news. He couldn't wait to tell his teacher he'd watched for Russian planes with binoculars and that he'd seen the president on television, but he'd barely slid into his desk when sirens started screaming.

"Children, get under your desks," Miss White said, her countenance serene despite the chaos in the classroom. Certain all the children were hiding, she tucked her trembling body into the knee space under her desk as the sirens continued to shrill.

Jimmy's heart pounded. *Is it a Russian attack?* He listened for airplanes. *Why aren't we going to the library?* To Jimmy, getting under their desks seemed pointless. He'd studied up. They'd need to be in a concrete bunker underground to survive the initial attack, and he'd read that the atmosphere and the ground would be "hot" for days afterward—maybe weeks. But he complied and clambered under his old wooden desk.

Cowering under the next desk, Katie had tears streaking down her cheeks.

"Don't be scared." Jimmy reached out and patted her on the shoulder. She gave a huge sniff, and smiled back.

The sirens stopped and he peeked out from under his desk. The silence was broken by two short bursts. He let out the big breath he didn't realize he'd been holding.

"Okay class." Miss White came out from her own desk and clapped her hands. "That's the *all clear*. It's safe to come out now. It was just a Conelrad Alert—a Civil Defense drill."

The children emerged. Some of them trembled and brushed away tears. Others ran to the windows and looked up at the sky.

"Back to your seats and get out your Crayolas." Miss White passed out blank sheets of paper. The best thing for her class was to keep them busy to get their minds off the alert. "Now, I want all of you to draw your favorite place. Is it your room? Is it under an apple tree? Maybe it's by a creek. What makes you feel good?"

Jimmy hadn't been scared, but Katie had, and he didn't want her to cry. He reached forward and patted her shoulder. She turned, brushing away her tears and smiled at him.

When the bell signaled the end of the school day, Jimmy looked back at Katie. "Can I walk you home?" He shoved the mess of papers, crayons, and a book into the cubby hole underneath the top of his desk. She only lived three blocks from him.

"Okay, but I have to go straight home or Mama will worry."

Jimmy usually couldn't wait to get home to his ham radio, but today he wanted to make sure Katie was all right.

"I'm sorry I ruined your blue ribbon." Jimmy kicked at a rock in his path and sent it tumbling ahead of him.

"It's not ruined. Mama washed it and the pencil came out."

"Oh, good." Jimmy was relieved. "Were you really scared today?"

"I try not to be, but I can't help it."

"Stupid sirens." Jimmy kicked the rock again.

He said goodbye to Katie at the gate to her house and then ran skipping and jumping home. For some reason he was happy. He raced up the steps and pushed open the front door.

"You're late." Phyllis stood with her hands on her hips and stared down at her young son. "Why are you late?"

"I dunno." Jimmy mumbled. He didn't want his mama to know he'd walked a girl home. "I'm hungry." Knowing he was ravenous when he got home, his mother always had an after school snack for him.

Jimmy's cousin April, who lived next door, rang the doorbell to her Aunt Phyllis's house. Born just a week apart, both the children were in the same class in school. She had seen him walking with Katie and appeared eager to tease him. April slipped onto a chair next to him at the table.

"Would you like some cookies and milk, April?" Aunt Phyllis reached into her cookie jar and pulled out two cookies and put them on a plate.

"Jimmy's got a girlfriend," April sang out. "Jimmy's got a girrrrrrl friend."

"What! Who?" Nelda seemed aghast. "Jimmy you're only seven. How can you be thinking of girls?"

"Katie. Jimmy loves Katie."

"Shut up." He doubled up his fist and hit April on the arm.

"Jimmy, don't hit your cousin."

"Mom, Katie was scared of the sirens."

"We're all scared of the sirens," Phyllis said. Her brows pinched together and she sighed.

"I'm not." Jimmy nonchalantly dunked a cookie in his milk. "Don't worry Mama, I'll protect you."

* * *

It was early November, and a heavy, wet snow had fallen overnight. Jimmy awakened early and looked out at the white carpet covering the lawn and couldn't wait to get outside.

"Don't eat the snow," Phyllis told him as she wrapped a woolen scarf around his neck. She worried because she'd heard that the radioactivity from the bomb testing was held in the clouds and would come back to earth in the first snowfall.

Large snowflakes fell as he dashed down the five concrete steps at the front of their house.

"And don't track snow into my clean house," Phyllis called after him as he fell backwards and waved his arms and legs to make a snow angel.

Phyllis had started keeping gallon jugs of water and cans of food stored away in her basement in case of a Russian nuclear attack. They had a large basement with a separate storage room that was heavily stocked with bottled fruits and vegetables she canned every year. Still, she wondered if she should ask Arden to build them a fallout shelter. Some of the families in town had

105

built them and stored the requisite two years of food the Mormon Church recommended.

One day, she was joking about needing a fallout shelter with her friend, Thelma, "If the Russians attack, we'll just come over to your shelter."

Thelma responded, "The door will be barred, so don't. We'll only have enough for ourselves."

This shocked Phyllis, who was generous by nature. As she poured the old water down the drain and refilled the gallon jugs from the tap, she wondered, *What good does this do if the snowflakes are contaminated? Maybe our water is, too. If we take a direct hit, then doing this won't make a bit of difference.*

* * *

Reese rarely drove as far north as Sevier County. It was only his second trip, since it was considered to be the farthest north that may experience fallout. His mission that day was unusual. He'd been tasked to visit a number of elementary schools in southern Utah to ask for baby teeth to be sent to the Atomic Energy Commission. The age group he met with was second graders. Researchers expected to be able to ascertain levels of radioactivity in humans by examining the baby teeth of seven-year-olds.

"How many of you put your baby teeth under your pillow and the tooth fairy took them and left you some money?" Every hand in the room shot up. "Do you think your mother saved any of those teeth?" A few children said their mother got the teeth from the tooth fairy and saved them. "Please take these instructions home and ask your parents if they will send us any baby teeth they have." Reese passed out the papers to the children.

Reese was unaware little Jimmy Christensen was shirttail kin to him.

* * *

That afternoon, Jimmy brought home the note from school about "Operation Tooth Fairy." It instructed parents to send their children's baby teeth to school. The school would then send the teeth to the Biology and Medical Division of the Atomic Energy Commission to measure them for levels of strontium 90, a lethal form of radioactive by-product from atomic explosions.

Phyllis had saved baby teeth from all her sons. Stored in baby food jars, she hid them under lingerie in her vanity. Each child's teeth rested on cotton in a separate jar labeled with his name. She had rescued the little pearly teeth

106

from under their pillows and replaced each tooth with a dime. She didn't want to part with her hidden treasure, but if it would help the government, she would. She only needed to send Jimmy's because the bomb testing didn't start until after Gerald and Bennett had their adult teeth.

With a sigh, Phyllis got up and went into her living room. She pulled a clean white envelope out of her desk drawer, wrote Baby Teeth, James D. Christensen, Born March 23, 1948 on it. Brushing away a tear, she carefully wrapped the teeth, placed them in the envelope and sealed it.

Chapter Twenty-One
1954
Fighting Back

After Reese learned that Oppenheimer had lost his security clearance for his repeated recommendations to stop testing atomic bombs, he wondered if he also was too vocal, that he would lose his job, too. Not that he wouldn't be able to get another job, but he still held out hope that he could help the people and persuade the Washington Warriors that atmospheric tests were too dangerous to continue. He sent letters proposing underground testing. The usual letter came back saying it was under consideration.

Reese was not alone in pressing the AEC. Early in January of 1954, Dave Clover, a sheep rancher, and Dr. Swenson Brown, the County Agricultural Agent in southwest Utah, met in the city council chambers with a panel of federal administrators led by Colonel Burt Fallstone.

"The problems with your livestock aren't caused by the A-Bomb testing," Colonel Fallstone said. "You sheepherders don't know how to manage your flocks." To Brown's ears—well sensitized by the arrogant professors he'd had in graduate school at Cornell—Fallstone managed to infuse both condescension and pity into that single sentence.

"Well, I may be just a dumb sheepherder," Clover argued, "but I'd like to ask some questions about the effects of radiation on internal organs." Clover, deputized by his fellow ranchers to be their spokesman, had a list of questions they'd collected from area veterinarians who had treated what clearly seemed to be radiation sickness in animals. Not only did they see a staggering number of burn cases, they saw sterility in good breeding stock and a high rate of aborted fetuses. The mortality rate often rose to fifty percent of an entire herd.

Vets were overwhelmed by the sheer number of cases. Recognizing they weren't getting truthful test results from government labs, they sent tissue samples to UCLA. Reports came back that there were high levels of radiation.

Even in rural Utah, medical professionals and veterinarians knew what happened to people and animals in Japan after exposure to radioactive fallout. Brown had shared his knowledge with Clover, who dug his heels in with more questions.

"Does radiation cause sterility in livestock?"

"No, the radiation from fallout isn't sufficient to cause sterility. The radiation your animals get isn't any more than they get from sunshine."

"Then how come the sheep are losing their wool and newborn lambs have short legs and pot bellies? What's causing that, if it isn't radiation? Their wool slides right off when we try to shear them."

"They must be malnourished," Fallstone said. "How can I explain radioactivity to you when you don't know the difference between fission and fusion? There's no way you can understand the effects of fallout."

Ranchers folded their arms across their chests. Some chins jutted forward in a gesture of defiance. Some slid back in their chairs and crossed their knees. It was evident his scolding tone galled the ranchers.

"I'll spell it out again. Your sheep aren't getting any more radiation from the bombs than they get from the sun."

Clover folded his arms across his chest. "I am listening," he said. "But I'm not convinced. You are saying it's coincidental. That just doesn't make sense. And, by the way, I do know the difference between fission and fusion. Briefly, fission is splitting atoms into two or more atoms and fusion is combining two smaller atoms." He narrowed his eyes. "I could be more specific and expand on that, but I'm not sure you'd understand." Clover knew he shouldn't have said that. It wouldn't help their cause, but he couldn't resist.

One of the administrators covered his mouth with his hand, but couldn't disguise a snicker.

Fallstone's mouth worked as his face reddened. He shifted gears, glancing pointedly at the American flag standing to the left of the dais. "Don't you know the importance of the bomb testing? We need these tests. The fallout has nothing to do with your sheep dying. In fact, I resent your saying that our government would deliberately harm your livestock. It's almost treasonous, that's what it is. It isn't our fault you don't know how to take care of your animals."

Clover stood his ground. "The vets in the area say they are removing cancerous tumors from the sheep. We've never had problems like this before," he pointed out. "Something has changed. The bomb testing is the only thing that's different. We want the nuclear testing stopped before we lose all our livestock." He looked down at the papers he'd brought, as though to check his facts. In reality, they were etched deep into his memory. "So far the sheep ranchers that wintered in Nevada have lost over 4,000 sheep and more are dying every day."

Clover picked up a stack of photographs and handed some to each of the administrators, finishing with several he handed to Fallstone. "This didn't start until after the bomb testing."

It didn't escape Clover that some of the administrators blanched. The large format photographs showed piles of dead sheep, hundreds of them being bulldozed into mass graves. The administrators grimaced at the photographs of lambs born without legs, without eyes, without wool—pale blobs of what should have been cute little lambs.

Clover continued, "If you were to lay the bodies of dead sheep next to each other, it would stretch two miles. That could only be caused by the bomb tests."

Fallstone clenched his fists on the tabletop and glared at Clover. "You people! You want us to lose the arms race with Russia? Do you want the Commies over here? Let me tell you, Mr. Clover—the day the Commies get here, you won't have to worry whether you have sheep or not. They'll take all of them away from you and distribute them to the people who don't have sheep." Saliva crept into the corners of his mouth. "Think about that before you go around accusing this great nation of causing you deliberate harm." He picked up Clover's file and slapped it shut. "Thank you for your time, sir." He nodded to Brown. "That will be all."

The other officials looked down, their embarrassment evident. It was clear to everyone present that Fallstone was blustering for the sake of intimidation. All the evidence pointed to radioactive poisoning.

Clover imagined if the Washington visitors were surprised by anything, it was by his and Brown's determination and their command of the facts of

110

animal science. He guessed that he was a far cry from what these D.C. city boys had been lead to expect from a Utah rancher, and likewise, he figured the panel hadn't expected to meet a country vet with an Ivy League DVM degree. However, it was all a pointless exercise, he realized. As he packed up his papers and slipped them into his battered briefcase, he was left with the solitary hope that if this treatment of decent citizens fit these bureaucrats' definition of "acceptable loss," it was ugly when they saw it up close.

* * *

In the back of the room, Reese sat in dismay and shame at how Fallstone had treated Clover. Prohibited from testifying, he inwardly nursed his growing anger. Not just his anger, when he analyzed it, but his growing disillusionment with his government. He questioned his role in working for the AEC. He'd studied nuclear medicine so he could develop a safe path between the dangers of this new science and the good it might do. He'd taken the AEC job to be a protector, a guardian. Now, it seemed his job was only to abet an enormous cover-up. As he rose to leave the hearing, a memory surfaced, one of that El Paso Post reporter who had written the lone true description of the White Sands test—at the time, Reese had considered the man foolhardy and nearly treasonous. Now he wondered at the man's bravery.

The thought stopped him on the courthouse steps. He stood lost in that thought, oblivious to the bustle of others exiting around him. *I am 31 years old, and I have accomplished exactly what? It's time for me to do some soul-searching*, Reese realized. What was his rightful duty as a citizen? What was his rightful calling as a human being? Were they anywhere near the same thing?

* * *

"Well, we didn't get anywhere with that," Clover said to Brown as he turned onto the highway to head home. "Unless you count it as an accomplishment," he added dryly, "to be called a 'Pinko'."

That afternoon, Clover met with bankers to plead for a loan to save his ranch. The bank refused him. Because the government denied responsibility for the loss of livestock, the bankers saw no chance of recovery of damages that would pay off the loan. He was a beaten man.

After picking at his supper that evening, Clover told his wife he felt tired and wanted to rest. Sometime in the night, he died of a heart attack.

111

*   *   *

A week later, a dozen angry farmers and ranchers faced men from the Atomic Energy Commission at a meeting in the Cedar City firehouse. There were an equal number of livestock owners to federal officials. Cyrus Brenner was among the ranchers.

"Ya gotta stop testin' those A-bombs. It's killin' our livestock," a rancher called from the back of the room.

Don Wheeler from the Department of Defense folded his arms as he answered, "We can't do that. We're in an arms race with Russia. We need the bombs in case they bomb us."

"My wife, she got cancer in her thyroid," said Orin Snow. "And her sister's kid in Parowan has leukemia, only six years old."

"Sounds like cancer runs in your wife's family," said Dr. Phillip Paulson, Chief of Biological Medicine with the AEC.

"Ain't had nothin' like it before the bombs," Snow said ignoring the harsh, unsympathetic response.

"We can't afford these losses," said Cyrus Brenner. "Something has to be done before I lose all my livestock."

Even as they denied any cause and effect between the tests and the ranchers' problems, the federal representatives called upon the ranchers' patriotism and asked for cooperation and "active participation." However, the participation they seemed to have in mind was for the ranchers to ignore the loss of livestock, to die quietly of cancer, and not make a fuss.

After hours of heated discussion, the livestock owners went away frustrated, disillusioned and betrayed by the government they'd always loved and given their loyalty. Most were furious, but some were almost convinced that they were wrong and the fallout wasn't causing their problems. For those, the government cover-up was effective.

Cyrus Brenner stomped out of the meeting. "Dammed sons-a-bitchin' bureaucrats."

He was still storming when he got home. Outraged by the government's position, he told his family he was going to take action. "Luke, you and Dad will have to take care of the ranch while I'm busy with this, I'm going to sue the Feds."

Brenner drove the six hours to Salt Lake City to hire the best lawyer he could afford. He was referred to Dan Warr, who cautioned him that he would have a tough time winning a lawsuit against the government. Nevertheless, Brenner sued the United States for the loss of his sheep. He thought he had enough evidence to win, confident that the findings from several veterinarians and Dave Clover's reports were sufficient.

A trial date set in six weeks at the Cedar City Courthouse brought out most of the ranchers in the area. They slapped Cyrus on the back and wished him well. If he won the case, they hoped they too would be compensated for the loss of sheep.

When the trial started, Brenner was shocked to hear veterinarians recant their findings under oath. Brenner knew these men. He'd grown up and gone to church with some of them.

He wanted to scream at them and call them on their treachery. Every time Warr presented documents, the government attorney said they were classified and inadmissible. Over the roar of protests in the courtroom, the judge pounded his gavel and complied.

Dr. Brown's report had been confiscated by the AEC. He was told to rewrite it and agents from the FBI made certain he removed any reference to nuclear fallout causing the ranchers to lose their sheep.

Under pressure from the head of the Atomic Energy Commission, scientists who had confirmed to Brenner his sheep had died from radiation exposure changed their story when they got on the witness stand, stating the sheep had died of cold and malnutrition.

Reese, though, had not recanted. He resubmitted his findings from the autopsy of Brenners' sheep and volunteered to testify. His report vanished, and convenient for the government's case, Reese was called to Washington for meetings during the trial.

Ranchers testified they had tried everything to save their sheep. When they knew a test was scheduled, they brought them into the feed yards and fed them corn. Rebuttal witnesses said the corn didn't contain enough protein to sustain the sheep. The sheepherders argued that when the sheep grazed, they ate white and black sage which was high in protein so they couldn't be undernourished.

Veterinarian Dr. Raymond Thompson had sent reports to the AEC that lesions on downwind sheep typified effects of beta radiation and that the A-bomb tests had been a factor in the mass deaths of sheep. Thompson had been instructed by government officials to rewrite the report and eliminate any reference to radiation damage or effects. He held out as long as he could, but finally caved in under extraordinary pressure from the FBI. Under threat of undermining the government during the Cold War and being branded a traitor, he recanted and rewrote the report.

Dr. Paulson told Dr. Brown that the federal government had no intention of being held accountable for the loss of herds. Under no circumstances could the AEC have a claim against it. To do so would establish a precedent.

The government denied anything was amiss, despite the fact that a herd sixty miles away from the test site had over twenty-five percent of new lambs die during the spring and summer of 1953. The Atomic Energy Commission denied that radioactive fallout from the bomb testing was at fault. They claimed malnutrition caused the loss of sheep. A claim the sheep ranchers found to be without basis. That spring and summer, over 5300 sheep perished from radioactive poisoning.

Brenner lost his case and his faith in the government. The betrayal was crushing, yet he told Luke, "We'll overcome this. We survived the war, so we can survive whatever they can throw at us." In his heart, he knew he'd never have the same trust again—not in his friends and neighbors, nor the country he'd loved and served.

Chapter Twenty-Two
The Children

Reese set aside a day to visit children with cancer at the hospital in St. George. It would be his sixth visit. On his way, he stopped in Las Vegas to shop for Teddy bears, dolls, comic books and board games. He picked out scarves and cute little hats for girls who'd lost their hair and baseball caps for the boys who were now bald. He knew most of these children wouldn't be leaving the hospital, but giving them some momentary joy made him feel better.

Today, screams permeated the air as he walked down the hall.

Two nurses held down a small, squirming boy while the doctor tried to insert an IV.

Reese paused to study the name on the door, William Brenner. *I wonder if he is a relative to Cyrus and Luke?* He had met William during his last visit, but didn't know his last name. Reese entered with a forced smile on his face. "Hi there, William. Having a rough day, I see," he said.

This greeting was met with more shrieks of, "No more needles!"

"Now be a brave boy," the doctor coaxed.

"I got no more brave," he wailed. "Got no more brave."

William's mother, Sherry, stood aside with the back of her hand pressed against her mouth. Giant tears coursed down her pale face.

"William, or should I call you Bill today?" Reese said when the boy stopped to gather his breath. "Someone told me your favorite thing in the whole world was orange Popsicles."

The boy's eyes focused on Reese's hand, and the bright paper wrapper.

"I have one here with your name on it. If you let the doctor put in the IV, you can eat it before it melts."

As William slowly nodded, the doctor slid the IV in and taped it down.

Reese handed William the treat. "That wasn't as bad as you thought it would be, was it? Here," he added. "I brought you a race car, too." He handed the child a miniature replica of a 1953 red Chevy Corvette.

"Are you Sherry Brenner? Luke's wife?" Reese asked the weeping mother.

"Yes," she managed between sniffles.

"I'm Doctor Reese Mayfield. I'm related to you through my mother, Donna Mayfield."

Sherry perked up. "Luke mentioned you—said you were trying to help with the sheep."

"I am. And investigating to see if there is a connection between the bomb testing and these children being ill."

The tears started again. "Little William is so sick."

"With your permission, may I ask the doctor for a copy of William's records."

"Of course. I'll tell him."

The Popsicle didn't stay down long. Within minutes William vomited it up, along with blood.

The sick little boy wrenched Reese's heart. He wanted to talk to the doctor privately and left the room to find him. When he caught up with him, he asked, "What's the prognosis, Dr. Swenson?"

"We've never seen a child this young with lymphosarcoma and acute leukemia. He may last another week. It has been less than a month since we removed a tumor. Now the cancer seems to be everywhere. This is the worst case we've seen. We've done blood transfusions, but he loses as much as we give him. He can't hold food down. His spleen is enlarged. His fever is high. We can't keep clothes or even a sheet on him. He throws it off. He's in constant pain."

Summoning his overt reason for being there, Reese tamped down his emotions and asked, "May I have copies of your reports on William? Mrs. Brenner said she would give permission."

"I'll check with her right now. If you can shed light on this outbreak of cancer in children, we'd be grateful. We've lost three children under the age of eight during the past month."

"Mrs. Brenner also gave me permission to photograph young William. Will you help me with my research by photographing him? I'll leave my camera with you. If you'll photograph the other children with cancer, it will help."

"Come with me. There's something I want you to see," said the doctor. He led the way to an elevator and pressed down. The basement of the hospital housed a pathology lab and the morgue. "In my thirty years of practice, I've never seen deformed fetuses and newborns like these." Large jars held unidentifiable specimens. "This fetus was aborted at five months." It was a tangle of tissue. "I'm surprised it didn't spontaneously abort earlier." He pointed to another larger jar. "This was a premature birth. I wouldn't allow the mother to see her baby." It was a grotesque head with flippers instead of arms and a tail instead of legs. Dr. Swenson went on to show Reese other horrifically deformed fetuses that should have been normal healthy babies. "Dr. Mayfield, this is too many abnormalities. Occasionally I would see a cleft palate or a club foot. Most of the women here are strong and healthy and deliver fully formed healthy babies. Is it fallout from the bomb testing causing this?"

Reese thought he'd toughened up, but what Dr. Swenson showed him caused waves of nausea to wash over him. He gulped hard to quell the urge to throw up. "I wish I knew for sure." In his heart of hearts, he knew it was from the bombs.

"Is it alright for me to photograph these too?"

"Sure, go ahead."

"It isn't only these. I'm seeing cases of bones so brittle, legs break upon standing, even with long term casting. The bones won't heal, and it isn't just the elderly, it is people who are in their prime. And, so many cancers. We've never seen a cancer epidemic like this before. As a matter of fact, cancer was rare before the bomb tests."

Reese told Dr. Swenson he would send in a report on what he'd seen, but didn't hold out much hope that it would stop the tests.

Each time Reese visited, another child had died. His heart lurched when he realized that without a miracle, William would be gone the next time he came.

Continuing his rounds, Reese dropped in to visit one five-year-old who had been in remission, but who now had returned for more treatments. Visiting her just after her readmission, Reese had complimented her on the lively pink polka dot bow in her hair. Having lost her hair during the first round of treatments, she had been proud that it had grown back. Now, mere weeks later, her hair was falling out again. A golden curl lay on the pillow next to her gaunt face. Reese picked it up and put it in his shirt pocket, saving it to analyze for radioactivity.

Reese guarded his affection for these children so he could be objective— an impossible feat. He loved them all and wanted to protect them. Often he thought about having his own children one day, but then he wondered how he could risk bringing a child into a world so radioactive it might die before becoming an adult. He thought of Rosa, so vibrant and vivacious felled by cancer. *We didn't know what would happen to people then, but now we do.*

Always, the question haunted him. What could he do to stop the tests? *These children are dying because of the fallout.* Again and again, he tried remediating measures. He stepped up his research, measuring hot spots of radioactivity in southern Utah. He submitted report after report proving the fallout was killing children and making urgent recommendations to stop the testing. He pleaded with AEC officials to warn people downwind. Why couldn't the AEC let them know to protect themselves when there was a test? Why not notify schools to keep children inside at recess? What was wrong with warning ranchers and farmers to get their livestock under cover? Sure, everyone knew about cloudshine, and parents had heard not to let children eat snow. But those were superficial measures. Reese knew it, and he was certain the AEC knew it, too. The cynicism of the government increasingly galled him.

He began to feel "watched." He couldn't put a finger on it, exactly, but it seemed to him there were people who didn't belong in his housing area hanging around near his house, or prowling around near his lab. A couple of them looked familiar, he saw them so often. He was tempted to introduce himself, but some warning signal inside stopped him. *If it's true,* he thought, *it's not funny.*

* * *

When Reese returned to his lab from visiting the children that day, there was a message for him to phone Dean, head of the AEC in Washington.

"Dr. Mayfield, we need someone with your qualifications to fly to Kwajelin in the Marshall Islands to evaluate the health of some of the islanders. A large number of them fell ill after our recent Bravo test there."

I'll bet they did. Reese had heard about Castle Bravo vaporizing three of the atolls, and seen in the files reports about tests on Bikini Atoll. The Bikinians had been moved along with their church, council house, and all their belongings to another island 168 miles away. They were promised it would be a temporary move. The Bravo test marked the eight year point. The Bikinians were still in "temporary" quarters.

"Is this about the people who were relocated from Bikini?"

"No. The problem now is with the people on Rongelap and nearby atolls. The winds shifted and carried radioactive fallout over those islands. We've evacuated the inhabitants, but many of them are sick."

"It will take me a few days to wrap up work here."

"Dr. Mayfield, I don't think you understand." Dean's voice had a distinct edge. "This is an order. We want you there within 48 hours. A military transport will pick you up at your quarters in Mercury, take you to Nellis Air Base and fly you to Kwajalein tomorrow."

Reese sucked in air through his teeth. "I understand. And what time will someone pick me up?" *This must be serious.*

"At 0700 hours."

"I'll be ready." *Somehow, I will.* "Have you notified my superior here?"

"Not yet, but as soon as I hang up, I will."

Angela overheard the conversation. "Going somewhere?"

"Yes. You'll have to hold down the fort while I'm gone."

"I'll get an Army doctor to fill in for you." As usual, Angela didn't pry for details.

"I'm being sent to Kwajalein. There are Islanders who are sick from the bomb tests near there. I wonder why they're calling on me." *Am I being sent there because of all the cancer reports I'm sending to the AEC?*

"You are the most knowledgeable, that's why. When do you leave?"

"At the crack of dawn."

"We'd better get busy then."

Angela pitched in and helped Reese gather lab equipment and supplies he thought may be scarce on Kwajalein, stuffing it in a duffle bag along with two

119

clean lab coats. At his quarters, he packed clothes, thinking his Nevada desert wardrobe wouldn't be much different from what he'd need in the Marshall Islands. He kept a couple of bags of penny candy around for when he thought he might be around children and tucked them in among his clothes.

After seeing those hospitalized children in St. George, Reese knew what was in store. He wondered how much fallout they'd been exposed to, and he wondered if he'd actually be allowed full information.

Arriving at the airport at Nellis, Reese was surprised to see he rated a jet—grateful that it wasn't a prop plane.

They must really want me there in a hurry.

After a six-hour flight, the plane landed at Hickam Air Base on Oahu for refueling. Reese was able to deplane and look around. As he stretched his legs while the plane was being readied, he admired the lush scenery—so different from Nevada. He hoped one day to return to Hawaii. Despite the speed of the jet, the trip to Kwajalein took almost twenty hours.

The plane landed at Bucholz Army Airfield in a tropical downpour. Reese's heart lurched when it slid sideways on the slick runway before coming to a stop. Met by an escort, he hurried down the steps and across the rain-drenched tarmac to a waiting jeep. He was in need of a shower, shave and a change of clothes. He didn't get any of that. He was whisked from the landing field to the Kawjelin Air Base Hospital.

On the way, his escort, a member of the AEC medical team, briefed him. "There was a design flaw in the Bravo bomb that resulted in an explosion two and a half times more powerful than expected. If that wasn't bad enough, Mother Nature had a hand in it. The wind shifted and the heaviest fallout fell on Rongelap—ash a little over three quarters of an inch deep coated the island. The shift in the winds hadn't been anticipated so the islanders weren't warned. Children played in the ash and ate it like it was snow. And—you've seen how that ash sparkles?"

Reese nodded.

"Women rubbed it into their hair."

Reese winced.

His escort continued, "236 islanders from Rongelap—that's the entire population—also people from nearby atolls were evacuated and brought here. All the Rongelapese are acutely ill. Every one of them. Those from the other

120

atolls are faring better. In addition, there are twenty-eight Americans who are sick. This is the worst we've seen." He swerved to avoid a rain-filled pothole.

No wonder the AEC sent for me. Reese learned from his escort that the crisis was so huge that he was part of a larger team of doctors, and may be the most experienced in fallout exposure illnesses.

After the test, it had taken two days for a team from the AEC to get to Rongelap to monitor the fallout. By that time people, were already suffering. The airlift to Kwajalein didn't happen until the third day, and meanwhile, people were living in thick radioactive ash."

The rain stopped, the sun broke through the clouds, and a triple rainbow arched through a cleansed sky. *God's promise.* Reese scanned the intensely green landscape.

"And the total exposure?" Reese asked. "What is the measurement?"

The medic's face was grim. "We estimate it at anywhere from 60 to 300 roentgens."

When Reese stepped out of the jeep in front of the hospital on Kwajalein, he was surrounded by children with huge brown eyes.

The escort said, "They heard another doctor was coming and wanted to be here to greet you."

Native women dressed in flowered muu muus approached him and put flower leis around his neck saying *yokwe*, hello in Marshallese.

"It would be appropriate for you to respond with *kommol tata* which means thank you very much," his escort said.

Reese smiled and repeated *kommol tata* every time another fragrant lei was placed around his neck.

"These natives are from other islands that didn't get as much fallout. Inside, you'll see the critically ill. It's pretty bad. The bomb was bigger and dirtier than expected."

The children took Reese's hands and led him toward the doors of the hospital chattering in Marshallese words he took to mean come inside. In the lobby of the hospital, they clustered around him, showing him beta burns on their faces, shoulders, arms, and feet. Most of the burns were starting to heal. He wondered how these children would be affected in the future: leukemia, thyroid cancer, or worse.

He inspected their wounds, felt their foreheads, and opened his mouth to indicate he wanted them to open theirs. With a serious look, he inspected their tongues then he smiled at each one and said, "Okay." A word the children seemed to know. Big toothy grins smiled at him. Some of the grins were missing front teeth, the adult teeth not yet having put in an appearance. Searching in his duffle bag, he pulled out a sack of candy and gave each of the children a Tootsie Roll.

Reese felt a tug on his sleeve. He turned to face a teenaged girl. "My sister Liana in there. You see her," she said in pidgin English.

He touched her lightly on the shoulder. "I will," he promised.

A native orderly approached. In Marshallese, he spoke to the children and shooed them off. In English, he welcomed Reese. After the children scattered, he said, "These are the lucky ones."

All the rooms were full. Cots holding desperately ill people lined the hallways. Here, too, on this lush, tropical island, the most sick were the children, the immune systems in their little bodies unable to cope. Patients vomited and bled from their ears and noses. Harried doctors and nurses rushed from patient to patient, attempting to ease the monumental suffering.

History told Reese that most of these islanders would experience permanent physiological changes, some severe. Five to ten roentgens ionized internally can alter blood chemistry and cause genetic damage. They'd been exposed to many times that.

Reese paused to examine a little girl. He picked up her chart. "Liana?" he said, smiling. Her eyes lit up and she returned his smile. The beautiful Polynesian child captured his heart with that smile.

"Your sister told me about you." He didn't know if she understood, so he gave her a reassuring pat on the hand.

The workload was staggering. The exhausted staff gave comfort to the dying and struggled valiantly to save as many Rongelapese as possible. Reese lived on coffee, taking an occasional shower to refresh himself, or sleeping for an hour or two when he couldn't stand any longer. He suspected half of population of Rongelap wouldn't make it. Here, as in southern Utah, the children were the most affected. Again, he tried not to become attached to these innocent and trusting islanders. However, there was Liana. Despite being sick, she was cheerful and her dark eyes sparkled. Her broad grin exposed an abundance of gleaming white teeth every time he approached her. He was sure the ten-year-old was improving. *I can save this one.*

It was two weeks before things settled down. Reese found an empty office, stretched out on the floor, and slept for six hours before a nurse wakened him. A patient had taken a turn for the worse. Liana.

Reese stayed by her bedside through the night. At four a.m., her hand went limp in his. Liana would never grow up, marry, and have children. Tears coursed down his face. He'd seen too much of this—too many young lives snuffed out by nuclear fallout.

It was daybreak by the time Reese could shower, dress, and go to find breakfast. Unable to eat, he took his coffee and walked the beach, deep in thought. To some, this was paradise, to others, a prison. To Reese, it was one more place where the Downwinders were losing.

Chapter Twenty-Three
1955
Las Vegas

Reese rested his arm on the door of his brand new, powder blue '55 Lincoln Capri and cruised Fremont Street in downtown Las Vegas. After seeing so many lives cut short at Kwajelein, he decided to treat himself. Life seemed so tenuous. *I'm around radioactivity all the time. Why not me?*

He'd spent $4,000, half of his savings. He had been unable to resist the new model with its V-8 engine and automatic Turbo Drive transmission. It had been years since he'd allowed himself such an indulgence. Now, the top was down and Reese sported a broad grin of self-satisfied pride.

Then he saw her. The most gorgeous girl he'd ever laid eyes on perched on the top of the back seat of a white Cadillac convertible driving toward him. She waved and blew a kiss his way as they passed.

Holy Cow!

He twisted his head to catch another look, and almost wiped out a parked car.

Shit! His heart pounded. He'd only had the car one day, and almost wrecked it, but he had to see that girl again. He whipped a U-turn right there, barely missing another car in the intersection.

Where'd they go? Damn, I've lost them.

He turned onto The Strip.

There they are.

He pressed his foot on the gas pedal and caught up. Reese beeped his horn to catch the girl's attention. His heart flip-flopped when she turned and waved at him. Since Rosa, nothing—and no one—had made him feel like this. He pulled alongside the Caddie.

"Hey, where are you headed?" he yelled at her.

"The Sands."

"You must be Miss Atomic Bomb, right?" Her mushroom cloud costume was unmistakable.

"You got it." She gave him a delightful grin.

He dropped behind the white car and followed them to the Sands Hotel and Casino.

What's the matter with me? I've never chased girls before. After Rosa died, he hadn't dated anyone. Well, there was Lisa, but one could hardly call that dating. *Must be my new car—no more Mr. Shy Guy.* His confidence soared.

Reese pulled into a parking space at the side of the Sands. He couldn't see the white convertible. Rushing into the casino, he saw a poster with a photo of the girl right in front of him. It advertised the "Miss Atomic Bomb Appearance" in the showroom. As he started into the entrance, an arm extended to block his path.

"Ticket, please."

Reese's face fell. He looked around.

"At the counter on your right."

Reese strode over to the ticket counter and slapped down a twenty, "A ticket to see Miss Atomic Bomb."

The usher accepted Reese's ticket with a knowing smile and pointed him toward the stage. There she was—gorgeous with thick, wavy, long blonde hair.

He went back to the usher. "What is Miss Atomic Bomb's name?"

The manager sighed, as if bored from answering this question. "Julie. Julie Carroll."

"How can I meet her?"

"You'll have to get in line."

"Will this help?" Reese pulled out a twenty-dollar bill and pressed it into the usher's hand.

The man raised his eyebrows a little and a sneer started to curl his lips.

Reese added another twenty. The sneer turned into a bright smile. "Right this way, sir." He crooked his index finger and started toward a door leading to the inner workings of the casino, and then backstage.

* * *

"Julie, this man wants to meet you."

125

Julie's smile was pleasant but guarded. "You were driving the Capri, weren't you?" *Persistent guy.*

Reese nodded and introduced himself as Dr. Reese Mayfield, hoping the title might influence her. Thrumming started in his ears and heat rose to his cheeks. "Will you have dinner with me," he blurted, then he gulped and thought, *Jeeze Louise, I'm no Joe Kool.* But he held a steady gaze into her eyes.

She shook her head. "Thank you for the invitation, but the pageant committee has plans for me."

"Then tomorrow night? I'm a physicist and a doctor. I work at the Nevada Test Site." The words spewed out. He hoped his resume would convince her to go out with him.

"I don't know." There was something about the timbre of his deep voice that attracted Julie, but she could tell he was much older that her twenty years. She wasn't sure.

"We can go to dinner and a show, if you'd like that."

Reese's gaze held Julie's captive for a moment causing her to blush. She bit her lip before throwing caution to the wind and said, "All right."

A rotund man who didn't come up to Reese's chin took Julie's hand and started leading her away.

"Where should I pick you up?"

"I'm in the phone book under Norman Carroll," she called over her shoulder.

Reese trailed after her. "I'll pick you up at seven thirty."

He drummed his thumbs on the steering wheel and sang Elvis Presley's *Love Me Tender* the entire sixty-five miles back to Mercury.

* * *

Reese took extra pains with dressing and shaving. He'd washed the car and vacuumed the interior. Being new, it didn't really need it, but he wanted to lavish attention on it anyway. Who was he kidding? He wanted to lavish attention on Julie. He allowed time to drop by a florist to purchase a small wrist corsage.

Standing on the front porch of the Carroll home, he straightened his tie and cleared his throat before he rang the doorbell. When Julie's father answered, he shoved out his hand. "I'm Reese Mayfield. I'm here to pick up Julie."

"Um, yes, she said you'd be here. She's not quite ready."

Reese stood eye-to-eye with Julie's father and endured some scrutiny before being invited in.

In the living room, the obligatory questions began.

"Yes, I work at the Yucca Flats Testing Labs for the Atomic Energy Commission in the Biology and Medicine Division. What do you do, sir?"

"I teach physics at the University of Nevada. Before that, I was with the Atomic Energy Commission at the Hanford Plant in Washington."

"Were you involved in making plutonium?"

"That I was."

"We used plutonium from Hanford at Los Alamos."

"You helped build the bomb?"

"Yes, sir."

"Don't you think you're a little old to be dating my daughter?"

"I'm thirty-one. Is that too old?"

"Julie's just twenty and still in college."

Reese was spared further interrogation when Mrs. Carroll came into the room. He sprang to his feet, as did Mr. Carroll.

"Hi, I'm Virginia Carroll." The lovely woman graciously extended a hand. "You must be Reese."

Reese clasped her hand. "Happy to meet you, Mrs. Carroll."

"Call me Ginny. Welcome to our home. Julie will be down in a moment. I hope my husband isn't giving you the third degree." She caught Norman's eye. "Oh, of course you are." A rustle drew her attention and she glanced at the staircase. "Ah, here comes your rescuer."

Reese caught his breath when his heart took an extra beat. The blue dress she wore accentuated her curves and intensified the color of her eyes.

"I've made reservations for the dinner show at the Flamingo." He tore open the cellophane covering a small white cardboard box and took out a white gardenia, which he slipped onto her wrist.

"Oh my. How lovely." She raised the flower to her nose. "And it smells so nice."

Ginny's smile of approval didn't go unnoticed by Norman.

Reese did all he could to dazzle Julie. With a few strategically placed dollars, he ensured they were seated at a table near the front and center. He showed off his knowledge of seafood from his San Francisco background and encouraged her to try lobster thermidor. He conjured up all his manners and charm to impress her, careful not to spend too much time gazing into her sea blue eyes for fear of drowning in them.

When he took her home, he resisted the urge to kiss her and instead asked her to take a Sunday drive up to Mount Charleston.

On the drive back to Mercury, a momentary sense of loss flitted through Reese's mind. He realized he was finally over losing Rosa. He puzzled over the feeling. He'd grieved so long for her, he wondered if he missed grieving. It was as though the clouds lifted and the sun shone through. He felt light as air.

* * *

The weather was clear and bright after a rare desert rain the night before. Reese had the top down and, despite the narrow winding road, he glanced over at Julie to admire the way the breeze toyed with her hair.

She talked effortlessly about her life and family, putting him at ease. Soon, he was talking about himself, his folks, the Los Alamos years, and why he became a doctor.

Reese realized he hadn't talked this much to anyone in years. Not even his parents.

Her infectious laugh burbled up from her throat and stopped just short of a guffaw.

It was cool at the 7000 foot elevation. As he helped her on with her sweater, she smiled up at him. If he hadn't already been smitten, that did the trick.

How can I win her over? I'm eleven years older, I have a bad leg, and I'm too serious. Reese, however hadn't reckoned with Ginny.

Ginny wanted a secure future for her daughter and didn't see the age difference as an obstacle. Ginny told Julie, when she asked what her mother thought, "You need to look to your future. You haven't met anyone you like. Reese is a man you can take seriously. He's nice and tall, educated, makes a good living, and not bad looking." She recognized a "good catch" when she saw it. Her instincts told her that her precious daughter would be safe with him.

Reese invited Julie to every new show that opened on the strip and all the movies in town. They dined casually and formally at almost every eatery in Vegas. He stayed at a hotel in town on Saturday nights so he could join the family at church Sunday mornings.

Reese became a regular at the Carroll home. Over Mr. Carroll's half-humorous protests that Reese was too old for his little girl, his wife invited Reese to dinner every Sunday.

To ingratiate himself with Julie's parents, Reese brought Ginny flowers, and vintage wines for Norman.

Reese started visiting jewelry stores three weeks after he met Julie. Although the convertible depleted half his savings, he wanted to marry Julie, and he wanted to present her with the biggest diamond ring he could afford. White gold was in fashion, but he wanted yellow gold to match her hair. After another month, he finally settled on a two carat diamond with three canary yellow diamonds set on each side and a matching wedding band. He carried the black silk ring box with him every time he saw Julie. He waited for the perfect moment, which included speaking with Mr. Carroll before proposing. He didn't know what kind of a response he would get, and spent time rehearsing what to say. Purposely arriving early one evening, he ratcheted up his courage and asked for Julie's hand in marriage.

"If you're going to marry my daughter," the older man said with a chuckle, "you'd better call me Norman."

"Yes, Mr. Car—" Reese began, then laughed at himself. "Norman."

Julie's father became serious. "Are you sure you want to marry into this family? I have a rather large skeleton in my closet."

"And what would that be, sir?" Reese couldn't imagine anything that would make him hesitate to marry this man's perfect daughter. He was expecting a joke, a leg pull, some kind of tall tale.

"I was investigated by Joseph McCarthy and his committee." Norman paused. "I see you're shocked."

Reese nodded. "Yes, sir, but…"

Norman held up a hand. "I want you to hear my side of the story."

"You owe me no explanation. I'm sure it was a mistake."

129

"That is not what you might hear once you're connected with me by marriage. It might not be good for your career."

"Tell me, then." Reese leaned forward.

"It wasn't a mistake." At the sight of Reese's expression, he said, "Oh, not the way you think. I'm not a subversive, but I believe the investigation was instigated by the AEC."

Norman stood up and poured them each a bourbon, neat. As Reese took his first sip, he thought about the occasional sense he'd had of being watched, followed, thought someone had gone through his papers in the lab.

Norman took the chair opposite Reese's. "As you know, I was a scientist at the Hanford plant in Washington. What you don't know is the circumstances surrounding my leaving." Carroll cleared his throat. "I was one of the protestors against continuing the manufacture and production of plutonium for bomb making. The war was over, and we had a surplus supply. Why did we need to continue when evidence showed we were polluting the Columbia River? My position was, as you can guess, very unpopular—so unpopular that my patriotism was questioned. Not only was I investigated by McCarthy, I was relieved of my position, and my security clearance was taken away."

"And then?" Reese looked around the lovely home. Certainly, the Carrolls seemed solvent.

"I was fortunate to get the position at the college here. Others who have been investigated have been ruined and unable to work because of the stigma. I was a university professor before the war, so I've had an easier time than most. Many academics are sympathetic, even if not public, with their views." He smiled a little bitterly. "Now, are you sure you want to be associated with the Carroll clan?"

"Sir, I love Julie and I want to marry her if she'll have me."

"Oh, I have no doubt she'll have you and so will her mother. When do you plan on doing the deed?"

"With your blessing, as soon as she comes down."

At that moment Julie appeared at the top of the stairs.

"I'll make myself scarce. Good luck."

Ginny came out of the kitchen and Norman wrapped his arm around her shoulders and guided her out of the French doors. "Come with me my love, I have something to show you on the patio." They disappeared as Julie reached the bottom step.

"Where are they off to?" she asked.

Reese reached out and caught her hand. "Come and sit next to me. I have something to ask you." He groped in his pocket and pulled out the black silk box. Kneeling before her, he said, "Julie, I'd like you to be my wife. Will you marry me?" He opened the box and offered the ring to her.

"Oh, what a stunning ring. I don't know what to say. We haven't known each other that long. I haven't thought about marriage." The moment Julie said that, she knew that was all she had thought about.

Reese's hopeful expression drooped. His worst fears might be realized. She might say no. He pulled the ring from its nest, took her hand and slid the ring on her finger and repeated, "Marry me?"

"Yes."

Julie's parents listened from the door they'd left ajar—Ginny with the back of her hand pressed against her mouth. Not being able to resist rushing into the room another moment, she went to her daughter and held her in a crushing hug while Norman pumped Reese's hand, issuing congratulations.

Chapter Twenty-Four
McCarthy

That night, Norman Carroll couldn't sleep. It wasn't just the excitement of having his only child engaged, it was talking about the McCarthy hearing. He slipped out of bed, taking care not to disturb Ginny. He poured a stiff belt of bourbon and went outside through the sliding glass door. Seated on the stone wall of his patio, he inhaled the warm calm desert air. It had been four years, but still it haunted him. His conversation with Reese brought all the buried memories back like they had happened yesterday. He remembered every detail just as he had related them to Ginny four years ago.

* * *

The man walked into my office unannounced. "May I help you?" I asked the unidentified man dressed in a black suit.

"Are you Norman Carroll?"

"Yes," I took off my reading glasses. "And you are?" I stood and extended my hand in greeting.

The hand was ignored.

"I'm George Hannon of the FBI. You are being summoned to appear before the McCarthy Committee on un-American Activities." He placed a manila envelope on my desk. "Your hearing date and other data are detailed along with your summons. I advise you to appear as instructed." Hannon's face showed no emotion as he turned and left.

I recall sitting and easing back into my chair, staring at the fat packet. I ran my hand through my hair before reaching for it. Settling reading glasses on my nose, I opened the envelope. My mouth went dry. Nobody wants to appear before Senator Joseph McCarthy. I knew what this could mean. My job, my security clearance, my career would be in jeopardy. Why, why me? But I knew. I'd been too vocal opposing the continuation of the manufacture of plutonium for atomic bombs. But I had no idea I'd been under the scrutiny of the FBI. My motives were pure. I should have been above suspicion.

Appear at the U. S. Senate at ten a.m. on June 7, 1951, the order read. I continued on and read the summons. Words like "disloyalty," "subversion," "treason," and "spy" jumped out, shocking me. My mind couldn't grapple with it and protested, *No I've never been any of these. I'm one of the good guys.* I sprang out of my chair and paced as I continued to read. *Rescind my security clearance? No! I'll be ruined. How will I support my family?* My eyes kept returning to the words, "disloyalty," "subversion," "treason," "spy." *Never!* I'd heard the rumors about Oppenheimer being investigated, but that was because he had Communist friends. Hmmm, Oppenheimer also knew the dangers of nuclear weapons, and as an advisor to the Atomic Energy Commission, suppressed the building, testing and use of them. *Pretty much how I've protested the ongoing manufacture of Plutonium. But I don't have any Communist friends.* Mentally I scanned a list of my former colleagues when I was a professor teaching at the university. I couldn't recall any of them ever being Communist Party members even though it had been popular during the 30s.

I arrived at the Senate offices in Washington D.C. half an hour before my hearing, fearful that I would be another victim of McCarthyism.

A little late. McCarthy appeared at 10:05 a.m. His thinning black hair with a prominent widow's peak made him look like the devil incarnate.

I stood, out of respect for the committee, and sized up McCarthy. *He has a wild-eyed look about him.* He was short and appeared bloated from, I surmised, his rumored alcoholism.

"Norman Carroll, you've been called before this committee to answer a few questions." McCarthy began. "Is it true that you are a scientist engaged in the manufacture of Plutonium at the Hanford Plant in Washington State?"

133

I leaned into the microphone on the table in front of me. "Yes."

"Are you, or have you ever been, a member of the Communist Party?"

"No, Sir." I felt dampness on my palms and forced myself to be calm.

"Before we go further," McCarthy continued, "I need to advise you that you have been under surveillance by the FBI for the past year. If you are found guilty of disloyalty, subversion or treason against the United States government, you will be stripped of your security clearance and relieved of your position at Hanford, possibly tried and imprisoned."

"I understand. I have nothing to hide." My mind reached back into my memory, searching for anything I may have done or said that could come back to haunt me.

"Have you ever attended a meeting of the Communist Party?"

I controlled my impulse to laugh. "No."

"Have you ever passed on classified information to a member of the Communist Party?

"No, sir." I didn't know whether it was my nerves that made me want to laugh in McCarthy's face, or the sheer audacity of the questions.

"Have you ever spoken against the continuing manufacture of plutonium and, if so, why?"

"Yes, we have an ample supply. The process of enriching plutonium for use in making atomic weapons requires a great deal of water. Water that we take from the Columbia River and return polluted with radioactivity. I believe it is a threat to our natural resources and the people who eat the fish and wildfowl."

"As great a threat as Communists in our midst? As great a threat as being attacked by Russia and not being able to use all the resources available to us to defend our great country?" McCarthy sputtered as saliva collected in the corners of his mouth.

"It's a different matter. As I said, we have sufficient plutonium."

"Are you qualified to determine that?"

"I believe so."

134

"Do you have any communist friends?"

"Not that I know of. My loyalty to my government is above question."

"Then why are you here? The FBI doesn't just pluck names out of a hat."

"I can't answer that. I've been a trusted employee of the Federal Government with a security clearance for the past eight years. My loyalty has never been questioned. I participated in the science of enriching uranium and plutonium for making the bombs that ended World War II. I've never discussed my work or what we do at Hanford with anyone outside the plant who doesn't have a security clearance."

"Thank you, Mr. Carroll. You are dismissed," McCarthy said with a wave of his hand.

Two weeks later I was relieved of my position at the Hanford Plant and my security clearance was revoked. McCarthy symbolically carved one more notch in his gun and ruined the career of another innocent man.

* * *

Even after this much time, Carroll's hands trembled in rage. He tossed back the rest of the bourbon. *I've got to get some sleep so I'll be fresh for work. I've got a wedding to pay for. Thank God I have work, I'm one of the few who were investigated that survived McCarthyism relatively unscathed.*

He ascended the stairs and slipped into bed, taking care not to awaken his wife.

Chapter Twenty-Five
The Wedding

Despite the horrors going on around Reese, his step was lighter, he smiled more often at his colleagues, and laughed at their jokes. They teased him and asked, "Who's the lucky lady?"

Although he hadn't talked about Julie, they knew by his demeanor that he had a girlfriend.

One of his buddies said, "I saw him out to dinner with Miss Atomic Bomb."

"Wooee," chimed in one of the Army guys. "Think you can handle all that radioactive energy?"

Reese blushed. "I hope so, because I'm going to marry that girl."

Before he could escape, his buddies slapped him on the back, shook his hand and congratulated him.

Voices swirled around him.

"Lucky guy."

"Invite me to the wedding."

"What does she want with an old man like you? Now me..."

"Ahh, you couldn't handle her."

Good-natured ribbing and well wishes surrounded Reese.

Reese even found himself whistling as he prepared to autopsy a pig which didn't survive the most recent blast. He'd already examined one that did, and it had trouble standing. These were all classic signs of radiation sickness. So ill was the live pig, Reese suspected it would die within a few days.

* * *

Over dinner one night, Reese said, "Julie, I want you to meet my folks. We have a long weekend coming up. What do you think about driving up to

San Francisco. We can make it in one day, stay two nights with my family and drive back in time for me to go to work on Tuesday."

"I want to meet your parents and I'd love the trip. I've never been to San Francisco."

When they returned, Julie and Reese set a wedding date for five months after their engagement.

Family gathered in Las Vegas to celebrate. In keeping with custom, Donna and Sam Mayfield hosted the wedding party and out-of-town guests at a dinner after the rehearsal.

Donna cornered Reese and pressed a piece of paper in his hand. "You have a cousin in Honolulu, Tom Miller. Here is his phone number and address. It would please me if you would take the time to get together with him."

"Yes, I remember Tom. He works at Pearl Harbor doesn't he?"

"That's right. Give him and his wife Carol our best. Now don't forget."

"I won't, Mother."

At five o'clock the next afternoon, Reese and Julie were married in an elegant ceremony at the Presbyterian Church, followed by a reception at the Carroll's home. Hung from wires strung from one palm tree to another, Japanese lanterns crisscrossed the area. Having congratulated the newlyweds, guests emerged from the reception line and loaded plates from a lavish buffet. They sat at small tables with white tablecloths and pink flower arrangements, eating while waiters circulated through the crowd, pouring champagne.

"Ginny, you really went all out. This is lovely." Donna said. "Julie's dress is beautiful. The flowers, the food—what a wonderful wedding. Our son is a lucky man." Sam nodded his agreement as he munched on hors d'oeuvres.

"Norman told me nothing was too good for his little girl—to spare no expense. He may regret it when he gets the bills." Ginny laughed and turned to greet another couple.

The arriving guests had thinned when a surprise guest showed up, J. Robert Oppenheimer. Reese broke formation and rushed forward to welcome his former boss. "I didn't think you'd be able to make it. Come and meet my bride." After the introductions, Reese handed Oppie a glass of champagne.

"Do you have anything stronger?" Oppie asked.

"Sure, come into the study. We'll raid my new father-in-law's liquor cabinet."

Having poured a half glass of Crown Royal over ice, Reese said, "I was so sorry to hear you lost your security clearance. Teller stabbed you in the back—a shame after all you did to support him at Los Alamos."

Oppie tilted his head, acknowledging Reese's empathy. "Are you happy at the Nevada Test Site?"

"I worry a lot about the damage fallout is causing. I do my best to try to keep our people safe, but my reports about radioactivity caused cancers don't seem to be making any difference."

"I'm not surprised, but this is your wedding and a time for celebration." Oppie raised his glass in a toast. "I wish you many happy years."

The men strolled back into the living room to rejoin the party.

"My happiness is standing over there in a white gown."

"She's a beauty and gracious. You're a lucky guy."

Julie caught Reese's eye and hurried over. "It's time to cut the cake. Please excuse us," she said to Oppie as she led her new husband away.

* * *

Left to his own thoughts, Oppenheimer reflected back to when he was hired to head up building the atomic bomb at Los Alamos.

"Call me Oppie," he'd said after the obligatory handshake with General Leslie Groves. "Everyone does."

"One thing I need to know, Oppie, is can you keep a secret?"

"If I need to." He kept his voice soft and persuasive while he waited to hear what was so important that the Army transported him from Berkeley to Travis Air Force Base and then flew him to Chicago to meet General Groves' train.

"Well, if you work on the project I have in mind, you'll have to. You're not a commie, are you?" Groves lifted the lid off a box of candy.

"No." Oppie hoped his serious but gentle grin assured his inquisitor. He lit a cigarette with a silver lighter.

"How do you get along with your colleagues? Do you work well together?" From the brief interview at Berkeley, Groves already knew the answer. Oppie could charm the bark off a tree. "Let me tell you what you'd be up against, and keep in mind what I'm telling you is top secret, but you need to know what you'd be getting into. I need a man to head up the building of an atomic bomb."

138

Pursing his lips into a low whistle, Oppie leaned back against his seat. He knew about the research being done in Germany. He knew scientists at the Argonne Labs in Chicago were working with fission and the Brits had scientists working on nuclear energy, but to head up a team to make an atomic bomb? Maybe to end this horrific war? Wow! Before the train reached D. C., he knew he'd accept the position if it were offered.

Oppie was jolted out of his thoughts when Julie tossed her bouquet to her contingent of bridesmaids and other single ladies. Julie had changed out of her wedding dress into a smart little navy-blue travel suit.

The newlyweds waved goodbye as they drove away in Reese's convertible with the clatter of tin cans bouncing behind.

* * *

Reese had chosen the honeymoon suite at the new Tropicana Hotel and Casino for their wedding night. Before the double doors at the entrance to their room, he swept her up in his arms and carried her across the threshold. He held her close as he settled her high heeled shoes on the luxurious carpet.

Reese's fingers trembled as he touched her cheek, then her hair. He stood back a bit as his eyes took in all of her. Mine, this beautiful girl is mine.

Julie's eyes looked up into his, questioning.

"I love you, Mrs. Mayfield."

"Mrs. Mayfield, what a nice sound. How about opening that bottle of champagne, Mr. Mayfield?"

"Of course, to celebrate our first night together."

He caught sight of an overflowing basket. Next to it, a bottle rested in a silver ice bucket. "The hotel went all out. Fruit, cheeses, and Dom Perignon." In truth, though, he wished for something stronger to calm his passion—a stiff belt of whiskey. He successfully popped the cork without showering himself, and poured two champagne flutes full. He handed one to Julie. "Here's to the Mayfield family."

"Oh, Reese, I hope we'll have children soon. I want a family. Four would be nice, two of each."

"That isn't possible unless we do something to make it happen."

Julie blushed. Her mother had had "the talk" with her, but she felt nervous with anticipation and a little scared.

139

He felt her shiver. "I won't do anything until you want me to. I'll be careful." He put his arm around her and gently pulled her to him. She melted into him as he began kissing her forehead, cheeks, the tip of her nose, her lips, her neck. Then he leaned back.

His experiences in the sex department had been few. A clumsy encounter in the back seat of a car in college—another at Los Alamos when he'd been seduced by an oversexed WAC. He and his beloved Rosa had kissed passionately, but that was all. He'd had a brief affair with his fellow medical resident, Lisa. He hoped those experiences would add up to a stellar performance.

After he refilled Julie's glass, he helped her out of her jacket and carefully hung it up. He stroked her arm and with trembling fingers, started to unbutton her blouse. A stirring started below his waist as he slid the cream colored silk blouse off her shoulders, exposing a lacy bra.

The champagne began to affect Julie and she giggled. "Not so fast, mister, Mom and I shopped all over Vegas for the most beautiful honeymoon nightie we could find."

"You won't need it." He nuzzled her mane of sweet smelling hair.

She ducked under his encircling arms. "Hold that thought." Julie shoved her glass into his hand and went to her suitcase. She snapped open the latches and produced yards of filmy stuff. Laughing, she shook out the wrinkles and disappeared into the bathroom.

"Not a chance of my losing that thought," he muttered to himself as he paced for what seemed like forever, restraining himself from gulping champagne. At last, she emerged in ivory lace and chiffon.

She twirled and asked, "Do you like it?"

"It is exquisite, but I don't think you'll have it on long." He pulled her close. He wanted this night to be perfect.

Julie yielded to his embrace and turned her lips up to his. He stroked her back until she relaxed against him. He picked her up and laid her on the bed, holding her closer, loving the excitement building within him—hoping she felt the same. She clung to him, her mouth exploring his. He touched her breast. She pulled her lips away to emit a tiny gasp. He pulled a ribbon and the peignoir fell away. Reese took her face in both hands and kissed her, then trailed his tongue down her throat. *My God, I could eat her alive.*

140

His thumb encircled a nipple through the chiffon nightgown before pulling it over her head and casting it aside. He slid a hand up her leg as his tongue left her throat, sliding lower, loving her smooth, fragrant skin.

Julie recalled the secret joy of touching herself in the darkness of her room. Then his tongue found the source of her pleasure. *This is the moment I've saved myself for.* Mindless, she became conscious only of the sensations rippling over her.

Involuntarily her back arched. Her voice was raspy as she gasped, "Reese, let's get under the covers."

* * *

The next day, Reese and Julie flew to Hawaii for their honeymoon. They stayed at the famous pink Royal Hawaiian Hotel. For the first two days, the beach was wasted on them. The third day they ate breakfast at the Surf Room on the beach.

After a leisurely Hawaiian breakfast of papaya, Portuguese sausage, and eggs, they planned their day. As they left the restaurant, two men in black suits caught Julie's eye. "It's strange to see people in suits when everyone else is in Aloha attire."

Reese turned to see who she was looking at, then said, "Probably bankers having a breakfast meeting." But he wondered if they were watching him. *Looks like FBI.*

"What time is it, Reese? I think we need to hurry if we're going to take surfing lessons."

They headed toward Kuhio Beach to meet their instructor.

Lessons over, and hair matted with salt water, the honeymooners lay on woven grass mats. They giggled at how clumsy they had been trying to surf as they smooched and rubbed coconut oil on each other.

"It's hard to be concerned about bomb tests and fallout here. I feel so far removed from work," Reese said.

"Mmm, it is lovely. Can we go to the Luau tonight? I saw an ad in the lobby. It's here at the Royal on that grassy area." Julie pointed a finger. "Look over there. They are setting up the stage now."

"This might be a good time to get together with Tom and Carol. I'll phone and see if they're free to join us."

* * *

Julie and Reese met his cousins in the lobby.

After introductions, Reese said, "Mom will be happy we got together," before leading his guests to the garden where he'd reserved a table near the stage.

The two couples sat at a long table with other tourists in Aloha attire. Coconut shells holding poi sat in front of each guest. After instructions from the MC on stage, they all twirled their fingers in the brownish goo, tasted, laughed, and pulled faces. A hula girl pulled Tom up on stage to learn how to do the hula. Everyone at the table whooped and cheered him on, but he hadn't drunk enough Mai Tais to enjoy making a fool of himself. He appeared grateful to escape from the stage and get back into his chair. Soon waiters in lava lavas carried the Kalua pig on a plank down the raised runway to be carved and served. The show and tropical drinks continued on until everyone was a little drunk and giggly.

As Reese and Julie's guests were leaving, Tom said, "I wish we'd got to know each other sooner, you work in the nuclear field and yesterday I made repairs on the nuclear reactor on the USS Nautilus. It came into port a couple of days ago. It's amazing that it can stay submerged for four months. I could learn a lot from you."

"Maybe not. I'm not very mechanical," Reese replied.

The valet delivered Carol and Tom's car to the porte cochere and they left, waving and calling, "Aloha, had a great time."

* * *

"Mom, We're back," Julie called as she and Reese walked in the door. The ten-day honeymoon had passed all too quickly.

Ginny Carroll rushed from the kitchen, wiping her hands on her flowered apron. "Sweetheart, how was Hawaii? Put your things down and tell me all about it." She wrapped her arms around her daughter and kissed her on the cheek. "Look at your tan. Did you learn the hula and how to surf?" She turned and gave Reese a squeeze around his waist. "I've been over at your new apartment all week getting it ready for you two."

"Mom, slow down. Sit by me and I'll tell you all about it. You and Dad must go and stay at the Royal Hawaiian. Everything was so wonderful. They have a show every night with dancers up high on pillars all around the room— and beautiful Hawaiian songs and music and hula girls—and the flowers.

Every night Reese brought me leis, plumeria and orchid and strands of these tiny little blossoms they call wedding flowers."

"Pikake," he filled in.

"It sounds like heaven." Ginny stood and untied her apron. "I can't wait for you to see your apartment. Let's go over there right now and get you lovebirds settled in."

As the three climbed into the convertible, a calm feeling of satisfied pleasure settled over Reese.

"Where's Dad?" Julie asked.

"Working. Where else? I'm sure he'll drop by later. We'll phone him and let him know you're home."

Ginny unlocked the door on the second floor apartment, turned and dropped the key into Julie's hand. "Ta da," she sang and spread her arms wide.

"Oh, Mom, it's beautiful. What a wonderful wedding present. I love the couch." She peeked around the corner into the bedroom. "A king sized bed? Reese's feet won't hang off the end. It's perfect—and the bedspread, powder blue, my favorite color."

Reese stopped exploring and turned to Ginny. "Thank you. This was wholly unexpected." Reese took Ginny's hand in both of his, leaned over and bussed her cheek.

"We wanted to do it." Ginny smiled. "And it's close to the university. You can walk to school, Julie. You do remember our agreement that you'd finish college?"

"Of course." *That is if I'm not pregnant.* Julie hoped she was.

* * *

Reese didn't relish the thought of returning to work. Hawaii had been the stuff dreams were made of. Now, back to reality. The first order of the day was to move his things to their new home. He'd already notified the Mercury housing coordinator that he was marrying and would be moving into Las Vegas. He didn't relish the hour drive each way, but with Julie going to the university, it made more sense than her moving to Mercury. It was a damned dismal place anyway. Besides, having lost Rosa to fallout, he wanted to protect Julie by keeping her away from the test site. She'd be safer in town.

While Reese was honeymooning, The Operation Teapot series of tests had been completed. Things at the test site would be quiet for a while, allowing

143

him plenty of time to finish his research and reports and send them off to Washington. He dove into his work, rested and content to be back in his lab.

* * *

Julie wasn't pregnant. She received her BA in Art History and walked with the class of '57.

"Reese, now that I've finished college, I want to get serious about having a baby."

"I'm ready for children, too, but, honey, we've never done anything to prevent your getting pregnant. Maybe you should see a doctor and make sure everything is all right."

"I'll make an appointment tomorrow."

Chapter Twenty-Six
1956
Disillusionment

Seated at the back of the courtroom, Reese watched, powerless, as the Brenner family lost their case in 1956. When the Brenners' attorney asked for reports, he was told the information was classified. All of the veterinarian's findings were deemed inadmissible when they mysteriously became classified.

Thompson's reports suddenly were classified, along with all the other evidence that would prove the Brenner's case. The Brenners weren't the only ones to lose sheep. Over five thousand sheep were killed by fallout. When the Brenners lost their case, the other sheep ranchers suspected there would be no compensation for any of them.

He admired the ranchers for fighting against a government in which they had once held unwavering faith. Reese recognized that it was the nature of the Mormon population of southern Utah to be hard working and soft spoken. They went to church, paid their ten percent tithe, stepped up to serve in the military, and raised their children to be good, God-fearing citizens. They put their hearts into making a better life for their young than they had. Up until the moment of the final refusal of compensation, they had believed the government would make it right with them.

It sickened Reese to see them shattered when, instead of receiving fair treatment by a nation that promised "justice for all," they fell victims to a vicious government cover-up. Many of them had to file for bankruptcy. The ranchers' disillusionment was total.

So was Reese's.

* * *

Tsk, tsk. You scientists thought you could control me. Foolish men, don't you know I'm a wanderer? When I was a little bomb, I only reached the winds aloft, but now that you're making bigger and bigger bombs, they can even reach the jet stream, and from there I can flit unfettered all the way around the globe. A little rain here—kids, don't splash in the puddles. A little snow there—kids, don't eat the snow.

I did wreak a little havoc all the way across the country after the Simon test. Who'd ever suspect that my cloud would rise to 44,000 feet? How could you predict a wind of 115 miles an hour would carry my fallout all the way to Troy, New York? What about that rainstorm? No one ever expected it would wash radioactivity out of the sky and the puddles would become radioactive. Dang, I'm sorry I made you sick, but what's a little cancer compared to my power? I must apologize for doing in all those sheep. But an atom's gotta do what an atom's gotta do. So Doctor Scientists, what's a little self-deception here and there? After all, you are doing the bidding of your government and it's the biggest deceiver of all.

* * *

Thoughts of the trial crowded Reese's mind the night after the trial. He tossed and turned as sleep evaded him. *I'm a reasonably smart guy. I ought to be able to figure out how to convince the powers that be that they must stop the bomb testing, that it's the fallout causing cancer and killing livestock. Even in these frightening times with our nuclear race with Russia, they should care about the people.* A voice in his head shouted, *They don't.* His mind resisted the denial and insisted, *Shouldn't they?*

* * *

Convincing D.C. powers was one problem. Rousing the people was another. Post-war patriotism blocked Reese's efforts to awaken concern—any criticism of the government was met with a change of subject, as though Reese had uttered a string of four-letter words. The Cold War kept people on edge.

The McCarthy hearings didn't help either, even if they didn't touch the people Reese knew in Utah. A person could implicate a neighbor, a business rival, or someone he just plain didn't like, simply by placing an anonymous phone call to the McCarthy Commission.

To Reese, it seemed that this wasn't a time of "innocent until proven guilty." With McCarthy, it was a time of "guilty until you were ruined." Most people who were investigated were loyal, law-abiding citizens. It was a witch hunt justified and perpetrated by one paranoid man.

146

Rolling it all together—the Cold War, the atomic threat, the Communist witch hunts—made Reese wonder if the nation's definition of patriotism was getting irreparably warped. Surely, these times were motivating people to ignore their own consciences under pressure to conform. He struggled with it himself. Every time he had the sense of being observed, it reminded him how fragile his own job security might be.

Regardless of his mounting frustrations, Reese's work continued. And so did the tests. He hated that the AEC researchers were using livestock at the Nevada Test site. There were three different locations where farms raised animals for the tests, some with pigs, chickens and sheep and others with larger animals such as cattle and horses. One even raised dogs. Pigs were favored because they most resembled the characteristics of humans. Biologists could get a fairly accurate picture of what might happen to people who were near an atomic bomb blast.

One of these farm factories was run by Hank Styller, a veteran of WWII who had earned the Purple Heart. Heavily scarred from burns, Hank was hard to look at, but he had a tender heart.

The animals Hank looked after were destined to be positioned at varying distances from atomic bomb testing during the Upshot-Knothole series of tests. As an experiment to test which fabrics provided the greatest protection during nuclear bombings, Hank's pigs would be dressed in uniforms made out of cotton, wool, nylon, or rayon. The idea of using animals sickened Hank, but he was grateful for the job.

It was one of Reese's assignments to accompany a veterinarian from the AEC who checked on the animals' health before the tests. They travelled from farm to farm. With a test scheduled for a month hence, it was time to make their rounds. As Reese and the veterinarian climbed out of the military Jeep, Hank met them with a handshake and a long face. He shifted his chaw of tobacco to his cheek and said, "I kinda hate to see you guys. It always means somethin's up. Usually you want to take my charges away for a test." He scanned the road. "No livestock truck today. Pigs'll be happy."

Reese realized it wasn't just the pigs that were happy. He suspected Hank tried not to become attached to the animals under his care, but sometimes the farmer just couldn't help it.

147

"Is that Pinky?" Reese asked, nodding to the young pig at Hank's heels. He'd seen the tiny eight-week old piglet nestled in Hank's arms when it first arrived at Hank's farm.

"Now, doc. You ain't sposed to notice, right?" Hank gave Reese a reluctant grin.

When the last litter arrived, the runt had captured Hank's heart. He'd allowed the tiny piglet to snuggle into his flannel shirt and root for treats from his pocket. He named him Pinky, and today, the runt looked way less runtish to Reese. He followed Hank like a pup. Reese hoped it wouldn't break Hank's heart to part with the animal. Reese had seen enough grief.

The vet was all business. After pronouncing the livestock fit, he told Hank, "We'll be back for a shipment in three weeks." He eyed Pinky. "We'll be taking all of them this time. That one, too."

Hank stepped between the vet and the pig.

Reese asked the vet, "May I have a copy of your report?"

"Don't see any reason why not."

He might have objected if he'd known Reese's motives. Reese wanted irrefutable proof that the animals were healthy and not malnourished, to present to the AEC, Congress and, if necessary, the president—proof it was exposure to radioactive fallout that was giving people cancer and killing livestock. Although those staked out closest to the blast would most likely die instantly, those farther away would be subject to fallout like the Brenner's sheep had been.

Hank appeared to be in a continual state of ambivalence about his work with the animals. In the last blast, all but two of the pigs were killed. The ones in the synthetic fabrics died horrible deaths with cloth melted into their skins. The two survivors came back with radiation burns, one blinded from the flash. Shortly after their return, they were transferred to labs for testing. He hadn't asked what happened to the pigs after that. He told Reese he didn't want to know, explaining that doubting the value of the research just plain went against his grain. "I was a soldier. I know we make sacrifices for our nation."

Reese found it hard to bite his tongue. Were such sacrifices truly necessary? He'd read the reports on animal testing on Bikini. Thirty five hundred animals had been staked out on the atoll and on abandoned ships from WWII and captured Japanese ships. There had even been a Time Magazine article about Pig 311, who survived despite insurmountable odds. It had appeared that he'd been blown off the ship, survived the blast, swam to shore, and survived the radioactivity. *It just wasn't his time*, Reese thought. He also thought Hank couldn't handle losing Pinky that way. Though not a devious man, Reese formulated a plan that may save Hank's little pet.

Two days after Reese's visit, extra rations of pies, cakes, cookies, sweet rolls, and breads began showing up at Hank's farm. After the third such delivery, Hank called Reese.

"Doc, it's kinda funny," Hank said. "I didn't put in for any increase in the requisition."

Reese answered with a noncommittal, "Hmmmm. Gosh, Hank. I don't know."

"What should I do with 'em, Doc? Do I have to send 'em back?"

"Considering where your animals are going...," Reese said. In his mind's eye, he was seeing Pinky doing what Hank would call "snarfing up" the extra food.

"You mean, given 'em the extras as a final send-off?"

"Maybe." Reese paused, calculating how to hint. "Or you could make sure some of the smaller ones..... The tests are hard on them, you know, Hank."

"Right. I get you, Doc." Reese imagined Hank smiling. Pinky would fatten up nicely. Maybe, Reese hoped, too nicely. Those pig uniforms were all one size. Medium swine.

Sure enough, Pinky grew fast with the extra food, faster than his brothers and sisters, although they were the fortunate recipients of his leftovers. As a result, they were getting fat, too.

The day of shipping the pigs arrived, but there was a problem. With unfavorable weather conditions projected to last several days, the test was delayed a week, as was preparing the pigs, which included fitting them into their uniforms.

* * *

"Ya got a reprieve, piggies," Hank crooned to them. "Bad weather may be yer salvation. Yer already pretty chunky fer them there uniforms." He chuckled. "And in another week, ya'll gain more weight."

149

When Army personnel came to dress the 250-pound pigs into their custom-made outfits, they could only squeeze two into the uniforms. Even Pinky was too fat for the loose boxer style pants. Hank turned his back to hide his laughter as the men wrestled pigs into their outfits.

"Ouch," yelled one of the soldiers as the pigs kicked, squealed, and pig poop flew.

"God dammit, I got pig shit all over me," said another.

"Who's idea was it to put pigs in uniform anyhow?" groused the first.

Innocence personified, Hank said, "Golly gee whiz. Guess that extra week made 'em gain too much weight."

Only two of the pigs toddled up the stock chute onto the truck and were taken away.

Knowing Hank loved the animals in his care, and sensing he could use a financial leg up, Reese bought Pinky and the pigs that didn't go to the test site. He didn't think Hank would accept charity and told him the Army was abandoning them because they were too big to be used for the tests, and he could thank Uncle Sam for the gift. Reese thought it would be more humane if they were butchered and sold for pork chops than to be staked out near the bomb site.

Chapter Twenty-Seven
Lisa

"Hey, Red," a sultry voice called out.

Reese jerked his head around. Nobody had called him Red since he finished his residency at L.A. County Hospital. He swiveled to scan the casino of the Sands, but couldn't see anyone he knew. He'd been in meetings in a conference room most of the day, discussing radioactive pollution in the Columbia River.

"Reese, it's me, Lisa Menninger." A waving hand appeared from a row of slot machines.

He caught sight of her. "Lisa, what are you doing in Vegas?"

"Just a little relaxation—been working way too hard. This doctoring is keeping me busier than I want to be, but I'm making a bundle of money."

"Probably a lot more than I am working for Uncle Sam."

"What do you do for Uncle?" She dropped a quarter in the slot and pulled the handle on the one-arm bandit.

"I'm with the AEC. Among other things, I do biological research on the effects of radioactive fallout from atomic bomb testing."

"Nobody's more qualified for that than you are, but it sounds boring. Come back to L.A. and work with me. You'll be rich in no time."

"Thanks for the offer. I'll give it some thought." He knew he wouldn't.

"We had some great times, didn't we?"

Reese felt his ears get hot as red crept up his neck.

She saw the blush. "Aw, still Mr. Shy Guy. I've got a room upstairs. How about an encore in memory of bygone days?"

"Lisa, I can't. I'm married."

"So?"

"Lisa, I love her. I couldn't—wouldn't."

"No surprise there. You always were a straight shooter, in more than one way. Good to see you, old buddy." She stood, threw her arms around him, and gave him a bear hug. "Don't lose touch. I'd think by now you'd be getting pretty pissed off at the Washington Warriors annihilating half the population of southern Utah."

"You mean the fallout causing cancer. You know about it?"

"Yeah, and I thought you'd be the last one to be a part of it."

Reese thought he was one of the good guys, but Lisa didn't seem to see it that way. He hadn't realized that was the opinion of a medical professional. *If Lisa thinks this, maybe I'm too insulated by the job to be objective.*

"You may want to take me up of that offer. I'm in the book." She sat and started dropping quarters into the slot machine. "About the job I mean—the other, too, if you're up for it."

As Reese walked away, his cheeks still burned from Lisa's suggestion when he heard the clang of bells announcing a winner and heard her scream of delight.

A twinge of shame washed over him. *I hope I never run into her when I'm with Julie.* Lisa was so outspoken, he wondered if she would keep their secret. *Secret? It wasn't so secret at LA County. What a jerk I was.*

His meetings over, he headed for home, still chewing on Lisa's comments. He hated the notion of being thought of as one of the bad guys—just another government hack doing its bidding.

* * *

Ah, Reese, you naïve fool, the Atom chortled. Don't you know you're just another pawn in a larger game? Do you think the Warriors would let all that ordinance go to waste? After all, they spent billions developing and building the atomic, then the hydrogen bombs. No way would they let that go to waste. So, a few thousand civilians are sacrificed, what's that compared to the money? It's always about the money, don'tcha know? The people are expendable in the face of big bucks. Manufacturing has been polluting the air and water for decades. Who is going to quibble about a few lives lost to bomb testing? Think about coal mine cave-ins and how many men are buried in the concrete at Boulder Dam. Is this any different? You can't fight it, Reese—better give in.

* * *

152

When Reese arrived home, he found Julie lying on the sofa with an ice bag on her forehead.

"Honey, what's wrong?"

Her eyes were red and swollen. She sat up, still holding the ice bag on her head. "I had the most terrible news."

"What? What happened?"

"I saw Dr. Noyes today. He doesn't think I'll ever have children." Tears started streaming down her cheeks.

"That can't be right. What makes him think that?"

"The tests he ordered showed scar tissue on my fallopian tubes and ovaries. He doesn't think I'll ever conceive. He said that he could be wrong, but he didn't think so." She started crying again.

Reese took her in his arms. "I'm sure he's wrong. Why didn't you call me?"

"I knew you had important meetings all day and didn't want to disturb you. Mom went with me. She left a few minutes before you got home."

"How could you possibly have scars? Did Dr. Noyes say how that could have happened?"

"He has no idea, but he did say that he's seeing an unusual amount of sterility in young women—women that are having the same problems I am."

Reese continued to hold her and stroke her back. *The fallout. Could it be the exposure to radioactive fallout?* A frisson of fear skittered up his spine. He couldn't help thinking about Rosa. *My fault, too.*

1957–Operation Plumbob

When Angela handed Reese the schedule of bomb tests, code named Operation Plumbob, his heart sank with every listing:

Boltzman, May 28

Franklin, June 2

Lassen, June 5

Wilson, June 18

Priscilla June 24

There were 24 more proposed tests to be completed by October 7—a total of 29, all in one summer.

"Angela, have you read this? He handed her back the file on Operation Plumbob."

"Yes, just before I gave it to you. Seems like overkill doesn't it?"

"Why do we need all these tests? And they are all atmospheric. When are they ever going to go underground with these tests? I've provided them with proof over and over that fallout is dangerous, particularly atmospheric testing, not just to the people of southern Utah, but it has far reaching effects. I wonder what I have to do to get them to take action."

"Perhaps if we resend some of the reports and recommend underground testing, demand stopping the testing all together. We can word it more strongly. All we can do is try again and again. Maybe if we send along the reports of new cancer patients in St. George and Cedar City, it will make them pay attention."

"Let's do it."

"I'll draw up a draft and gather all the information for you to go over."

"Thanks Angela. You're a gem."

*   *   *

Priscilla hung from a balloon, an ominous black canister. Below, over 900 pigs staked out at varying distances squealed in protest, some behind glass to test possible damage to humans struck by flying glass.

Trenches scarred the landscape, burrowed among desert shrubs that had survived the winds of prior tests. A few brittlebush bloomed an optimistic bright yellow. Marines nervously awaited the moment to crouch down.

"If we aren't in harm's way, why are the officers five miles behind us?" queried one of the men to his buddy.

Then it came: the flash, the deafening boom, the powerful wind. When the wind passed, troops emerged like locusts and hundreds marched toward ground zero. Tanks overturned with their tracks blown off. Mannequins dressed in military garb lay strewn around, some burning, some in pieces littering the landscape. Surviving pigs with glass shards impaled in their flesh and others burned over eighty percent of their bodies shrieked in pain. Still the men marched, their orders to secure the area. When they arrived, the only thing to secure was scorched earth and a giant crater.

Reese could only worry about those men. He had stood twelve miles away in the control tower behind the scientists who detonated the bomb. The size of the blast had been underestimated. It blew the metal door off the tower and shook him so hard he had to hang onto the wall to keep from falling. Plate glass windows in Las Vegas shattered. What was supposed to be a fourteen-kiloton bomb was, in reality, thirty-eight. When the reports reached Livermore Labs, scientists scratched their heads, wondering how they could have made such a major miscalculation.

Chapter Twenty-Eight

The end of further experiments with atomic bombs would be like
early sunrays of hope which suffering humanity is longing for.

From Albert Schweitzer's "A Declaration of Conscience"
speech given in Oslo, Norway April 24, 1957

Reese returned from spending a day in the field gathering samples. He was hot, tired and thirsty. Angela handed him a special delivery letter. He gulped down water, quenching his thirst as he opened it. A smile spread into a broad grin as he read it.

"What is it?" Angela asked.

He handed her the letter to read. "What an honor." She handed back the letter.

"Angela, I'm taking off. I want to tell Julie."

"Congratulations," Angela called after him as he dashed out the door.

Reese floored the gas pedal and sped past slower vehicles in his rush to get home.

"Julie, I've been invited to join Albert Schweitzer to conduct an environmental impact examination of the Columbia River." The words tumbled out as he loped into the kitchen. "We're going to study the impact of the radioactive waste from the Hanford Site."

"You'll be going to Washington? Will you be staying in Richland?" Julie wiped her hands on a dishtowel.

"Yes, we'll be working out of Hanford. I've never been there, but isn't it about half an hour north of Richland?"

"That's about how long it took Daddy to get to work. May I tag along? I'd like to see some of my old friends there."

"Julie, don't you get it? I'll be working with Schweitzer. This is an honor. And yes, I'll make arrangements for you to accompany me."

Julie had been preoccupied since her bad news from the doctor. "I'm sorry, honey. I can see how excited you are about this trip." She flipped the dishtowel over his head and around his neck, tugging on both ends to bring his lips down to meet hers. "When are we going?"

"Next week."

* * *

At seven a.m. Monday morning, Julie and Reese met an army transport plane at Nellis Air Force Base and flew to Richland where they were met by a driver. When they arrived at their hotel, the driver told Reese he would wait for him and take him to the Hanford Plant.

After taking the elevator to the ninth floor, Julie walked through the door of their room and peeked around another doorway to the bedroom with a king sized bed covered with a green silk bedspread. "Oh my, this is nice. I didn't know we'd have a suite."

"Nothing but the best for my beautiful wife. I wanted you to be comfortable since I'll be away working all day." Reese settled the suitcases on luggage racks, turned and grazed her cheek with a kiss.

With Julie settled, Reese grabbed a pair of jeans and stuffed them into his briefcase, then headed off to the Hanford Site where everyone involved would meet. Impressed as Reese was meeting Schweitzer, the noted humanitarian and peace advocate seemed honored to meet Reese. After an orientation meeting with biologists and environmentalists attached to the Atomic Energy Commission, they caravanned in three army jeeps northeast to the river. Reese had not realized that approximately fifty miles of the Columbia River bordered the Hanford Site. He was surprised to see cooling towers next to a bend in the river.

Clad in knee-high rubber boots, the men tramped through reeds and grass on the river bank.

"Look at that duck," Reese said. "It has tumors on its feet."

"Can you catch it?" asked Schweitzer. Despite his advanced age, he was robust, sporting a bushy white mustache and a full head of unruly silver hair.

Reese approached the duck as quietly as he could. The duck teased him. As soon as he got within arm's reach, she waddled and flapped her wings,

157

leading him on. "She must have a nest near here that she is leading me away from," he whispered to Schweitzer who was moving the grass aside with his gloved hands.

"*Achtung*, what's this. Mayfield, I think I found her nest." He carefully scooped up three speckled eggs, wrapped them in tissue, laid them in an egg carton and gently placed it in a net bag attached to his waist. Mama duck came squawking back toward him. "Sorry, mama, no babies for you this year. I need your eggs for research."

She was so busy trying to protect her nest that she didn't see Reese on her tail. He caught her with both hands and in a single motion shoved her into his net bag. She squawked her protest and tried to take off a finger or two, but just got a beak full of leather glove. "I won't hurt you. I just want to take a sample of those lumps on your feet. You'll be free in a couple of days."

"*Gut gemacht*, Mayfield," Schweitzer praised Reese.

The AEC biology men came back with three silver salmon tails hanging out of their creels. "It was a good day for fishing," one of them said. "Hate to be doing research on these fish, they'd make good eating."

"You may change your mind if they have high levels of radioactivity in them." Reese said. "Did anyone get mud and water samples?"

"We have both," the biologists said in unison.

After a day on the river tromping through mud and grasses in the March chill, Reese relished the thought of a hot shower and a good dinner in the hotel dining room. He was tired and barely warming up, even though the car was toasty enough. He bade his driver goodbye and said he'd be waiting in the lobby at eight the next morning. He rushed to the elevator and tapped his toe impatiently as it ground its way up to the ninth floor.

"Hi, sweetheart," Reese said when he got to the room. "Did you have a nice lunch with your friends?"

"It was good and bad," Julie said

"What was bad about it?"

"All of them have babies—it's all they could talk about. I felt left out, and, I hate to admit, jealous."

"That's tough. I'm so sorry. We'll start adoption proceedings when we get home."

"Oh, Reese, I don't know."

"Let me get cleaned up and we'll talk about it over dinner."

"I did meet someone interesting today."

"Who?" Reese called from the shower.

"A lady doctor who's here for a family reunion. It seems her mother's maiden name is Buchanan—an old family of Mormons here, but her name is Menninger.

Reese stopped mid scrub. *Holy crap! Is Lisa Menninger here?* A wave of apprehension spread over him.

"I gather her mother's the black sheep in the family. Her father is Jewish."

"Where did you run into her?"

"In the lobby, she's staying here."

Damn. Although, I don't think Lisa will say anything. He knew her motive as far as he was concerned was to have him work at her clinic.

At dinner, he was relieved not to see her in the dining room. But he was more concerned about Julie's sadness about not having a baby so she would be fulfilled and fit in with the rest of her friends. He ordered Chateaubriand for two with Chateau Margaux wine. Halfway through dinner, Julie was giggling—the wine had the desired effect. Reese was happy to see her lighthearted again.

* * *

The next morning, half of the team stayed in the lab to test the salmon, the duck, and the eggs they'd collected. The rest of them took off to drive a hundred miles downstream to get more samples of river mud and water, and more fish and waterfowl. They had even better luck, capturing a Canada goose, gathered several eggs—taking one from each nest they found—caught a few salmon, a coot, and even a seagull that had made its way inland.

The next day Reese and the biologists worked in the lab while the environmentalists and Sweitzer made an excursion upstream to collect samples.

Late that afternoon, Sweitzer and the team of environmentalists delivered their samples. "Well Mayfield, we went almost fifty miles upstream," Sweitzer said.

The team dropped off more fish, water fowl, and eggs.

"Do you have any results?" Sweitzer picked burs off his pants leg.

159

"As we suspected, the amount of radioactivity is well above the allowable limits. The eggs are contaminated with radioiodine I-131." Reese went to the sink and began washing his hands. "The flesh of the birds and fish show both radioiodine I-129 and I-131." Shaking water from his hands, he reached for a towel. "I excised a tumor from Mama Duck, which I'll have to send to my lab in Nevada for testing, but it appears to be malignant. I think that's why there are so many lumps on her feet. The cancer seems to be spreading."

The team advised state and federal authorities to caution people living in the area not to swim in the river and not to eat the fish or the game birds. The information was contained in a small article buried near the back of the local paper. Again, the Atomic Energy Commission downplayed the dangers of radioactivity.

* * *

Reese spent his evenings at home the next week preparing his report on the Hanford plant. He became angrier as he listed his findings. At work, he phoned the other team members to compare notes. Sweitzer was the most vocal about the Columbia River being contaminated with radioactivity—he wanted Hanford shut down.

Chosen as the team's spokesman, it was up to Reese to present their findings to the Atomic Energy Commission. He wanted to have all the ammunition available to him to persuade the commission to close down the plant. He knew a lot of people would lose their jobs, but considered that a small price to pay for the lives the closure would save. At last, satisfied with the power and depth of their case, he phoned the AEC and made an appointment with Director Gordon Dean. He packed a suitcase and put copies of all the reports in a briefcase, kissed Julie goodbye and flew to Washington D.C. There, after the introductions and initial pleasantries, he made his presentation in front of a committee made up of members of the AEC and Congress.

He laid out the evidence, explained the science so the congressional representatives would understand. He complained about the cover ups and lost reports from prior investigations. Reese was not a confrontational man, but he'd contained his anger long enough. "Gentlemen," he concluded, "I want action."

Senator Dawson spoke up, "You know what the Department of Defense says? 'The people in Utah don't give a shit about radiation.' How do you answer that, Dr. Mayfield?"

"I've seen parents hold their child who had just died from leukemia. They don't give a shit? Have you ever lost a child? Have you ever seen your wife lose all her hair and turn into a yellowed skeleton? Have you stroked her scarred chest after her cancerous breast has been cut off? Don't tell me they don't give a shit."

"I was just repeating what I heard," Dawson snapped back.

"Gentlemen, gentlemen," said Dean. "Let's calm down." He cleared his throat. "Dr. Mayfield, you worked with Oppenheimer at Los Alamos, didn't you?"

"Yes." Reese wondered where this would lead.

"And you socialized with him?"

"From time to time."

"Were you aware of his communist leanings?"

"I'd heard rumors."

"Did you know his wife, Kitty, was a member of the Communist party?"

"I'd heard that."

"Have you ever attended a Communist party meeting?"

So that's where this is going. "Gentlemen, if this is an attempt to discredit me, keep in mind, this report expresses the findings of an entire team—a team of some of the brightest scientific minds in the world." Adrenaline raced to Reese's heart, sharpening his anger. "Their reports and mine have nothing to do with politics." Sensing he was going to lose this round of the battle, he said, "I'm not a communist. If you want to cast doubt upon me, it would be a fool's business, and that's up to you. But I beg you to consider the collective scientific findings of the team."

Dean picked up the sheaf of papers in front of him, tapped them into a neat stack, and set them aside. "Thank you for meeting with us," he said. "We'll take your report under advisement. Considering the import of this matter, it will take some time to get back to you. Enjoy your stay in Washington."

That's it? That's all? Deflated, Reese gathered up his documents, stuffed them into his briefcase, went through the formalities of shaking hands, then

161

left. Had he made a difference? Considering the panel's attitude, he doubted it.

* * *

After Reese left, Dean leaned back in his chair. Eyebrows knitted together, he said, "I don't like what that Mayfield guy had to say. He bears watching. He's too opposed to our nuclear program."

"But what he says does concern me," Dawson said. "If we are killing our own people, we can't continue the bomb tests."

"We're in a war, albeit a cold war. There are always innocents killed during a war."

"But not in our country."

Landon shrugged. "An acceptable loss. Those people in Utah are considered to be a low use segment of the population."

Dawson persisted. "Then there are also the reports of Schweitzer and the rest of the Hanford investigating team."

"Do we know that Mayfield's report truthfully represented their reports? He seems like an extremist to me," Congressman Warren said.

"Exactly my point," Dean said. "Let's keep an eye on him. I'm going to phone Hoover and ask for FBI surveillance." Privately, he would ask J. Edgar to make the surveillance obvious. Mayfield wouldn't be the first scientist silenced by a little intimidation. Did the man have a family to protect? Hopefully so.

Dawson nodded. "No point in taking chances. He did work with Oppenheimer, and we all know he was a pinko."

"I'll never believe that," protested Warren. He paused, in thought. "But I suppose it doesn't hurt to err on the side of caution."

Chapter Twenty-Nine
Under Surveillance

Still fuming from the pointlessness of the hearing, Reese left the capitol building. He stopped by his room at the Willard Hotel to freshen up and phone Julie.

"It's done," he said. "Nothing left to say."

"You did your level best, Reese."

"Well, fat lot of good it did. At least I'll be home tomorrow. No sense lingering here."

As long as he was in Washington, Reese wanted to tour the National Gallery. He'd never been a big aficionado of the arts. Maybe it was time to get a little culture under his belt, but not before he had lunch. He was starving after the stress of the committee's questioning.

As Reese left the elevator, he bumped into a man. After apologizing, he made a beeline toward the hotel dining room. He ordered a bourbon and water and the chicken pot pie special. As he waited for his lunch, he sipped his drink, hoping it would take the edge off his nerves.

He thought back on the meeting. Could he have made the case differently? Better? Second-guessing was inevitable, he supposed, but no, he didn't see any place in the presentation that might have been more convincing. Those men didn't want to make any changes, and that was the flat, unassailable truth. He wondered if he would lose his security clearance and his job. The job didn't worry him too much, he could always get another, but being thought of as a subversive did. His mind went to Oppenheimer. After all that great man had done for his country, he was now treated like the enemy.

Glancing around the room, Reese saw the man he'd bumped into sitting at a table talking to another man. They seemed to glance his way a couple of times. *Are those guys watching me? Probably not. I'm just a little jumpy.* That day, his bad leg ached and he had a headache. He massaged his temples, gulped his drink, and signaled his waiter to bring him another. He thought about the TV shows he'd seen and mused that those two looked just like plainclothes men on TV. The theme song from "*I Led Three Lives*" played in Reese's head. That thought and the liquor finally mellowed him. An unexpected smile curved his lips.

The waiter served his plate with a flourish. Reese put his concerns to rest for the moment and dug into the steaming dish. Fully sated after coffee and a dessert of cherry pie à la mode, Reese paid his tab and left to walk to the National Gallery. It was a hot day and he shrugged off his coat, hooked it on a thumb and hung it over one shoulder.

D.C. was a handsome city, the green and lush grounds everywhere contrasting with massive white stone buildings and monuments. The beauty of the nation's capital made him proud to be an American. Then his pride diminished as he reflected back on the plight of the people who were so sick from radioactive fallout, and the callous manipulation by the powers in government. Shaking the thought from his mind, he determined to enjoy what Washington had to offer outside of politics.

Awed by the Whistler, Rembrandt, and Gainsboro paintings his education had given him only a nodding acquaintance with, he took time reading the descriptive tags. For a while, the art absorbed him completely, but while he was in front of a portrait of George Washington, he had the prickling sensation of being watched. He turned, but saw no one looking at him. He resumed his tour and left the building only when they announced it was closing.

His cultural desires fulfilled, he strolled back to the Willard, musing on the art he'd seen. It was a new experience seeing the real thing instead of a bad reproduction in a book. He wanted to keep this familiarity fresh in his mind.

At a crosswalk, Reese looked around to see if it was safe to proceed. Again, he saw the two men from the restaurant. *I do believe they are following me.* He joined the crowd of pedestrians scurrying across the street. After he was halfway up the next block, he chanced another look behind him, but the men weren't there.

Reese thought back on his days at Los Alamos and how everyone had been under suspicion, watched, and their phones tapped. He wanted to confront the men, but didn't think it was wise. *It's almost as though they want me to know they are watching me.* Still he had his doubts. That is, until he returned to the hotel. There they were again. Not even disguising their interest in him.

Later, when Reese left the hotel, there was no sign of the watchers, nor did he see them as he checked in at the airport, walked to his gate, and settled into a seat in the waiting area. There they were. The same black suits. Both pretending to read newspapers, but peering over them from time to time. After a while, one put his paper aside and sat openly staring at Reese. *Intimidation— won't work—not on me.* He returned the stare causing the bolder of the two to avert his eyes, pick up his paper, and duck behind it again. Surreptitiously, the suits continued to watch as he boarded his flight. *I wonder if I'll be under surveillance in Las Vegas.*

Belted into his window seat, Reese worried. *What will I say to Julie?* He tried to distract himself by gazing down on flat clouds so dense he thought he might be able to take a stroll on them, but even the beauty of the monochromatic whites and grays couldn't keep him from fretting. He finally came to the realization that his thinking was faulty. He could not, as he had once believed, be more effective working from within the government. Over and over he had come up against "Cold War Logic."

The potential devastation of these horrific bombs was such an important deterrent against war that testing would continue—regardless of how thoroughly he proved the tests were killing thousands of America's own citizens—killing them from direct exposure to high radioactivity or indirectly and insidiously over a period of time by exposure to lower levels. The almost endless loop of horrendous effects began to replay itself in Reese's mind: the lethal exposure caused by eating fish and waterfowl with high levels of radiation in their flesh. The innocent children exposed by wading in the river and making mud pies along the banks, among the swampy cattails. Deformed livestock. Cancer everywhere. He felt the despair of true helplessness.

The plane touched down in Las Vegas at last. The sight of Julie waving as he made his way into the terminal lifted his black mood. She ran to him and threw her arms around his neck. "I've missed you."

He bent down and buried his nose in her hair. "It's good to be home." *This is what's real. This is what's important, not that political bull crap.* He draped his arm over her shoulders as they walked toward baggage claim. "I went to the National Gallery." He glanced over her shoulder then looked down

165

at her with a smile. "As soon as I can arrange it, I'm taking you to D.C. You'll love it."

At the carousel, Reese looked around again. No one in sight.

"What are you looking for?" Julie glanced around, too, in reflex.

"Julie, has anyone been watching the house?"

"I don't think so. What do you mean?"

"I thought I was being followed in Washington."

Julie giggled. "Dum, da, dum dum," she sang the *Dragnet* theme. "Why would someone follow you, much less watch our place?"

"Sweetheart," he started, putting his hands on her upper arms and looking square in her face. "Because I don't think they liked my position on continued nuclear testing."

She frowned. "But surely you're entitled. You're the scientist, after all."

"My report was pretty damning. And that panel didn't like it one bit." Reese shook his head. "They've got their Cold War concerns. Now, they think I might be a commie."

"Uh-oh. You know what happened to Daddy. Do you think they'll take away your security clearance?"

"One never knows. I don't want to worry you, but if you see anyone who looks suspicious, let me know."

"Reese, now you're scaring me."

"That's the last thing I want to do." He pulled her close. "Don't be frightened, nobody will hurt you. Ah ha, there's my suitcase." He sprang forward to snatch it from the carousel.

* * *

Two days later, Hood, a two-stage thermonuclear bomb the government said they wouldn't be testing in Nevada was scheduled. This was the largest atmospheric test done in the U.S. Like Priscilla, Hood hung from a balloon, but this one rose 1,200 feet in the air. Reese chewed on the back of his knuckle as he read about troop maneuvers by 2,500 Marines and air operations using 124 aircraft.

Reese had observed the trenches located two and a half miles from the bomb site on one of his trips to check on some of the animals staked out near a mock village. How could those marines be okay in five and a half foot deep trenches? Would they survive? All the commanding officers would be five

166

miles away. Their mission was to determine how troops would react in an atomic war.

A medical team stood ready to treat the marines with radiation sickness. Reese suspected most of them would be ill to a greater or lesser degree. After the blast, he would drive over to the hospital to help.

It was two hours after the test when marines showed up at the hospital. It was evident they hadn't been prepared for radiation sickness with vomiting, burns and fever. Some had to be carried in on stretchers. Many complained about aching like from a bad flu bug. Even tough, battle hardened warriors were no match for Hood.

Reese questioned one he treated about his experience. Reese recorded the marine's words:

"'Turn around and hunker down. Cover your head,' ordered our commanding officer.

"I crossed my arms over my helmet and scrunched down in the trench as low as possible, praying the sides didn't cave in and bury me. A blinding flash, burning heat on the back of my neck, arms so transparent I saw the bones. How can that be? I didn't have time to dwell on it as I was knocked back and forth in the trench, then the boom and roar of wind—dirt showered down on me.

"When the wind subsided, I turned to my commanding officer and asked, 'What are our orders, sir?' He stood staring into space. He didn't hear me. The boom had deafened him. Again, I posed the question, 'Sir, what are our orders?' He roused from his shock and brushed fine white ash from his uniform.

"'March toward the blast site. Evaluate the condition of animals, equipment, mannequins, and structures,' the officer barked. We hauled ourselves out of the trenches, shook off ash and dirt, controlled our shaking legs and started our march toward ground zero.

"Mannequins lay flattened, some still burning. Tanks flipped over, their tracks ripped off and lying nearby. Trucks, a mass of twisted metal, dead animals—the lucky ones—screeching pigs, dogs, and horses, some horribly burned, but still alive, wooden structures gone. In their place, wood scattered around like matchstick houses that had been kicked. Concrete buildings half

167

blown apart. I'd been in Korea for two years, but I'd never seen anything to equal this."

The next day, reports came in from Las Vegas about plate glass windows on casinos shattered and houses damaged.

Reese imagined scientists saying, "Oops." Then they'd huddle. A buzz of conversation, notepads and pens would come out, and the calculations begin.

Reese recalled one of the scientists at Los Alamos saying, "A bomb has no conscience. It doesn't know or care who it hurts."

That same day, Reese renewed his efforts to stop the bomb tests. He wrote to the resident.

> *Dear Mr. President,*
>
> *I'm Dr. Reese Mayfield, a medical doctor and physicist working in the field of Nuclear Medicine at the Nevada Testing Grounds.*
>
> *I'm making an appeal on behalf of humanity, and most especially for the people downwind of the atomic bomb testing in Area 51 in Nevada. This is genocide. We are murdering our own people with radioactive fallout. Children are dying of leukemia. Women are getting breast and uterine cancer. Families are losing their livelihood because of the loss of farm stock. I've seen horses with radiation burns on their backs. Open sores that ooze—so painful they can't be saddled and ridden. Even if they could, men won't, for fear of becoming sterile. I've seen sheep so exhausted they will not move. Ewes will not claim their young. Many lambs are still-born or born deformed with pot bellies or without wool. The death toll is up to fifty percent of an entire herd. I've tested milk from cows. It showed traces of radioactivity and people are giving this milk to their children—children who now have cancer. When cows eat grass that has radioactive ash on it, radioactivity concentrates in their milk. Then when children drink the milk, it becomes more concentrated.*
>
> *Also, I'm seeing thyroid cancer in both men and women.*
>
> *We can't continue to place our military so close to the blast. None of our men should be within fifty miles of the blast*

site, and even that isn't a safe distance. To put men in trenches two miles from the site is certain death. Not immediately, but I'm seeing men die within two years, and most of them will contract cancer within five years.

Out of concern for their employees, the owners of Bride's Mine, thirty-eight miles from the test site, have shut down their operation. Mrs. Stevens, wife of the owner, died of cancer, a direct effect of exposure to radioactive fallout. I've been to the hospital in St. George and seen little children so thin, I marveled that they were still alive, their vacant eyes huge in their sunken faces. Parents have lost hope of saving their little ones. There is no cure for them.

The Federal Government has been sued for relief by the people of Cedar City, Utah. The Federal Government won, but this doesn't make the case any less relevant, nor does it alleviate their suffering. In fact, the fallout doesn't stop there. It is directly affecting people as far north as Sevier County in central Utah. When I say I'm appealing on behalf of all humanity, I truly am. When radioactive fallout gets into the winds aloft, which it does during atmospheric testing, it circumnavigates the globe within two weeks. Anywhere there is rain or snow, that precipitation delivers contamination.

Essentially, our atomic bomb testing conceivably could terminate all life on the planet. It is incumbent upon us, as the most powerful nation on earth, to protect, not just the people, but all life forms.

I realize the tests are in the interest of national security, however we cannot continue to inflict this pain on our people. Please meet with the Atomic Energy Commission and your Secretary of War and find a solution that will protect the people. I do encourage moving the tests underground. That should be practical and keep the testing at Area 51. I will be happy to meet with you here or in Washington to provide further information and assist in any way I can.

169

I realize the importance of nuclear testing. I understand we are in a race with Russia, but in all good conscience, we must find another way—a way that will protect the people. I recommend that we stop atmospheric testing and develop a method of underground testing. If this isn't possible, we need to find another test site that will not impact people.

I'm requesting that you make a trip to southern Utah to see firsthand what the tests are doing to these people.

These are our people, Americans, and we are exterminating them.

Very truly yours,

Reese Mayfield, M.D., Nuclear Medicine, Ph.D., Theoretical Physics

* * *

Three weeks later, Reese received a form letter from the Office of the President, thanking him for his concern and promising the president would take his suggestions under advisement. Reese snorted after he read the form letter. *I'll bet the president didn't even see what I wrote.*

Reese fretted about Julie. Most of all, he wanted to keep her safe. She had been nervous since he told her about being followed in Washington. He wished, now, he hadn't said anything.

Reese decided to put out feelers for a new position. He felt his growing bitterness toward the government, and he didn't want to live that way. He wanted a place where he wasn't reined in by a government agency and ignored by the highest offices in the land. He wanted a place that honored his findings and the science supporting them.

Chapter Thirty
Lisa

It hadn't been a week since Reese started scouting around for a position in the private sector when the phone rang in his office.

"Hey, I heard through the grapevine that you're leaving the AEC." It was Lisa Menninger.

"That's right. I thought I could make a difference working within the system, but experience has proven me wrong." *How did she find out so soon?*

"My offer's still good. Come and work with me, Reese. I need someone who is skilled in research. I've expanded my office practice to a clinic. You wouldn't have to see patients if you don't want to. I've been successful in obtaining private and government grants that will keep us in the chips for several years. The clinic has a state-of-the-art research lab and we're working extensively with cancer patients. That's right up your alley. I don't know of anyone who has the background you have. You'd be working to cure people. What do you think?"

After a long silence, Reese spoke, "I'll give it some consideration."

"Well, that's progress. You can reach me at the Menninger Clinic in Beverly Hills."

"That's impressive."

"Only the best. Your beautiful wife will love L.A., and I promise to be a good girl and never reveal our little secret."

Reese blew out air. In his heart, he knew Lisa wouldn't. "I'll appreciate your discretion." She was a shrewd, clever woman. She respected him and wanted him on her team. Tough as nails, Lisa would never give into emotion.

"You'll be free to pursue research into cancer cures."

Reese chewed on his lip during another long silence.

Lisa didn't speak. She knew the old salesmen's trick—the first one to talk loses.

Reese finally broke the silence. "I'll have to talk to Julie."

Lisa knew she had him. "I'll get with my attorney to draw up an agreement. You'll be able to see what I have in mind in writing. It should be in the mail by next week."

Reese's heart raced when he hung up. *What am I thinking? I've always been a government hack working on one project or another. Still, maybe it's time for a change.*

* * *

Over dinner that night, Reese said, "Julie, how would you like to live in Los Angeles?"

"I don't know. What do you have in mind?"

"Lisa Menninger has opened a clinic with a cancer research center. She asked me to come and work with her, but before I looked into it, I wanted to talk to you." Reese shoveled a forkful of mashed potatoes into his mouth.

"Lisa Menninger. Isn't that the lady doctor I met in Richland?"

"The same."

"You never said you knew her."

"Didn't I? We went through residency together."

"Why didn't you tell me you knew her when I told you about meeting her in Richland?"

Reese's mind scrambled for a plausible answer. "I don't know, honey—I was so wrapped up in the whole thing with Schweitzer and radioactivity in the Columbia River."

Julie narrowed her eyes. "Was there something between the two of you?"

Reese's cheeks reddened.

"There was, wasn't there? That changes the whole picture."

"Julie, it was nothing, and it was a long time ago. We just worked together."

"Just worked together? Then why do you look so guilty? Should I be jealous?" Julie's usually sunny face clouded with distrust.

"Of Lisa? Absolutely not. She's all business." Reese stood and walked around the table. He pulled her to her feet and took her in his arms. "There's no other woman in the world to compare with you."

172

Still angry, Julie pulled away from his embrace. "Better not Mister. Did you love her?"

"Love Lisa?" Reese wrinkled his brow. "I don't think people love Lisa, at least not in the way you mean. Respect her, admire her brains, maybe even fear her. She's a dynamic woman."

"So you admire her. How much?" Standing with her arms folded, she glared at Reese.

"Not as much as I admire you. Know that I'd never look at anyone else." He gently unfolded her arms and wrapped her up in his. "I love you and only you." Reese nuzzled her hair, lifted her chin, and gave her a lingering kiss.

Relaxing in his arms, she returned his kiss, then leaned away, still chewing on the thought of moving. "It would mean leaving Mom and Dad. I've finished my docent training at the art museum and started conducting tours. I hoped as a docent I may be in line for a position. It'll be a big change." Julie fell silent.

"Let me fix us a drink and we can talk about it," Reese said.

Seated on the sofa with her legs curled under her, Julie sipped a martini. "It sounds exciting—Hollywood with all its glamour. There is so much to do there. I've always wanted to tour the studios. Oh, and the beach. We can have picnics at the beach on Sundays. I wonder what my folks will say? I think we need to sleep on it." She toyed with the toothpick holding an olive in her drink. "What do you think?"

"Sure, honey." Still in persuasion mode, Reese said, "There may be an unexpected upside to living there. Perhaps we'll have better luck adopting a baby."

"It is disappointing that we haven't been successful through the local adoption agencies." Julie fell silent for a full minute. "Well, if there really isn't anything between you and Lisa," she said. "I still want to sleep on it, but I think I'd like to live in Los Angeles. Before we make a decision, let's talk to Mom and Dad about it. I want them to be the first to know we're considering a move."

"Of course. We have time. We need to drive over to Los Angeles and meet with Lisa. She said she'd send me a letter with the details of the position. After that, I'll phone her and make arrangements to visit."

* * *

173

Now that Reese was exploring other options, he was antsy at work. He didn't want to leave the Utah people he'd come to care so much about, but felt he'd done all he could to protect them—which was precious little. Angela noticed his restlessness and questioned him. He wasn't ready to share his plans with her and evaded her queries.

Time seemed to drag until it was time to meet with Lisa in Los Angeles. Much to Reese's relief, Julie and Lisa hit it off. Lisa poured on all her charm and diplomacy to win Julie over. Julie told Lisa about her hopes to adopt a baby.

Lisa said, "I know an attorney who arranges private adoptions." She poked around in her purse and found a small address book and wrote the name, Mary Fleming, and noted the phone number. She also gave Julie the name of a realtor, telling her, "Just say the word, and I'll have her line up some houses to look at.

After some negotiations, Reese accepted the position at the Menninger Clinic.

* * *

When Reese submitted his resignation, the AEC seemed relieved. They'd never liked his position on the dangers of radioactive fallout and considered him a troublemaker. They'd kept a close eye on him for years. Reese's innocence and trust of his government, despite all the evidence pointing to their deception, protected him from the knowledge that he was under constant surveillance. That was, until his visit to D. C. Then he knew he wasn't exempt from Big Brother's eye.

He packed up his personal belongings and bade farewell to Angela, his lab, and office at the test site. He hoped he could make a difference working outside the AEC. He certainly hadn't been successful working on the inside. He wondered what ever happened to the hundreds of pages of reports he had written. *Did anyone even read them? How can my government be so indifferent to the suffering of its own people? Wonder who the black suits will watch now.*

174

Chapter Thirty-One
Los Angeles

Lisa was true to her promise. The lab boasted all the latest equipment, even better than Reese's pristine lab at Oak Ridge. "This is where I'm meant to be," he told Julie as he showed her around the Menninger Clinic and his new laboratory.

"I'm happy for you, Honey. Now, we need to find a house. We have an appointment in an hour with a realtor.

Julie and Reese bought a charming little Spanish casa with a red tile roof, a swimming pool, and palm trees all around. Its close proximity to the Menninger Clinic was a boon after years of driving the hour from Las Vegas to Mercury. Reese considered that its finest asset.

While Reese was busy settling into his new position, Julie packed up her oil paints, brushes, and an easel and headed to the beach to paint seascapes. She decided to go three times a week in the morning after Reese left for work. Wearing sunglasses and a broad brimmed straw sun hat, she became a regular figure on Venice Beach and the Santa Monica Pier. Seeking other vistas, she ventured south to Laguna Beach. Once or twice a week, she visited the museums and set her heart on becoming a docent at the Los Angeles County Museum.

In the soft warm evenings, poolside, they shared their days, happy with each other, content in their new home.

Reese was in his element when involved in research and solving problems. Right away, he became engrossed in his work. He had his eye pressed to a microscope when a phone call interrupted him.

"Yes, this is Reese Mayfield. Who's this?"

"Ward Porter, old chap, remember me? From Los Alamos."

"Of course, how could I forget. How the hell are you?"

"Jolly good. Hard at work for the AEC. Do you still have your security clearance?"

"They haven't notified me that it has been revoked."

"Good. I need your help to check out a radiation leak at the Santa Susana Field Laboratory. You're pretty close to them?"

"I think it's located about thirty or forty miles from here in Simi Valley."

"We need someone knowledgeable to check out the problem today. I'll be out there in two days. Right now I'm tied up in D. C. What will it take for you to go over there and assess the situation."

"Not much, I'll cancel my afternoon and drive right over. What information are you looking for?"

"Primarily the impact, if any, it will have on Los Angeles and the surrounding areas, and can it be repaired quickly."

"I can assess the possibility of radioactive fallout, but the repair needs an engineer. They should be on site. I'll interview them."

"Consider this a verbal contract. I'm authorized to pay you $100 an hour, plus expenses, to provide us with an impact statement. I'll get a contract drawn up and in the mail. Phone me as soon as you have anything." Ward rattled off his home and work numbers.

Fingers of dread skittered up Reese's spine. He feared something like this might happen. Not so much for himself, but for the people. After all, he'd survived the Trinity test, and numerous others, at the Nevada Test Site, but he'd seen how the Downwinders had suffered.

* * *

Ha, you thought you were rid of me. Quitting the Nevada Test Site isn't an escape from my power. Fickle little old me, I pop up everywhere. Nuclear power plants, laboratories, even medical facilities. Now, it looks like you're back in the game. Your buddy Ward has seen to that. Good luck at Santa Susana, but you are probably too late to do much good. The personnel there are beyond naïve about my dangers.

* * *

Prompted by Ward's plea, Reese sped to the lab. Once there, he scanned the laboratory and shuddered at the chaos as workers frantically tried to clean up radioactive water spilled by overheated reactors. They wore no protective clothing and used sponges and mops with their bare hands to sop up the lethal liquid.

Reese met with the head of the lab who said, "I was expecting you. I received a call from Ward Porter at the AEC. I really don't have much time to explain the situation. We're doing the best we can. Every time we start up the reactors, they overheat." Frustration and fear laced his voice.

Safety of the workers his primary concern, Reese said, "The men cleaning up should be wearing protective gloves and clothing. Do you have any?"

The manager yelled at his assistant to take care of it.

After nosing around, Reese discovered they were releasing gases under cover of darkness every night. Radioactive gases for the wind to strew over homes, schools, and cities in the San Fernando Valley. He found a phone and called Ward. "I recommend the plant be shut down until repairs can be made. This is critical, much more serious than a simple leak. The staff is getting too much exposure. Fallout will endanger the entire Los Angeles area. I suggest immediate action."

"I'll do what I can. Thanks, old chap."

As Reese drove home, he thought, "I've got to get Julie out of here—send her to her folks for a visit." His mouth twisted in disgust. "There's really no safe place." In his judgment, Las Vegas was safer than Los Angeles at the moment.

Reese didn't go by the clinic, but drove directly home. He briefed Julie on the possibility of radioactive fallout over Los Angeles. "Please pack a bag and go visit your parents. They'll love to see you. I'll let you know when it's safe to come back." When Reese left the house the next morning, he noticed a black sedan parked across the street. The hair on the back of his neck stood at attention. *Is that the damned FBI?*

Working in the private sector, Reese thought he would be of little interest to the Feds, but it seemed investigating the Santa Susana Labs kicked a sleeping dog. *Here we go again. Let's see how far they take this. How did they find out so soon? Have they been watching me all the time?*

* * *

That morning Lisa paid a rare visit to the lab. "Reese, I don't mean to pry, but where were you yesterday?" She wrinkled her nose at the smell of formaldehyde.

177

"I had some business to take care of. I left a message for you."

"Yes, I got the message. Late in the afternoon, two FBI agents came by the office asking for you. What's going on?"

Reese hadn't intended to say anything to Lisa and didn't think he should, but this changed things. He pulled up a stool for Lisa.

"You may want to be seated." Reese pushed back a microscope that was near the edge of the countertop. "Lisa. This needs to be between us. There is a radiation leak at the Santa Susana Field Laboratory. It may or may not be serious. The AEC asked me to investigate."

Lisa emitted a low whistle. "So why is the FBI after you? Seems to me you're on the side of the good guys."

"I was much too vocal trying to get the AEC to stop the bomb testing. They started watching me after I presented a report in Washington."

"You're the last person on the planet I'd be suspicious of."

"Yeah, but apparently not Uncle."

"By the way, Mary Fleming phoned and left a message for you to call. Who knows, she may have a baby for you. Still interested?"

"Yes, of course we are, but Julie's out of town for a while—visiting her parents."

"I see. Send her away, but don't tell me so I have a choice whether to stay or go? Thanks, old buddy." Lisa slid off the stool. "Anyway, here's Shields's phone number. Give her a call." She turned to leave, pausing at the door. "Are we safe here?"

"Lisa, we aren't safe anywhere."

Chapter Thirty-Two
Protesting

Reese had retained copies of all the reports he'd written while at the Nevada Test Site. He wondered what would happen if he turned them over to a newspaper. He needed to think this through. *How would it impact Julie? Would he still have a job if he did?* That day, it became evident the FBI was still interested in him. How interested, he didn't know.

A chill washed over Reese. *We haven't been in Los Angeles for ninety days. We're barely settled in, and now we may be Downwinders.*

On the weekend, Reese drove to Las Vegas. He needed to talk to Julie about his plans. He'd done some research on reporters for the *Los Angeles Times*. He identified one whom he felt he could trust to give copies of his reports. Shielding himself and his family was critical. He wanted to remain anonymous.

Initially, Reese planned to contact the *Washington Post* until he learned that the CIA's Operation Mockingbird manipulated the press and might quash anything he sent there. He wasn't all that certain about the *L. A. Times.* He thought the West Coast would be less scrutinized. From what he'd read, their position on bomb testing was to stop it.

* * *

Reese took Julie to dinner at the hotel where they'd spent their wedding night, the Tropicana. He wanted to keep their conversation private. No need to worry her folks.

"My, what a beautiful dining room." Julie looked up at the crystal chandeliers casting a full spectrum of colors that reflected off their wine glasses.

Reese pulled out a chair for her. "They really went all out, didn't they? We didn't see this room when we stayed here before."

A waiter appeared, and Reese said, "Scotch and soda for me and a glass of Chablis for the lady."

Reese explained to Julie what he wanted to do. "If I do this, I may be arrested. I may go to prison."

"If you become an activist, I'll become an activist. Painting and being a docent at the art museum isn't so important that I can't put them aside to protest with you."

"What if Irene Shields does have a baby for us? You can't take care of a baby if you're in prison."

"Right now, we don't have a baby. We'll cross that bridge when we come to it."

"I need to phone her. What would you like me to say?"

"Let's see what she has to say first."

* * *

Reese phoned Shields on Monday morning. She apologized and said the mother had decided to keep the baby. "I'll let you know when I hear of another one."

When he told Julie, she cried a little, dried her tears, and straightened her shoulders. "Maybe children aren't in the cards for us. Maybe we are meant to be activists with those inherent risks."

Reese held her close. "As long as we have each other, we'll be fine."

* * *

Reese met with the chosen reporter to turn over his documents. He asked to remain anonymous, reasoning that he would be ineffective as an activist if he was in prison. He suggested August sixth as the date to break the story. It was the twelfth anniversary of the bombing of Hiroshima.

On that date, protestors gathered outside the gates at the Nevada Test Site and the *L. A. Times* broke the story. Headlines screamed, AEC DECEIVES FALLOUT VICTIMS.

* * *

Reese and Julie stayed with the protestors until the ninth, the anniversary of the bombing of Nagasaki. They held signs saying, "Stop bombing our people." Two of the protestors gained entrance to the test site and were promptly arrested.

Watching this, Reese said, "I helped build that weapon, and now I'm protesting our using it. I worked here, now I'm protesting what goes on here." He saw the two men being dragged off to a waiting military police vehicle.

"I believe we're doing the right thing," Julie said.

"It may be the right thing, but there are some who don't think so. The issue of continued testing divides the scientific community."

Before the three-day protest was over, eight people were arrested.

On the way back to Los Angeles, a black Lincoln swerved in front of Reese's car.

Julie gasped and grabbed onto the dashboard as Reese braked.

"Idiots!" Reese yelled.

The Lincoln swerved side to side, forcing Reese to brake again. "What the hell are they doing?" he muttered.

The car sped up and turned sideways across the highway, blocking their passage.

Reese slammed on the brakes, throwing Julie forward. When the car came to a stop, mere inches from the Lincoln, he asked, "Are you okay?"

"Yes. Scared out of my wits, but fine. What's going on?"

Two men in dark suits got out and strode toward his car.

After he caught his breath, Reese jumped out and confronted them. "What the fuck! You could have killed us."

One of the men flipped out a shield. "FBI. You need to come with us Dr. Mayfield."

Reese crossed his arms. "Why? I want your names and badge numbers. And how do you know who I am?"

The second agent said, "Never mind how we know you. We're taking you in for questioning." One hand pulled his jacket aside, revealing a gun. His stance indicated he meant business.

"Julie, drive back to your parent's and stay there."

"Wait! Where are you taking him?"

They didn't respond. Instead, they grabbed Reese by the arms and pulled him toward their vehicle.

* * *

181

Angered by the rough treatment of her husband, Julie defied Reese's instructions and followed them to the Federal Building in L.A. She couldn't just sit at her parent's house and do nothing. She'd go crazy with worry.

Running into the building, she searched for Reese, asking for him at each desk she came to. Nobody seemed to know anything. Frustrated, she looked for a pay phone. When she found one, she called Lisa and told her what had happened.

"My attorney will be right over," Lisa assured her.

"I'll wait for him at the front door." Julie found a bench and waited. After an hour, a man approached her. "Are you Mrs. Mayfield? I'm Michael Weems, Lisa Menninger asked me to see Dr. Mayfield. Do you know where they have taken him?"

"No, and I can't find anything out."

"Let's see if they'll talk to me," Weems said and motioned for Julie to accompany him.

* * *

Reese was sequestered in a windowless room with a table and three chairs, and no water. *Oh shit, what have I gotten myself into? Will it be worth it?*

The door opened. "Reese, old chap, what the bloody hell are you doing here?"

"Ward? What are you doing here?" Reese stood and shook Ward's hand.

"Trying to save your arse. I hear you've been up to mischief. Have a seat."

"How did you know? How can you help?"

Ward plopped down on one of the chairs and crossed his long legs.

"I work for the FBI in tandem with the AEC, covering matters involving nuclear energy, bombs, power plants, etc. I've been in L.A. since I arrived to work on the Santa Susana problem."

"When you phoned me to go out to Santa Susana, I thought you were still a lab rat. The FBI? That's a stretch."

"I was burned out after Los Alamos. Hated being confined in the lab, so I cast about for something more exciting." Ward stretched out his arms to indicate 'so, here I am'. "And you? How'd you end up in here?"

"Protesting at the Nevada Test Site."

182

"Are you off your trolley? Well, never mind, let's see what we can do to get you out of here. Ever since I saw them bring you in, I've been talking a blue streak to convince the suits you are okay. By the way, your wife and a fancy solicitor are out there. What a doll, how'd you rate her?"

"Just lucky, I guess. You think you can get me out?" *Now, why didn't Julie do as I asked?* Nonetheless, he was grateful to know she was just a few steps away.

"The suits were told to aggravate you a little to keep you in line. There wasn't any real reason to bring you in. We do still have freedom of speech in this country, but I suggest you keep a low profile and not participate in protests. Give me five minutes and you'll be out of here."

"Thanks, Ward. I'm in your debt."

"Don't thank me until after you walk out of this building."

Good to his word, Ward returned in five minutes and escorted Reese to the front of the building. Julie ran up and hugged him.

"Is this what being an activist will be like?" she whispered in his ear. Turning, she introduced Lisa's attorney.

"It doesn't look like I'll need your services," Reese said. "Thank you for coming." He told them that Ward had arranged for his release. The attorney wished Reese well and handed him a card before leaving.

"Julie, I promised Ward a dinner."

"Ward, I'm so grateful. Are you free tomorrow night? I'm not a bad cook. Come at seven."

"She's beautiful and she cooks, too?" Ward grinned at Reese. "I'll be there. Where do you live?"

Julie fished in her purse for a pen and paper and gave him the address.

"Got to get back to work." Ward kissed Julie's hand and slapped Reese on the back. "Cheerio, until tomorrow."

183

Chapter Thirty-Three
Dinner with Ward

The next morning, Reese dropped by Lisa's office to thank her for sending her attorney, but she was tied up with a patient, so he went on to his lab. An hour later, the door burst open.

"What in the hell were you thinking?" Lisa looked furious. "Am I going to have to bail you out every time you decide to protest? And involving Julie? I didn't think you were that sort of man. Here you have a cushy, and, I might add, safe job, and you stick your neck out like that."

Taken aback by her verbal assault, Reese said nothing until she wound down.

In a soft voice, he responded, "I'm afraid there was no stopping Julie. I appreciate your support, but you didn't need to send your attorney. My old buddy, Ward Porter from Los Alamos, got me released. But thank you anyhow."

Rare tears moistened Lisa's eyes. "Reese, I'm sorry. You just scared the crap out of me."

"I'll be more careful in the future. I didn't mean for you to get involved."

"Well, I had to." She gave him a playful punch on the arm. "I've always had a soft spot for you. If you plan on any more shenanigans, will you let me know in advance?" She headed for the door. "I hate being caught by surprise."

"I promise." He called after her. "Come to dinner tonight?"

"Can't. Got a date."

* * *

Ward arrived promptly at seven, with a bottle of French wine in hand, and presented it to Julie. "Something smells brilliant. Hope Burgundy goes with dinner, luv."

"Perfect. I've made beef stroganoff. Reese will you open this?" Julie asked, handing him the bottle.

"How far are you going to take this activist stuff?" Ward took a sip of wine.

"I don't know. This was my first protest. I can see there must be better ways to go about it."

"How so?"

"To start with, I'll go back to the sheep ranchers and get them to write their congressmen. If I can get a big enough group involved, maybe it will help."

"There's a lot of noise in Washington about an atomic test ban. If they see a grass roots movement, that may move it along. Eisenhower is pushing for an international ban, now that Russia, Great Britain, and France have the bomb." Ward tasted his Stroganoff. "Umm, delicious. My compliments to the chef."

Julie smiled.

"Yeah, one hothead with his thumb on a button could start World War Three and we'd all be annihilated," Reese said.

"Oh Reese, don't even think that way." Julie frowned.

"None of us like to think that way," Ward said, "but it is possible, and it's the fear of a lot of people, in particular scientists, the bloody blokes who know the worst."

"Coffee anyone?" Julie cleared away dishes and headed for the kitchen.

"I read a report from a Dr. Knolls that says the measurable strontium 90 in children's thyroids exceeds 400 times the acceptable levels," Ward said.

Reese emitted a low whistle. "Where were the tests done?"

"St. George, Utah."

"I saw a lot of those children when I was at the Nevada Test Site. Those little kids didn't have a chance, given the levels of exposure. Heartbreaking."

"Another report says they are exhuming children's bodies to measure radioactivity in their bones, still another says they are doing radioactive experiments on prison inmates."

"What we hear gets worse every day," Reese said.

There was a long pause in the conversation before Ward said, "It gets too frustrating to think about."

Reese changed the subject. "Did you get married?"

"Yes. Jeannine and I had a great couple of years. We lived in D. C. My work involved a lot of travel. She got lonely—dumped me for her for her high school beau. Haven't been serious about anyone since."

"Too bad, I know you were crazy about her."

"One bright note. I did get my U. S. citizenship."

"Really, congratulations. What prompted you to do that?"

"I don't have any family left in the U.K. No reason to go back. I had a good position here. Besides Jeannine kept after me to do it. They would have fast-tracked me when I first arrived at Los Alamos, but I wasn't ready. It didn't seem quite patriotic. Then after the war, being patriotic to England didn't seem to be so much of an issue anymore."

"I can see it would free up more job opportunities to have citizenship."

"That it does." Ward pulled out his pipe. "Mind if I smoke?" As he tamped tobacco into the burl wood bowl, Ward asked Reese about Rosa.

"Bloody shame," Ward said after he'd heard the story. "But you have a beautiful wife."

At that moment, Julie came in with coffee. Ward added. "You'd better keep a close eye on her, or someone may steal her away." He winked at Reese.

* * *

Julie spent the next two weeks composing letters to Utah, Nevada, and Arizona federal and state congressmen. Together, they made copies and addressed envelopes, including putting stamps on them. All the people had to do was sign the letters, put their address at the bottom, and mail them. In order to get groups of people together, they put personal notices in each local newspaper they planned to target. Some wouldn't participate, fearful of reprisal, but those most affected, those who had lost family and livestock, those who had cancer, were eager to join the cause.

* * *

Reese read a report from a biologist in Chicago who had done extensive research on the amount of radiation the people in St. George had been exposed to. Children had received 850 times the amount considered to be safe.

This was even worse than the report Ward had told him about.

Armed with statistics like this, Reese appealed to parents, community and church leaders, to put pressure on their congressional representatives. People

186

who had never thought they could write the president, with Julie and Reese's help, did. They began to realize they had power—the power to cause change, especially when they read about the proposed nuclear test ban. Reese assured them that it was their letters moving it along.

* * *

"Good morning, darling," Julie placed a cup of coffee in front of Reese and laid the morning newspaper on the table.

"You're all dressed up early. Where are you off to?"

"Women Strike for Peace is marching down Sunset Strip today to protest atomic bomb testing."

Reese put down his newspaper when the doorbell rang. "Now, who could that be this early.

"That must be Mom." Julie headed for the front door.

Ginny put a small suitcase on the floor. "Hope you don't mind an overnight guest, Reese."

"Not at all. Ginny, are you going to march, too?"

"That's the plan. Julie, you'd better put sensible shoes on. You'll never make it in those high heels, and wear a hat so you don't get sunburned."

"You gals behave yourself. I don't want to have to bail you out of jail."

Julie leaned over and kissed him on the forehead. "Silly, all we're doing is walking down the street. What kind of trouble can we get into?" She went to the bedroom and came back wearing a white picture hat and ballet flats. "Are we off, Mom? Have a good day, honey," she said as she left.

"Drop by the lab when you're finished. Be careful."

"We will," drifted back to him as the door closed behind them.

When two o'clock rolled around and Reese hadn't heard from Julie, he began to worry. *Maybe they went to lunch.* He picked up the phone and dialed home. No answer. At four o'clock, he called again and still didn't get an answer. *They can't be marching this long, can they?* Reese decided to go over to Sunset Strip and see if they were there. As he took off his lab coat, the phone rang.

"Reese, I don't want to alarm you, but Mom and I are in jail. We're okay, but can you come and get us out? Maybe Lisa's attorney can help."

Reese wasn't the only concerned husband at the jail. A cluster of men stood around the desk sergeant's area. One blustering man demanded the

187

release of his wife, saying, "You don't know who I am. I'm the chairman of the board of the Beverly Hills Country Club. Release my wife right now."

"Mister, there are half a dozen other husbands before you. I'll take care of you when I'm finished with them. If you don't settle down, you'll join your wife in lockup."

"Well, I'll be. The mayor will hear of this."

Reese decided he'd have to cool his heels after seeing this exchange.

Half an hour later, the desk sergeant beckoned him. "Okay, who belongs to you?"

Reese gave him Julie and Ginny's names. "What's the charge, officer?"

"Disturbing the peace, blocking traffic, resisting arrest...shall I continue?"

Reese stifled a snicker.

"Frankly, we just want to get rid of them," he said as he waved over an officer to escort Reese to the holding cells. "But there is a fine."

"How much is the fine"

"Fifty bucks a head. That's one hundred dollars to spring them."

"Okay, I'll pay it."

There were at least forty women in a row of cells chanting, "Stop the bombs." White-gloved women in hats, dressed in the latest fashions, had taken off their shoes, setting up a racket banging on the bars with them.

"Cut the racket," a drunk laying on a bench in one of the cells shouted. "You're giving me a headache. Damned bitches." When the noise didn't stop, he covered his ears.

"Okay, you and you, you're out," the officer said after Reese pointed to them. "Nothing worse than a bunch of women on a rampage," he muttered.

Once outside, Julie said, "I'm sorry, Reese."

"Protesting can be risky business, Julie. Are you all right?" Reese held her at arm's length, searching for an injury. Did they hurt you?"

"No, but I fell and ruined my nylons when they pushed me."

"I'll buy you a new pair. Let me see your knees."

Julie hiked up her skirt. "See just a couple of strawberries."

"We'll get some iodine on those when we get home.

Ginny massaged a bruise on her arm.

"How did you get the bruise? Did they hit you?" Reese asked.

"They just manhandled me." She broke into a smile. "Most fun I've had in a long time." Her smile became a chuckle.

"Ginny, this isn't funny. You could have been hurt." Reese inspected her arm. "We'll ice that when we get home."

Ginny suppressed a giggle. "And will you prescribe a martini to numb the pain, doctor?"

Reese lightened up. "Martinis are pretty good for pain management. We'll all have one. You girls don't look too bad, considering. Let's go get your car Julie. Where is it?"

"I parked at the Sunset Tower Hotel."

Chapter Thirty-Four
Trip to England

Without a warning knock, the door to Reese's lab opened. "Hi, mate. How the bloody hell are you?"

"Ward, what a surprise. What brings you to California, and to what do I owe the honor of this visit?"

"I've bloody well missed you. Have lunch with me?"

"Sure. Let me wash up and get my jacket. I'm in the mood for tacos. Sound okay to you?"

"As long as I can have a Corona, I'm fine with that."

Seated on hard wooden chairs at Reese's favorite taqueria, the men drank their beers.

"Reese, I'd like you and Julie to come to London. There is a meeting I'd like you to attend with me. A group of concerned scientists, academics, journalists, religious leaders, and ordinary citizens are launching the Campaign for Nuclear Disarmament. A public meeting is scheduled in February to help form the organization."

"Sounds interesting. How involved are you?"

"Some of my mates in England have been after me to speak. I'd like you to speak as well, since you've seen firsthand the effects of radioactive fallout."

"Have you quit the FBI?"

"Yes, I'm weary of the intrigue."

"And the AEC?"

"I can't very well protest if I'm still with them, now can I, old chap? I've given this a lot of thought. I'd like to join you at your protests." Ward finished his beer and ordered two more.

"Actually, I'm in a position now to quit and work full time as an activist to stop bomb testing. With my American citizenship, I can stay in the U. S. California seems to be a good place to live. Maybe I'll look for a home here."

"What inspires you to go to the meeting?"

"The knowledge we now have, that if exposed to 450 roentgens of radioactivity for one hour, we'd be dead within twenty-four hours." Ward squeezed a wedge of lime into his Corona.

The tacos arrived, and Reese took a bite before saying, "When I was called to Kwajalein to treat the Marshallese natives, the team that took measurements figured the people on Rongelap atoll had received up to 300 roentgens. They were 75 miles from Bikini during the Castle Bravo test. The AEC has been monitoring the survivors ever since."

"We Brits exploded a hydrogen bomb over Christmas Island. We've done all our testing on islands off the coast of Australia. Beyond that concern, the U. S., Russia, and England have enough nuclear weapons to wipe all life off the face of the earth. Somehow, we have to stop it."

"I'll tell Julie to buy a winter coat and we'll go with you. Neither one of us has been to England. Maybe we can take in some of the sights while we're there."

* * *

Ward picked up Julie and Reese when they cleared customs and immigration at Heathrow Airport. "You won't believe who is here for the meetings: Joe and Ann Pope. You remember them from Los Alamos?"

"Of course. What a coincidence. Haven't heard from Joe in years."

"Julie, you'll like Ann, and it'll give you some female companionship," Ward said. "They live in Los Angeles, too."

"Is he working there?" asked Reese.

"Says he's working at the UCLA Radiation Labs."

"Well, I'll be darned," said Reese.

"Are they involved in protesting, too?" Julie asked.

"I think this is their first foray. Joe said his participation in building the bomb has haunted him all these years."

"I know about that," Reese said.

Ward pulled up in front of the Grosvenor House. "The meetings are going to be held here."

After a week in London, attending meetings to help with the formation of Campaign for Nuclear Disarmament, the trio flew home to California, promising to return for the Aldermaston protest march at Easter.

* * *

Reese phoned his parents to tell them he and Julie were home.

"We just walked in the door," Donna said. "We've been in Utah at a funeral. My cousin Phyllis and her husband Arden were killed in a head on collision. A drunk driver hit them."

Shocked and saddened, Reese said, "I'm sorry to hear that." He didn't know his Utah cousins well, so his mother filled him in.

"Phyllis and Arden have three sons. Two are in college, but the youngest, Jimmy, is only eight." Donna's voice broke, betraying her emotion. She cleared her throat before continuing. "Can you imagine losing both parents at such a young age?"

"A terrible tragedy," Reese murmured.

"There was enough insurance and inheritance for all the boys to complete college so money isn't an issue. Gerald and Bennett are attending BYU, but Jimmy has nowhere to go. There is an aunt, Elva, Phyllis's older sister, who might be willing to take in Jimmy, but she has a disabled son she cares for."

"And the older brothers? Can't they take care of him?

"They need to complete their undergraduate education and go on to higher degrees. They aren't in a position to raise him," Donna said.

"I don't know how to ask this, so I'll just say it right out. I know Julie wants a child. Would she consider adopting the boy? And what about you?" Donna's voice became soft. "Reese, he's a sweet boy. He'll be lost without his mother and father. He needs parents and we *are* family"

The idea his mother tossed out took the wind out of him. He was quiet.

"Reese? Are you still there?"

"Yes, just astounded." Reese hadn't even considered this possibility.

"Would you like me to inquire if you could adopt the boy and raise him?"

"Let me talk to Julie. She may want to. We'll need some time to think."

"I don't mean to put pressure on you, but realistically, there isn't much time. Jimmy will need a home soon, so Gerald and Bennett can go back to school. I hate the thought of him being passed around from relative to relative after losing his parents."

192

"I'll get back to you soon."

* * *

Reese fixed himself a scotch and soda and poured a glass of Chablis for Julie. He seated himself opposite her to gauge her reaction.

"Mother has proposed an adoption for us to consider."

Julie perked up.

"An eight-year-old boy who is my relative."

Julie leaned forward and picked up her drink. "An eight-year-old? What happened to his parents and how are you related?"

"His parents are Phyllis and Arden Christensen. Phyllis is mother's cousin." Reese went on to tell her about the accident.

"My goodness. I'll need to think about it. What's his name?"

"James. They call him Jimmy. Mom thinks we'll be the ideal parents for him. He's a bright child with a scientific mind. She thinks my influence and your nurture will give him a solid home."

"I never thought about a child other than a baby. Do you think he really needs us?"

"I don't think Mom would have suggested it if there wasn't a need. Yes, Julie, the boy needs a home."

"Well we haven't been able to adopt a baby, I think I'd love to raise a little boy. Would you?"

"Let me find out more. I wanted to check with you before I looked into it further."

Julie leaned forward and looked Reese in the eye. "I don't need to think about it. The child needs a home, and we need a child. Phone your mother."

Reese didn't wait. He called his mother right away and told her they would adopt Jimmy if it were agreeable with all concerned.

After numerous phone calls talking to Gerald and Bennett and agreeing to raise their brother in the Mormon Church along with a promise that Reese and Julie would make sure they didn't lose contact, the older boys agreed that Reese and Julie could adopt Jimmy.

Reese hadn't been raised in any religious denomination, but Julie was Presbyterian and knew little about the LDS Church. She thought about her friends who were Mormon. She'd gone to events with them from time to time

193

when she was growing up. She rationalized that she didn't have to be Mormon to make sure Jimmy went to Church and the children's primary programs.

The prospective parents flew to Salt Lake City, rented a car, and drove the 150 miles south to Redfield. They followed directions to the Christensen family home—a compact yellow brick house with lawn, still brown from winter frost. Before they got out of the car, the three brothers came down the front walk, the youngest hanging back.

Reese introduced himself while opening the car door for Julie. "Please accept our deepest sympathy. You must be Gerald." He extended his hand.

Gerald shook it and said, "This is my brother Bennett, and, come here, Jimmy." He put protective hands on the child's shoulders. "This is James."

Before greeting the older brothers, she leaned over and took Jimmy's hand. "I'm Julie. I'm very pleased to meet you, James." She smiled her most engaging smile.

The child puffed out his chest. "Everyone calls me Jimmy."

"Jimmy it is then," Julie said.

"Come in." Gerald led the way into the house.

The Christensen boys were polite and gracious as they offered punch and cookies.

Julie had brought photos of their home in Beverly Hills and postcards that showed the beaches, hoping it would make Jimmy more comfortable. She handed them one by one to Jimmy. She had even driven by the Mormon Church closest to their home and taken a snapshot. "This is the church you'd go to."

Jimmy leaned in toward Gerald and whispered. "I don't want to go with them. I want to stay with you and Bennett."

Gerald put his arm around Jimmy's shoulders. "Jimmy, you need a mother and father. These people are family. Reese is a scientist, like you, and he's your second cousin, Donna's son. You remember Donna and Sam from the family reunion last summer? And they came to Mama and Daddy's funeral last week."

"I think so." Jimmy stared at his feet.

Julie leaned forward so she was eye level with Jimmy. "We'd love to have you come to live with us. Los Angeles is right on the ocean. We can go to the beach," she persuaded.

Jimmy asked, "Will I be able to swim in the ocean?"

"Of course. We can go on weekends," Julie promised.

"We'll take very good care of you," Reese said. "I think you'll like California."

Jimmy began warming up, and agreed that Los Angeles might not be all that bad.

With Gerald and Bennett assuring him they would write letters and come to visit, Jimmy got his suitcase and said he was ready.

Reese invited the brothers to spend time in Los Angeles during the summer, Christmas and spring breaks. They were welcome anytime, he said, adding, he would arrange for Jimmy to visit in Utah during the summer, reiterating that Julie and Reese didn't want to separate the family.

"I packed your ham radio and equipment in this box," Bennet said. "Maybe I'll find someone at BYU who has one and we can talk." He carried the box to the car and stowed it in the trunk with Jimmy's suitcase.

A girl that looked to be Jimmy's age came running toward them. "Jimmy, you're not going away?"

"Katie, I have to."

"I don't want you to go."

"I don't want to go, but now I'm an orphan, and I need new parents."

Tears streamed down Katie's cheeks.

Jimmy reached out and patted her on the arm. "Don't cry. I'll write to you."

As they drove away, Jimmy turned to look back. Everyone he loved was standing there waving goodbye. Everything familiar to him vanished into the distance.

* * *

As it often was with the young, it didn't take long for Jimmy to settle in. He accompanied Julie to the beach, helping her carry her paints. Soon, he was playing in the water and, not long after, testing his swimming skills. The freckles on his nose and cheeks deepened as his skin tanned, intensifying the blue of his eyes. One Saturday, Julie painted a sun splashed portrait of Jimmy and Reese building a sand castle.

Based on Jimmy's grades from Redfield Elementary, the counselor at his new school gave him a test to determine what grade he should be in. The counselor recommended fourth grade, even though he hadn't finished third. It was no surprise to Julie and Reese that he fit right in and had no trouble with the schoolwork.

One evening, Julie heard soft sobs as she passed his room. She silently opened the door and went to Jimmy's bedside where she reached out and pulled him into her arms, stroked his back and wept with him. That was the night he cried out his loss in great wails of grief. Until then, he'd been the brave young man he'd been told he should be. That night, he was a brokenhearted little boy.

Chapter Thirty-Five
1963
Going Underground

Contentment settled over Julie. At last, she had a child to lavish affection on. "Jimmy get ready for school and come to breakfast," she called.

Reese was already at the table having his morning coffee. An article in the Los Angeles Times caught his attention. He set down his coffee cup. "Well, Julie, maybe our protests and letters are finally bearing fruit. There's an article here that says the atomic testing in Nevada is going underground. I've been agitating toward that goal for ten years. I'd hoped it would happen after President Eisenhower announced a limited test ban after his speech in 1958."

"That's good news." Julie put a plate of scrambled eggs in front of him.

Jimmy dashed to the table, pulled out a chair, and sat. Eyeing Reese's plate, he said. "I'll have eggs and toast, too."

"Coming up, sweetheart." Julie buttered a slice of toast and scooped eggs onto a plate. "Here you are. Hurry and eat. We need to get you off to school."

Absorbed in the article, Reese absentmindedly said, "Good morning, son," then continued. "I wanted them to discontinue the tests all together before they made the entire planet radioactive, but this is a step in the right direction. I want to see if there's anything on TV about it." He picked up his plate and fork and headed to the living room.

Flicking on the television, he scanned the channels until he found news. A reporter in New York, located on Fifth Avenue, interviewed people at random. He stopped a fashionable looking blonde in a navy blue suit and asked, "What do you think of the International Ban on Atomic Bomb Testing?"

"The what?"

"Russia, England, and the United States want to stop testing atomic bombs. Are you for or against it?"

"I guess I don't know anything about it."

"You aren't aware of the bomb tests going on in Nevada?"

"Oh, yes of course, but it doesn't worry me. That's so far away." She glanced at the jewelry in the window at Tiffany's.

"Do you know that the Russians, also, are conducting bomb tests?"

Turning her attention back to the reporter, she said, "I've heard about it."

"Are you aware that Russia detonated the biggest hydrogen bomb? A bomb they called 'Tzar Bomba.'"

"Umm. No."

"There is a conference going on right now to draw up a treaty to ban testing nuclear bombs, because scientists and doctors believe radioactivity is causing cancer."

"I really don't know anything about it." She glanced at her watch. "I've got to run."

The reporter turned and looked into the camera. "Well, there you have it, TV viewers. The average American doesn't seem to be worried about bomb testing. This lady isn't aware of the dangers or its potential to affect her. Back to the studio for more on the International Test Ban."

* * *

Reese snorted his frustration. *Why are people so laissez faire? How can they not be aware of the dangers?*

While he chewed on his angst, across the country, a man in Miami sat at the bar in his favorite watering hole watching TV and sipping rum and Coca Cola. "What's this stuff about an International Test Ban Treaty?" He gestured at the TV.

"Beats me," says the bartender.

"Looks like they are going to ban atom bomb testing." The man put down his drink.

"Doesn't affect me one way or the other." The bartender picked up a glass and started drying it.

"Guess those Mormons out in Utah kicked up a big stink about radioactive fallout." The man took a sip of his rum and Coca Cola. "That's a wacked out cult, anyhow."

The bartender placed the glass he'd been polishing on a shelf. "They're good, hard-working people, and they may have a point. I remember seeing films after we nuked the Japs. Pretty bad."

"Serves 'em right for bombing Pearl Harbor." The customer twirled ice in his drink.

The bartender leaned back and looked up so he could see the TV, too. "Yeah, but I don't think government wants to hurt our own citizens."

The man tossed back the rest of his drink. "There aren't that many of 'em out west, so how many could it hurt, I mean, not like here in Miami or in New York."

"Want a refill?"

At the man's nod, the barkeep poured rum and topped it off with Coke and a wedge of lime. "So you think they'll stop the bomb testing?"

Picking up his fresh drink, the man said, "Looks like it. The announcer says Russia, England, and the U.S. are negotiating a treaty now. Wonder if that'll end the Cold War. I don't trust those Ruskies. Do ya think they'll keep the agreement?"

"I haven't the foggiest notion how they could make it stick if they didn't," the bartender said as he wiped a wet ring off the top of the bar.

"The Cold War has kept the weapons manufacturers busy. Wonder if they think they'll have to use those stockpiles of arms." He stood and laid a ten dollar bill on the bar. "Gotta go. Don't work too hard."

"Hardly workin'. Not like the place is crowded at two in the afternoon. See ya tomorrow. The bartender looked up at the television to see President John F. Kennedy signing the test ban treaty. What he signed was a partial test ban. Nuclear testing would continue underground.

* * *

Ha. You think going underground is such a great idea? Have you thought about the aquifer? My radioactivity is so strong, it will make the ground water unsafe. I was successful in making the air deadly, now it will be water. Humans don't know what they are doing when they mess around with my power.

* * *

Reese and Julie threw a dinner party to celebrate the end of atmospheric nuclear testing. Reese had connected with Ann and Joe Pope while they were at the protest walk in England. The party was a reunion of the people he

199

worked with at Los Alamos. Inevitably, the conversation was about the bomb tests.

"It doesn't look like going underground is solving the problem," said Ward as he puffed on his ever-present pipe.

Joe said, "I was on assignment at the test site last week. There seems to be a lot of problems."

"Such as?" Reese asked.

"The great pressure created by the explosion makes cracks in the earth. Radioactivity spews high into the sky. If it doesn't do that, it seeps into the atmosphere."

"I've heard craters are formed when the earth collapses," Reese said.

"I saw the craters when I was there. There's another concern too— radioactivity seeps into the ground and may contaminate the ground water."

Julie interrupted. "Aren't you guys ever going to stop solving the world's problems and come and eat?" She'd prepared a lavish dinner of roast beef and Yorkshire pudding, with trifle for dessert.

Ward's eyes widened when he saw the spread. "You're stealing my heart, luv. All my favorite foods."

"I made Yorkshire pudding and trifle especially for you, Ward."

"Well, this seals the deal. I'm moving to Los Angeles. I've had a job offer that I've been considering. I think I'll accept it."

* * *

Reese was pleased to have his old friend, Ward Porter, living in Los Angeles. It had been years since he'd had a buddy to talk to. Every week, they met over drinks at Ward's favorite watering hole, or he came to dinner. Now, with Joe Pope working at UCLA, he and Ann living not even five miles away, the old Los Alamos crowd would often get together.

After work, Reese met his buddy at what Ward called his second home, The Old English Pub.

Seated at the polished mahogany bar, Ward said, "I have been trying to figure out how to tell you this, old chap."

Reese was puzzled by Ward's demeanor. Usually exuberant and confident, Ward perched on the edge of his barstool and fidgeted with a cocktail napkin.

"Why don't you just spit it out?" Reese prompted.

Ward braced himself with a big gulp of his scotch and soda. "You know how Julie is always talking about wanting to adopt a baby? Even after you got Jimmy, she wanted a sweet little girl." Ward paused, took another swig of his drink.

"Yes, yes, go on. What are you getting at?"

"Well, I thought it was odd that two well off and eminently qualified and educated people wouldn't be top of the list of eligible prospective parents, so I did a bit of digging."

Reese swiveled his barstool to face Ward, who avoided making eye contact. "What do you mean?"

"When you told me the FBI had been following you...I began to be suspicious about how much they were interfering in your life. Since I was no longer with the bureau, I enlisted the help of a chap that still worked for them. I asked him to see what he could find out about their intimidation techniques." Ward paused and motioned the barkeep to bring them more drinks.

Reese began to piece the sketchy information together. "Do you think they did something to injure our chances for adopting?"

"I not only think it, I'm bloody well sure of it." Ward pushed his empty glass forward, retrieved the fresh drink and took a sip. "The way I see it, they passed the word on to the adoption agency in Las Vegas that you were a subversive and not to give you a child."

Reese turned to face the decorated mirror behind rows of liquor. Leaning his elbows on the bar, he rested his head in his hands and mumbled, "Son of a bitch. I should have guessed." He stared at the reflection of the bartender polishing glasses. "I can't tell Julie this. It will crush her. Do you think they got to Irene Shields, too?"

"Is she the attorney who had arranged an adoptive baby for you, then said the mother had changed her mind?"

"The same."

"Yes. They got to her, too."

The two men sat in silence for a while before Ward looked around and broke the stillness between them. "Looks like the place is beginning to fill up."

As Ward's information sank in, Reese allowed the waves of rage to wash over him and subside before he twirled the ice in his half empty glass and said,

"I need to go home. Julie will be fixing dinner." He chugged the rest of his drink.

"What are you going to do?"

Reese wasn't sure if he was glad Ward told him. He needed time to think. "I don't know." He slid off the stool and clapped his friend on the shoulder. "See you around."

"Oh bugger. Maybe I shouldn't have told you."

Reese didn't answer. With the sagging shoulders of a beaten man, he walked toward the exit, his limp more pronounced than usual. *I've failed Julie. I vowed to protect her, but I can't protect her from the government's henchmen. How could they?* This was a question he'd mull over for a long time.

Chapter Thirty-Six
Grandparents

Reese never told Julie what Ward had said about FBI interference with their adoption procedures. She was too happy being mother to Jimmy, and both of them were in their element as parents. They had a transmission tower built at the back of the house to make sure his ham radio worked, so he could keep in touch with his brothers and radio operators all over the country. True to their promise, they sent airline tickets to his brothers to come for Christmas and spring breaks and as long as they could stay during the summer. Julie made sure the boys had as much beach time as they wanted. She took her easel and paints along and painted water scenes with the three brothers playing in the surf. Both Disneyland and Knott's Berry Farm were near. They went every summer as a special treat.

Jimmy excelled in school and had an aptitude and an avid interest in science, which pleased Reese. They placed him in an accelerated education program where teachers challenged him. Jimmy aced every test. He outgrew being a bit on the chubby side as a child by thinning out and topping six feet. He graduated at sixteen and went to UCLA for his undergraduate studies.

One day after classes, Jimmy asked Reese. "Why did you work on the bomb?"

"It was the times, son. We were in a battle to save our country. Tens of thousands of our men were dying. We needed to stop the war. That was our goal. We were breaking new ground working with atoms. We had no idea the power we were unleashing. Once we'd opened Pandora's box, we couldn't get it closed again."

"I want to work with neutrons and fusion—maybe go into research," Jimmy said. "Work toward peacetime uses for nuclear energy."

"It's a fascinating field. I think you'll do well."

After two years, Jimmy asked his adoptive parents if he could transfer to Brigham Young University in Provo, Utah. Katie Hatch planned on attending there in the fall and he wanted to be near his love. Initially Reese was opposed, but with Julie's gentle persuasion, he came around. The boy they'd raised had become a man. Although not his biological child, he resembled Reese. Equally as tall, blue eyed, with the same slouch and mannerisms.

* * *

Jimmy had loved Katie Hatch since first grade. He wrote letters to her every week and, when he was older, phoned her often. Reese and Julie made it a point to take Jimmy to family reunions, weddings, and funerals in Redfield. On these occasions, he spent as much time as possible with Katie.

Reese and Julie hated to see him leave, but they helped him with his transfer to BYU. As promised, Jimmy came home for Christmas vacation. He wanted his folks to know Katie and asked permission to have her spend the holidays with them.

Julie wanted the young lady to be comfortable and fixed up the spare room with new curtains and bedspread and put flowers on a bedside table. She suspected an engagement announcement. On Christmas morning, she wasn't disappointed. Jimmy gave Katie an engagement ring. A year later, a wedding was in the works.

Julie saw an opportunity to negotiate having them near. Jimmy wanted to go on to graduate school and Katie wanted to finish her undergraduate degree. She talked to Reese and asked if he would pay for their education if they both transferred to UCLA. He agreed. He too wanted to have the young man home. Julie found an apartment near their house and furnished it. She knocked herself out endearing herself to Katie, thinking, *This may be the family I've hoped for.*

* * *

The day Katie graduated, she announced she was expecting.

On New Year's Day, Katie gave birth to a baby girl. Julie was over the moon. At last, a baby to hold and love. As Julie held the newborn, she cried tears of joy. When she reluctantly placed the infant back in her mother's arms, she left the hospital and went shopping. No little girl ever had more pretty, frilly things than Grandma Julie lavished on her.

Jimmy finished his doctorate and went to work at the UCLA Radiation Laboratory. Although he worked under Reese's former colleague from Los

204

Alamos, Joe Pope, his work on neutron research took him around the word to meet with physicists in other countries.

When Jimmy was away, Julie spent as much time as possible helping Katie with the baby. On one of these days, Katie announced she was expecting again.

She had twin boys and further gladdened the proud grandparents.

Chapter Thirty-Seven
Three Mile Island, 1979

We have homicide, genocide, suicide, lotsa cides—now we are committing ecocide.
Definition—the murder of the environment.

"Something's wrong. The reactor isn't cooling."

"The gauge on the valve says it's closed. Maybe it isn't working right. Let's put eyes on it."

"It isn't closed!"

"Holy shit. We're in trouble.

At four a.m., March 28, 1979, the core of nuclear reactor number two at the Three Mile Island Nuclear Power Plant near Harrisburg, Pennsylvania began to melt down.

"If we don't let some of the steam escape, the reactor will blow."

"The gasses are radioactive."

"What's the alternative?"

The engineer on duty said, "Notify the manager. He needs to get over here, right away."

To prevent a bigger nuclear disaster, the plant manager said, "Release the steam." Radioactive gasses leaked into the environment.

It was eight a.m., and Reese had just arrived at his lab, when the phone rang. It was the head of the Department of Energy, the new and more politically correct name for the Atomic Energy Commission. "We need someone with your expertise to fly here immediately and help with the health assessments. I can have a car pick you up at your home in two hours and take you to LAX where a jet will have you here in less than five hours."

Reese spoke to Lisa about taking time off and went home to talk to Julie. "Of course you should go," she said.

During the flight, Reese wondered why they had called him. His security clearance had expired years ago, but he didn't think he needed it for a power plant. There were other doctors in the field of nuclear medicine, most of them younger. Maybe it was because they didn't hold doctorates in physics, too.

It was 7:15 in the evening when Reese arrived at Three Mile Island. He was escorted to the plant manager's office. The frazzled man spoke in shorthand. "Not sufficient cooling. One faulty valve. Rods overheated. Vent the gasses or have the reactor explode." He ran his hand over his face as if he could erase the disaster. "Valve gauge gave wrong reading." He escorted Reese upstairs to a viewing area overlooking the reactor.

Reese experienced a flash back to Santa Susana, when he saw the cleanup crew mopping up radioactive water. *At least this time they're wearing protective suits.* "I'll need to examine all of them. Are any of the personnel sick? Vomiting? Fatigue?"

"Not to my knowledge. I know it's paramount to protect the safety of the public, so I notified the governor when radiation began leaking. He immediately ordered the evacuation of children and pregnant women. I'm to keep him advised on an hourly basis."

"Do we know how many roentgens are being expelled?"

"One of my men went outside with a Geiger counter. It registered twelve.

"Let's hope it doesn't go any higher," Reese said.

The meltdown of the reactor cores took place over a two-day period. Always in cover-up mode, the head of the Department of Energy bragged about the containment of contamination.

A cynical thought crossed Reese's mind. *What else would he do when the lobbyists for the manufacturers of nuclear equipment and the utility companies wanted to smother all negative aspects of nuclear power plants for electricity?*

Hearing the cover up and seeing the cleanup methods, Reese shook his head and said, "Nothing ever changes."

Fortunately, there were no immediate deaths. However, Reese knew from his experience with the Utah and Marshall Island Downwinders, cancer would be rampant in the area. It might take ten, twenty, or even thirty years, but the insidious, tasteless, colorless, odorless radioactivity would be there, lurking, awaiting the moment to manifest itself—and kill.

Nuclear had become the hope of the future for unlimited electric power. However, in forty-eight hours, a million-dollar asset became a billion-dollar liability—the cost of cleanup and repair. It was a black eye for nuclear power plants around the world.

When Reese arrived home, he told Julie, "I'm beginning to believe there is no such thing as safe nuclear." Then he recanted, "Except for its use in medicine, and even that carries risks."

Chapter Thirty-Eight
1983
Pearl Harbor

Since their honeymoon in Hawaii, Reese and Julie had wanted to return. They looked forward to the laid-back atmosphere of the islands and planned to go to the outer islands to spend time on Maui and Kauai. While on Oahu, they wanted to see Tom and Carol again.

The USS Enterprise was in Pearl Harbor for repairs. Along with a coworker, Tom was assigned to repair a valve inside the nuclear reactor. He had arranged for Reese and Julie to tour the nuclear powered aircraft carrier. He would join them after he finished his work. It was a small job and he didn't expect it to take more than an hour or so.

Tom was one of the only qualified mechanics who had the natural ability to identify mechanical problems on the ships. He could sniff out faulty equipment and fix it in half the time of his colleagues. He proved to have an unusual skill working inside the gloves to repair mechanical problems in nuclear reactors.

For the past four years, he'd been questioning his role in maintaining weapons of war. As he neared his fifties, his values changed. It wasn't just a job he wanted. He wanted to make a difference—a difference dedicated to peace. Or, at least, he didn't want to contribute to the maintenance of ships and submarines whose sole purpose was war and destruction.

He'd heard about Reese and Julie protesting against nuclear bomb testing from his mother after she'd visited with Reese's parents. He made it a point to stay in touch after their visit during Reese and Julie's honeymoon. He wanted to get better acquainted. Other than the evening at the luau at the Royal Hawaiian, they hadn't spent time together since Tom quit college and joined the navy. During that time, their only contact had been secondhand through their mothers who passed information on.

After Tom served four years in the Navy, he went to work at Pearl Harbor and had lived in Hawaii ever since.

The morning of the tour, Tom entered the tent inside the nuclear reactor, along with his co-worker, Bud Torres.

Tom put his hands into the gloves attached to the tent. Bud gave him a grin and shoved his hands into his set of gloves. His lack of care caused a rip in one of the gloves. Tom saw the terror in Bud's eyes.

"Let's get the hell outta here," Tom yelled. The radioactive material had touched Bud's bare hand. He sprinted for the scrubber. After ten minutes of scrubbing, his skin was raw and throbbing from the intense washing. The radiation clean-up team hustled him off to the base hospital for evaluation. They were only allowed so many roentgens of radioactivity per day. Bud had received a year's ration.

The clean-up team, dressed in protective suits, replaced the tent and Tom went back to finish the repair, exercising extreme caution.

The accident caused Tom to be late meeting Julie and Reese. They were leaning against the rail, gazing into the ocean when he approached them. The sun gleamed off Tom's chestnut brown hair as he apologized for the delay and related the reason why. "Bud's exposure has made up my mind. I've been wrestling with a decision. I want to work in a field that benefits mankind, not weapons of war. Moreover, I think I've had enough radioactivity for a lifetime. It's time to get away from it."

"I know what you mean. Let me know how I can help out," Reese said.

Tom began sending out feelers for a job on the mainland the following week.

* * *

To his relief and delight, Tom secured a position with the Bureau of Reclamation on a project in Utah, Jordenelle Dam. He would be on the ground floor, planning and construction of the water storage dam. "Right up my alley," he claimed.

Having been raised in Utah, his wife Carol said, "It seems like I've come full circle." They moved into a ranch house in the small town of Heber City, Utah, near Park City.

"I wonder how I'll fare living in a predominately Mormon community again." Carol worried, while Tom helped her unwrap china and put it away. "We've been in Hawaii for twenty-five years. The good news is that I have family all over the state and I have a high school reunion coming up this summer. It'll be the first one I'll ever attend." Carol pushed her streaked blonde hair behind her ears.

"Let me know well in advance and I'll put in for time off to take you. Where will they have it?" Tom picked up an empty box.

"I have the invitation, but it's still packed away. It's in July at Fish Lake, my favorite place in the world."

"Thought that was Hawaii."

"It's a toss-up. There's a lot more to do in Hawaii. I guess Fish Lake is a nostalgia thing, from camping there as a child. Once I've been there again, it may not rank as high as Hawaii."

"Do you suppose we could entice Reese and Julie to meet us there? It's probably not as fancy as they are used to, but we can rent one of the two bedroom cabins at Lakeside."

"You get me the information and I'll phone Reese to see if we can arrange that."

Fish Lake, Utah

Carol Miller inhaled the clean, high mountain air. She hadn't been to Fish Lake since one of her mother's family reunions the year before she moved to Hawaii.

Deep blue water formed a natural. seemingly bottomless glacial lake. It was rimmed on one side with tall pine trees. One end was thickly wooded with aspen groves. Streams trickled through the trees. At the other end, lime green meadows swept to the shoreline. A road ran the length of the lake by a hundred-year-old lodge, and on to another resort with a restaurant at the lower end.

"Tom, did I ever tell you that two of my great uncles helped build that lodge?"

"Nope, you never did."

"They came up in wintertime when the lake was frozen over and cut pine trees on the other side, and teams of horses dragged the logs across the ice."

"Yes, I read the history of the lodge that gives the descriptions," Tom said.

"They've reproduced an old tintype photo with my uncles."

"That would be a nice tidbit of information to tell Reese and Julie when they get here." Tom had arranged for his cousins to stay at the Lakeside Lodge with them.

"I love this place. It brings back so many fond childhood memories."

It was where Carol had gone to 4-H camps. Her family spent a week at Fish Lake almost every summer. She remembered the good times fishing with her brother, Richard and her dad. But, now she was here for her 35th high school reunion.

Carol left her home in Redfield right after graduation from high school. She hadn't seen most of the people since then. *Will I recognize them?*

After they had checked into their cabin and left word that they were expecting company to join them, Tom said, "Ready to go?"

They drove to Twin Creeks, where classmates with motorhomes were camped. The men had built a fire in an open pit that had seating logs circled around it. After meeting and greeting all the classmates, Carol and Tom found a place to sit. Kim Hales offered each of them a stick with a marshmallow on the end. "I haven't roasted marshmallows since high school," Carol said.

"Have a ball," Kim said as he sat by her. "It's been a long time."

"Living in Hawaii made for a long trip to get here, but now that we're back on the mainland, we'll be around more often," Carol said. "How have you been?"

"Lost my wife from cancer." Kim picked up a stick and drew a fish in the soft dirt.

"I'm sorry."

"It's been three years now. I'm over it. Well, I'll never be over it, but I'm used to it." Kim added a line of waves under the fish.

"You know, Sharon Hansen just died a coupla weeks ago."

"No, I didn't. What happened."

"Cancer."

"She never had children, did she?" Carol asked.

"Nope. You didn't either did you?"

"Uh uh. Guess it wasn't in the cards. I tried but it didn't happen. I find it odd that so many of the girls in our class couldn't have kids."

"Karen Morgan died from cancer about ten or twelve years ago. She'd had to have a kidney removed 'cause it was malignant," Kim continued. "Johnny Riggs wife died of cancer too."

"Seems like we're dying off fast. Tom's cousin, Reese, says it's from the atom bomb tests they did in Nevada," Carol said.

"That's what we all think. Shhh, look over there." Kim pointed at a nearby aspen grove with the stick. Several deer were walking along in the shadows of the trees. "They're going down to the lake for a drink."

As the deer sneaked along the edge of the aspens, Kim lowered his voice and continued. "We graduated with forty eight in our class. There are only thirty three of us left. Fifteen have died, most from cancer. It seems like a lot."

"It really does. That's almost a third. I'm not ready to die."

"Me neither." Kim stood and stretched. "Think I'm going to turn in."

"We need to be going, too. We invited Tom's cousin and his wife to spend time with us here. They should be waiting for us at Lakeside Cabins"

"See you tomorrow at breakfast?"

"We'll be there and probably bring our guests. Think that will be all right?"

"Sure, the more the merrier. It'll make the restaurant owners happy," Kim said.

* * *

Having met up with Reese and Julie at the cabin, the couple drove the mile to Bowery Haven. Seated at a wooden table across from Julie in the rustic café, Carol said, "Reese, do you think exposure to fallout causes infertility in women?"

Reese was taken aback by the question. He mulled it over for a minute before saying, "Nobody has proven that it does, however, we humans are mammals. Fallout caused infertility in livestock, so it's conceivable. When the bomb tests were going on in the fifties, cowboys and sheepherders wouldn't ride horses that had radiation burns on their backs for fear it would make them sterile." Reese was visibly uncomfortable. He had never told Julie that he suspected her inability to conceive a child was because of fallout.

213

"Well," said Carol. "I think it caused my infertility."

Julie's eyes widened. "Reese, do you believe that?"

"I'm not positive, however, indications suggest that may be the case."

The air seemed to have been sucked out of the room as the two couples sat in silence.

Tom said, "On a lighter note, the trout here is reputedly caught this morning and delicious. Let's order."

* * *

Nestled under heavy quilts, Reese sensed Julie had tears sliding down her cheeks from an occasional sniffle. He reached a comforting arm around her. "I'm so sorry, sweetheart."

"I wish you had told me," Julie sniffled and reached for a tissue.

"It wouldn't have changed anything, and I didn't know for sure. Still don't."

She turned toward him, snuggling into his comforting arms. "I know."

* * *

Too bad, Julie. But you can only blame your husband and his cohorts. Before Trinity, only the ambient radiation from the sun and occasional hot spots from uranium deposits existed. Now, within two weeks of one of my atmospheric explosions any place in the world, radioactivity can blanket the planet, circumnavigating the globe in the winds aloft. Ninety days later, carrots from a vegetable garden anywhere on earth may show measurable radioactivity. I love it. Ah, the power, the power. There are babies everywhere. So you didn't get one. That's the breaks Julie.

* * *

The first official day of the class reunion dawned with golden sunlight and bluer than blue skies.

Carol was up early and put a pot of coffee on to perk. "We're going to have to take turns in the shower," she said when she saw Reese.

"I've already showered and been out for a walk. Beautiful lake." Reese settled himself onto a camp chair.

"Coffee should be ready in about five minutes. I'm going to take a quick shower and be right back." Carol disappeared through the screen door.

"I'll be here on the porch admiring the scenery," Reese said.

When Carol came back, both Tom and Reese were sitting on the porch, nursing big mugs of coffee. She poured a cup and joined them. "My favorite time of day," she smiled as she admired the lake shimmering in the sunshine. Reese said, "I'd better see if Julie's up." He stood and went inside.

* * *

As soon as they arrived at the restaurant, Carol started introducing Tom and their guests, wresting almost forgotten names from her memory. Once seated, they perused their menus when Kim and another man walked up. "Carol, you remember Aaron."

Carol scanned her memory for a moment before introducing everyone, "Aaron, good to see you, this is my husband Tom and his cousin Dr. Reese Mayfield and his wife."

"Dr. Mayfield? That name is familiar to me. Mayfield, Mayfield, now it comes back to me. You're the doctor that was at the hearing in Cedar City that worked at the Nevada Test Site. I was just a teenager, but I remember. And, I remember you were supposed to testify for the ranchers at the trial and didn't show up."

"Yes, I was called to Washington."

"Well, wasn't that convenient." Sarcasm laced Aaron's voice. "You sons-a-bitches. You and the rest of you lying bureaucrats killed my mother. We lost our sheep and our ranch. You and your damned bomb testing."

"Aaron, this isn't the time or the place." Kim tried to steer Aaron away.

Aaron shrugged off Kim's hand. "Yes, it all comes back to me. You. You helped build the bomb."

"It ended the war," Reese said.

"Yeah, and it almost ended the lives of half the people in Southern Utah."

Kim got between Aaron and Reese. "Aaron, cool down. C'mon, let's get a cup of coffee and go outside for a while." He nudged Aaron away.

Reese stood, losing balance on his bad leg. He grabbed the back of the chair.

Aaron saw and said, "You're a damned cripple. I could take you, but I can't beat up a crip."

Trying to get distance between the men, in a firm, level voice, Kim said, "Come on, let's go outside." He grabbed Aaron's arm and maneuvered him out of the door.

The room buzzed, classmates trying to figure out what the ruckus was about.

"I'm so sorry," Carol said. "Let's go over to the lodge and have breakfast there."

"No, Julie and I will leave. You can't miss visiting with your classmates," Reese said.

"Oh, yes I can. We'll all go." Carol grabbed Julie's arm and pulled her toward the exit.

As they were driving, they saw Aaron pacing around the marina, yelling and waving his arms while Kim hung his head, dug the toe of his shoe into the dirt and nodded occasionally.

A few minutes later, Tom pulled into a gravel parking lot.

"My, this old lodge is wonderful," Julie said.

Glad for a way to diffuse the pall that hung over them from Aaron's tirade, Carol launched into the story about two of her uncles who helped build it.

*   *   *

Huddled under heavy quilts that warded off the chill, high mountain air, Reese said, "I should have done more."

"What do you mean?" Julie came alert.

"Aaron was right. I should have done more. I should have made an excuse when they called me to Washington and stayed to testify on behalf of the ranchers." Reese propped himself up on an elbow. "I knew what was going on. I was one of the few who knew that radioactive fallout was causing cancer and loss of livestock. I watched as children died painful deaths. I saw their mother's grief. Why didn't I do more?"

Julie sat up. "Reese, you did everything you could. I remember your reports and the trip to Washington to try to stop the bomb testing. You can't fault yourself."

In the quiet, darkened room, Julie felt Reese's sobs. She sat up and pulled him to her. She was used to him being the strong one, the brave and solid man who always took care of and supported her. Now she held him and stroked his back. "It was the times, the Cold War, the constant threat, the need to protect our country."

A great shudder shook the bed. "I can't excuse myself and I can't blame the times. I lacked the courage to go up against Uncle and the military."

216

"But you did, over and over again. I remember, even if you don't. You were strong and you did stand up against the AEC and a very powerful military. And they did stop atmospheric testing. You did succeed." Julie felt her husband's body relax. She pulled up the covers and curved into his body. "You can go to sleep knowing you'll always be my hero."

"Thank you, Mrs. Mayfield." But, that night, his old demons returned to haunt him.

Chapter Thirty-Nine
Chernobyl

The baritone voice of the television newscaster caught Julie's attention. "April 26, 1986, the nuclear reactor at Chernobyl, in the Ukraine, exploded, raining fallout over thousands of miles."

Julie ran outside where Reese sat by the pool reading. "Come in and watch the news. They're reporting a nuclear disaster."

Reese closed his book and walked into the house with Julie, who continued "The reporter said fires are burning out of control and they're calling in hundreds of firemen to quench the flames."

Transfixed, Reese watched as the story unfolded. The urge to go there and help popped up in his mind. *No!* Then to emphasize, "Not only no, but hell no," he said aloud to convince himself. Then he mumbled, "I'm too old to go."

Julie's brow knitted in concern. "You aren't thinking of going there?"

Reese didn't realize he'd been talking out loud. "No, just reminding myself that those years are behind me." He returned his attention to the TV. "This is really serious," he murmured.

"Worse than Three Mile Island?"

"Oh yes. Much worse. According to this report, twenty-eight people died of acute radiation exposure, and..." Reese's voice trailed off as he listened to more news. "...and there are over 200 hospitalized—God only knows how many more will die or be sickened."

Over the course of the next weeks, Reese learned that a radioactive cloud had drifted over Russia, Belarus, and the Ukraine. Most of Europe, and as far away as Canada, were affected.

Russia withheld news of the Chernobyl explosion from surrounding countries. The evidence of radioactivity was discovered by the Swedish when personnel at their nuclear power plant discovered radioactive particles on their clothing. They had no leaks in their plant and traced the source. That was the first hint of serious nuclear problems in the Western Soviet Union.

Health officials predicted that over the next seventy years, there would be a twenty-eight percent increase in cancer rates in a Ukrainian town near Chernobyl.

* * *

Julie invited Katie and Jimmy over to dinner. "How are the children?" Julie asked.

"Doing well. They are off doing their own thing, one on a date, the boys at a movie."

Julie had difficulty imagining they were already grown. The time went so fast.

Katie helped Julie with dinner by tossing the salad. "Nothing tastes good to Jimmy. He doesn't want to eat."

Jimmy had been diagnosed with cancer and was being treated with chemotherapy.

Convinced if she cooked some of his favorite childhood dishes he would be inspired to eat, Julie spent the day in the kitchen preparing. She baked a magnificent three-layer chocolate cake. She was certain that even if he didn't eat the southern fried chicken with mashed potatoes and white gravy, he would succumb to the cake.

Katie set the table while the men visited.

"We've got to do something. The Department of Defense is planning a bomb test in Nevada. We can't have 700 tons of explosives set off at Frenchmen's Flat. It will stir up the old radioactivity." Reese's face reddened with anger. "Hummph, a nuclear 'bunker buster' warhead they are calling Divine Strake. Wonder how they came up with that name. We have to warn the people of St. George and Cedar City. They're still feeling the effects of the atomic bomb tests from the fifties and sixties. People who were children during those times are dying."

With bitterness, Jim said, "Tell me about it."

"Ouch, son. That was thoughtless of me. I didn't mean to strike a nerve." His shoulders slumped as if the anger had been pumped out of him.

Jimmy had been through surgery, months of radiation, and chemotherapy. He had become emaciated from his battle with cancer.

Jimmy struggled not just with cancer, but being sick from the treatment, the nausea, fever, dizziness, and deep bone aches that accompanied *the cure*.

Reese considered himself lucky. Still, the old guilt gnawed at him. All the years he had worked with nuclear materials, he'd escaped getting cancer. He thought it was because he was fully grown and not fond of milk. At eighty-four, Reese had added twenty pounds to his waistline and his slouch had become more pronounced. Other than using a cane for his lame leg, he was robust and healthy.

It broke his heart to see Jimmy so sick. *Why not me?* he thought. *I've been subjected to unbelievable amounts of roentgens.*

But, Reese knew the answer. Jimmy was a little boy downwind of the fallout when he was the most vulnerable. Reese was grateful that Jimmy was able to grow up, marry, and raise a family.

* * *

Jimmy turned in his hospital bed, tangling the sheets in his legs. Through the morphine haze, Jimmy's thoughts went to his family. *I don't want to die. What will Katie do?* He realized he'd never hold her in his arms again, he'd never play with his grandchildren, never see them grow up. An unbidden tear slid down his cheek. *I'll never see my future.* He knew he was feeling sorry for himself, but fifty-eight was too young to die.

Five years earlier, when the doctor gave him a diagnosis of colorectal cancer, a chill raced over him, but then he thought, I'm young and strong, I can beat this. But all his prayers, all his good works and thoughts couldn't save him. Not even his youth and strength. *Strength, what strength. I can't turn over without tangling myself in these sheets, and I don't have the strength to untangle them.*

First it was surgery, they took his colon and gave him a colostomy bag. He would never again be able to go to the bathroom in the normal way. Months of pain, and becoming accustomed to the bag. Second, being put into a saddle, the entry spots for the radiation tech to follow to administer radioactive rays to the tumor area marked on his skin. The object was to kill any and all cancer cells the surgeon couldn't excise. Third, chemotherapy that made him deathly ill, vomiting and unable to eat without throwing everything back up. The chemo was meant to kill any elusive cancer cells that surgery and radiation didn't get. Jimmy considered the treatment barbaric, but a necessary evil to save his life. It didn't. He knew he was dying.

Another tear slid down his cheek. He brushed it away, chastising himself for indulging in self-pity.

Mercifully, a nurse came in to give him another shot of morphine. He drifted away into a dreamless sleep.

* * *

Katie had shed most of her tears during the downward spiral of Jim's cancer. At the memorial service, she was devoid of emotion as she sat among her children with Reese and Julie flanking them. Jimmy's brothers, Gerald and Bennett, and their families, filled the rest of the pew and the one behind them.

Jimmy had been a high priest in the LDS Church. Katie and his children closely followed the Mormon religion. They wanted the funeral to be personal, and prepared the service according to what they knew he would like. Each member of the family spoke, sharing their memories.

Gerald approached Reese and said, "On behalf of Bennett, myself, and the Christensen family, I want to thank you and Julie for taking Jimmy in as your own."

"We loved him as if he had been born to us." Reese's eyes misted. "I was proud to know him and be a part of his life. He was a remarkable man."

At the reception after the funeral, family friend and Jimmy's former supervisor, Joe Pope, approached Katie. He took her hand and covered it with his. "Please accept my deepest condolences." He let go of her hand. "Katie, UCLA Radiation Labs would like to hold a symposium as a tribute to Jimmy. He's made so many seminal contributions to neutron research. We want to honor his life's work."

"Thank you, Joe. That will be nice. What can I do to help?"

"Nothing, we'll take care of everything. The lab is compiling a tribute book. We would like you and your family to attend a dinner at the end of the symposium for the presentation."

"We are taking Jim's body to Utah tomorrow. He wanted to be buried in the family plot in Redfield. I won't be back for about two weeks."

"We haven't set the date for the symposium yet. It'll take some time to put it together. We want it to highlight progress in both science and instrumentation. We're inviting leading scientists and colleagues from all over the world who Jim interacted with both as a scientist and as a person."

* * *

After the funeral, Jimmy's cousin April pulled Katie aside. "Have you considered applying for the $50,000 Downwinders compensation?"

"No, I didn't know money was available."

"I think you would be eligible. Sevier County is the farthest county north to receive compensation. If memory serves me, the type of cancer Jimmy had qualifies."

"I wouldn't even know how to go about getting it."

A fellow mourner in blue jeans and a plaid flannel shirt standing near them interrupted. "I have the name of an attorney in Salt Lake who can help you." He pulled a small notebook and a pen out of his breast pocket and wrote down the name Irene Shields. "She helped me. I applied after my wife died and received $50,000. It paid her medical bills. Otherwise, I would have had to take bankruptcy. It sure helped. We didn't have medical insurance." He tore off the lined sheet of paper and handed it to Katie.

Katie knew Jimmy was a Downwinder, but hadn't considered applying for compensation. She contacted Ms. Shields. After reviewing the case, Katie was notified that she was eligible for Radiation Exposure Compensation (RECA) from the government. Still a bit skeptical, she decided if she actually received the money she would donate it to the Downwinders organization.

222

Chapter Forty
Retirement

"Julie, I don't know if I'm ready to retire."

"Well you'd better make up your mind. Lisa has spent a fortune reserving the Beverly Hills Hotel to throw you a magnificent party. And, people you've worked with over the years are already in town." Julie walked over to help Reese tie his bow tie. "Your tux still fits, and I'm two sizes up from my wedding dress. Not fair."

"You will be the most beautiful woman at the party."

Julie had shopped all over L. A. for the perfect black gown. She twirled. "Do you like it?"

"I love it. If we didn't have to leave in ten minutes, I'd ravish you right now."

"Down, boy. Help me with this necklace." She held it out for him to fasten around her neck.

Dr. Russ Howard, who worked with Reese years ago at Oak Ridge, approached Reese. "Congratulation on your retirement"

"Russ, thank you for coming. It's been a long time."

"Now that you are retired, will you be available to speak at our conference about educating doctors about the effects of radioactivity on the human body?" Russ had recently been voted in as the president of the American Medical Association. "They've already heard everything I've had to say, but you were right there at the Nevada Test Site."

Reese's ears perked up. *Maybe there is life after retirement.* "When is it?"

"Not for another four months. It's being held in Seattle. I heard you worked with Schweitzer researching pollution from Hanford. We'd like to hear about your research and experience and a little about Schweitzer."

"I'll give it some thought. Where can I reach you?"

223

"I'll need to know right away to include it in our literature," Russ said.

"May I get back to you by the end of next week? Is that enough time? I want to talk to my wife."

"Sure. We'll pay all your expenses, plus a $5,000 speaking honorarium."

"That ought to convince Julie." *Being paid to speak, plus expenses. Can't be all bad.*

"Bring her along. We'll arrange a tour of Seattle at our expense."

A grinning Reese approached his wife. "Julie, come with me. I have something to tell you."

*   *   *

After Reese spoke at the AMA conference, word got around. Requests for him to speak about the hazards associated with nuclear power plants and the problems with nuclear waste poured in from all over the country and abroad.

"This is hardly retirement," Julie said as she zipped up a suitcase in preparation for a trip to Chicago. She accompanied him on most of these speaking tours and participated in protests.

In most of his speeches, he said, "Now, we get to the problem of nuclear waste. Nobody wants it, but if we are to have nuclear weapons, medicine, power plants, ships, etc. there will be nuclear waste. The people of Nevada feel as if they've had enough radioactivity and are refusing the storage of any more nuclear waste at Yucca Flats. New Mexico was a likely candidate. After all, it was already radioactive from the Trinity test, and it is a big, largely unpopulated state, but New Mexico doesn't want nuclear waste.

"If you have a nuclear power plant in Pennsylvania, the waste has to be transported across the country. How? Train? Truck?

"The reactor in the Nautilus submarine is estimated to burn out in 2012. What will we do with the burnt out, highly radioactive reactor? If we shoot it into space, it could come back, if we sink it in the deepest trench in the ocean, that area of the ocean and the sea life become radioactive. If we bury it, an earthquake could crack open the sealed storage bunker and release radioactivity."

Julie and Reese had devised a signal if he was getting too preachy. Julie decided it was time and leaned her head to the right and tugged on her ear.

Reese paused and took a drink of water before continuing. "All isn't doom and gloom, though. Now, scientists are looking at the possibility of recycling

224

nuclear waste, which, next to abandoning the use of nuclear energy, would be the best solution.

"Countries will argue for nuclear power plants. It is cleaner than power made from fossil fuels, such as coal—no argument there until you try to figure out what to do with the waste or water pollution from cooling the reactors.

"And great good has come from nuclear medicine. What kills can also cure. Radiation is used to destroy cancer cells. Its uses in medicine from mammograms, x-rays, radioactive injections to show tumors, or other problems in the body during imaging tests can't be denied."

After his speech at the conference, Reese was mingling with his audience and answering questions when he heard a familiar voice. "Good speech, Reese." He whirled and saw his old Los Alamos buddy. "Joe, Joe Pope, how in the world are you? It's been a long time."

"The last time was at your son, Jimmy's funeral, and that was a sad occasion."

Reese drew in a long breath. "I still wrestle with guilt over building the bomb, do you?"

"Sometimes, but I keep in mind how many lives were saved at the end of WWII."

"I think about that, too, but my beef is that we did over a thousand tests that injured and caused the deaths of so many of our own. I feel responsible for Rosa's and Jimmy's deaths from cancer."

"You're doing what you can, educating and increasing awareness of the dangers of nuclear power."

"Where's Ann? Is she here with you?"

"Over there visiting with Julie—probably comparing notes about grandkids. Do you ever see Ward?"

"Not recently." Reese wouldn't say why he no longer saw Ward. They drifted apart after Ward told him about the FBI interfering with their adoption applications. It seemed as though Reese held Ward responsible, though he knew it was an irrational supposition.

"How long are you in town? Can we get together tomorrow night for dinner?" asked Joe.

"Darn. We're leaving in the morning. How long are you staying?"

"A couple more days. I want to visit some of my old Argonne buddies."

225

"Let's make it a point to get together back home."

"You got it. Maybe Ward can join us."

Reese nodded, but would he phone Ward? Probably not.

But Julie did. She invited Ward and the Popes for dinner. At first, Ward and Reese were a little formal with each other, but after a couple of cocktails and a nice dinner with good wine, they loosened up and reminisced about the days at Los Alamos, London, and how Ward came to his rescue to get him released from FBI questioning after a protest.

* * *

After dinner, the ladies cleared the table and disappeared into the kitchen. Reese reached for his cane. "Let's have a brandy." He stood and gestured toward the den.

Ward collapsed onto the cozy sectional. "Well, old chap, the scuttlebutt is that they want to test some of the A-bombs in storage to see if they are still viable."

Joe shook his head. "What are they thinking?"

"Maybe they don't think. The bloody warriors don't seem to be able to handle the idea of not blowing things up," Ward said.

Reese shook his head as he poured brandy into snifters. "We can't let that happen. Wonder if the Downwinders will protest."

"If they do, count me in." Joe accepted the brandy, swirled it, and inhaled the aroma.

* * *

The next morning over coffee, Reese told Julie about the rumor of a new bomb test. As he was relating the men's conversation of the night before, the phone rang.

"Hello, Reese, it's Ward. I have the skinny on the proposed test. It's scheduled for next month at the Nevada Test Site. Not only have those wankers scheduled one or more nuclear tests, after that, those fools plan to explode old ordinance just to get rid of it. What radioactivity the nuclear bomb doesn't put into the winds aloft, those bombs will."

"Thanks, buddy. I'll get back to you after I've contacted the Downwinders. I'm sure they'll form a protest."

"I'll wait to hear from you. Toodle-oo."

Reese smiled at his friend's British farewell as he went to his desk to look up the contact phone number for Downwinders.

* * *

Two weeks later, a thousand protestors lined up ten deep and faced the gate to the Nevada Test Site carrying signs: "No More Nukes," "Don't Kill Our Children," and "Fallout Causes Cancer." Reporters interviewed the people as TV cameramen filmed the crowd in between focusing upon interviews.

On the opposite side of the gate, over a hundred soldiers in camouflage held assault rifles at the ready.

"This is pretty scary," Julie said to Ann.

"I couldn't agree more, but surely they won't open fire with the world watching on live TV."

"I'm counting on that." Julie waved the sign she carried that said, "Fallout Killed My Son."

A caravan of army jeeps sped up the road, screeching to a halt behind the soldiers. A two-star general with a megaphone jumped out. He shouted into it, "Disperse or you'll be arrested."

Julie said, "Have you ever been arrested for protesting, Ann?"

"No. I wouldn't like it, but I'd tough it out for our cause."

"Reese had to bail me out along with my mom and his mother, several years ago. It wasn't too bad, but this looks more serious than the street protest we did in the 60s."

"I hope not." Ann cast a worried glance at Joe, who grinned back at her.

Another blast from the bull horn threatened arrest again. This seemed to antagonize protestors further, who shook their fists in the air and shouted back, "You and who else?" and "I'm looking forward to it."

A slight man with sparse white hair wended his way through the crowd. He talked to everyone rallying them to keep up the pressure. "We can't let them get away with killing our children again." His baritone voice rose to a crescendo. "The government used us as guinea pigs, but not again—not on my watch."

"Who's the guy who looks like he's at death's door?" Joe jerked his head in the direction of the agitator.

"He probably is at death's door, but he's only in his 50s. He's the founder of the Downwinder movement. He has cancer attributed to fallout." Reese waved his sign and shook his fist. "I hear it's all over his body—now attacking the pancreas. Probably doesn't have much longer."

"He knows how to whip up the crowd," Joe admired the man for his vigor.

* * *

Protesting? Protesting! Surely you jest. You have the nerve to protest me? You and your Downwinder allies? No more nukes—fat chance of that. Pandora's Box is open. The world is enamored with me and drunk with power. Power, the greatest aphrodisiac after money. True the Nevada and Pacific testing was my heyday—over a thousand tests by the United States alone, but then Russia, England, France, and others joined in bringing the total up to twice that. My single finest hour, though, was Tzar Bomba, Russia's hydrogen bomb. It was the biggest of all. I even surprised myself. The activity was so great around the world, I couldn't keep up. So, you think protesting will make a difference? Not as long as someone wants something that another country has, land, minerals, or a religious difference. The warriors and the politicians will start a war over something, or perhaps nothing—just because they can.

* * *

After hours in blistering Nevada heat, the TV crews loaded up and took off in their vans, presumably to get back and prepare for the six o'clock news.

Reese said, "Looks like we'll get a lot of coverage. Do you think we've done any good?"

"Well, we've done our best." Ward lowered his sign. "I wonder if the TV stations will send crews tomorrow."

"I hope they do. The public needs to know." Reese leaned on his cane.

The Downwinder's intended to protest every day until the proposed date of the bomb test.

Ann and Julie joined the men. "Are we going to do this again tomorrow?" Ann asked.

"Yes, if you are up for it. It's late, we're going to pack it in for today." Reese rubbed his bad leg.

"My feet are killing me," Ann said, "but if you'll be here, I'm up for it."

"That's my girl," Joe reached his arm around Ann's waist. "Let's all go to dinner."

With dusk nearing and the crowd thinning, they headed for Reese's SUV.

228

"Las Vegas, here we come. How about dinner at Ballagio? My treat," Reese promised.

"I could use a double Scotch on the rocks," Joe said.

"I have cold beer in the car if all the ice didn't melt. Will that hold you until we get back to town."

"My parched throat thanks you," Ward clasped his neck with both hands.

* * *

In an uproar over the protests and negative news coverage Congress called a special session. Although the crowd lost size and enthusiasm over the next ten days, they were heartened to hear they had Washington's attention. The nuclear test was cancelled. Nobody was arrested and the Downwinders breathed a sigh of relief amid celebrations.

Chapter Forty-One
Divine Strake
2006

"Reese, telephone," Julie announced from the kitchen.

Reese hoisted himself out of the comfy recliner in the study, steadying himself with his cane. He met her halfway into the living room and took the phone.

"It's Joe Pope. Have you heard about the planned explosion of ordinance at the old Nevada Test Site?" He was shouting into the receiver.

"No, not yet. An atomic bomb? What's going on?"

"Not an atomic bomb, but it may as well be. It will be powerful enough to stir up all the old radioactivity, and you know that's plenty."

"That's for sure." Age having worsened his bad leg, Reese leaned heavily on his cane as he eased himself onto the living room sofa.

"What I read, it is a high yield explosion is to be set off June second this year. I don't think they should do that considering what happened to all the people exposed to fallout." Joe's voice sounded less agitated.

"I couldn't agree more."

"They've code named it Divine Strake. Odd, since strake is a nautical term."

Reese pulled the word strake from his memory and recalled a synonym was stringer. He'd seen stringers from the atomic bomb's mushroom clouds as winds aloft carried off the cap of the mushroom-shaped explosion. Maybe it made sense, but there was nothing divine about it. "As I recall, a strake is metal or wood that holds the hull of a ship together. I think it refers to aircraft, too."

"Yeah, I recall now. What can we do to stop it? They sure as hell aren't using their heads. Do you think they'll go ahead, despite what it may do to the Downwinders?"

"Not if I can help it. If we can generate enough public outrage, maybe it can be stopped."

There was a moment of silence before Joe said, "I wouldn't know how to begin, but I know it's right up your alley. Let me know what I can do to help out."

"I will. Thanks for the head's up." After he hung up, Reese called out to Julie. "Hey, honey, want to get back into the protesting business?"

"Not tonight. It's too late. How about looking into it in the morning?"

* * *

With the threat of radioactive fallout from Divine Strake, and obsessed with stopping all explosions at the Nevada Test Site, Reese got onto the Internet and checked out the flights to St. George. He wondered who would still be around that remembered how bad things were during the bomb tests. He researched the city councils of Cedar City and St. George and made a list of the members' names.

"We'll need some clout. Humm, Orrin Hatch, the senator from Utah. Julie do you supposed he will help?"

"We can always ask."

"I'll contact him. I wonder if he's aware and what his position is."

"I'll bet he's opposed." Julie put down the needlepoint she was working on. "My guess would be that he's already working on it."

Julie was right, Senator Hatch was already responding to pressure from his constituents, who were privy to sensitive information. They wanted him to persuade Congress to cancel Divine Strake.

When Reese phoned Hatch, he was put right through. Hatch said, "The people of Utah had suffered enough. I'm doing everything in my power to stop any and all bombs being set off at the Nevada Test Site."

* * *

"Damn. Julie, I've been digging to find out more information about Divine Strake. The reports say there isn't a health threat. It appears to be another cover up. They know it's dangerous. Makes me fighting mad."

"Mad enough to join another protest?" Julie cocked her head and raised her brows. She already knew the answer.

"Absolutely." Reese's mouth set into a hard line.

* * *

Reese and Julie joined members of the Western Shoshone Indian Tribe and Downwinders from southern Utah to protest Divine Strake.

Protestors held up signs that said, "Uncle Sam is a Trespasser." A steady drumbeat provided background to shouts of, "No More Bombs." A hundred and fifty angry protestors faced a wall of soldiers bearing arms at the Nevada Test Site check point. In defiance of security, they crossed the boundary onto the site, ignoring the threat of arrest or possibly worse. Reese and Julie were among forty protestors arrested for trespassing on Federal Lands.

"Well, sweetheart, here we go again. Arrested," Reese said in a low voice.

"We knew it was a possibility when we made the decision to join the protest," Julie whispered back as she clung to Reese's arm in apparent apprehension. "What do you suppose will happen next? Wonder how much trouble we're in." After a few hours, they were issued citations for civil disobedience and released.

"That wasn't as bad as I thought it would be," Reese said as he folded the citation and stuffed it into his blazer jacket. "Come along, Julie. Freedom is a beautiful thing."

"I'm grateful we didn't land in a jail cell. I'm getting too old for bare-bones accommodations." Julie curled her arm through Reese's.

* * *

The Western Shoshones reminded the Federal Government that the lands where they were accused of trespassing were part of the Western Shoshone Tribal lands—that the government was in violation of the 1863 Treaty of Ruby Valley. The Tribal Council claimed the government had contaminated and abused their land. The Shoshones sued the Federal Government to stop the explosion. One tribal leader said, "There's nothing divine about a bomb."

* * *

Julie and Reese attended town meetings and joined protests in Idaho, Utah, and Nevada. With the help of Senator Hatch, the Shoshone Nation, and dedicated Downwinders, in 2007 Divine Strake was cancelled.

People in the southwest breathed easily again. Downwinders *finally* had the attention of the United States Government.

At last, Reese's claims were heard—radioactive fallout kills, but it took a senator, the Downwinders, an Indian nation, and ultimately, Congress.

The LDS Stake Center in Cedar City became the venue for a victory celebration, barely holding most of the citizens in the surrounding area. While Reese was drinking fruit punch from a paper cup, a silver haired woman approached him. "Remember me? William Brenner's mother, Sherry?"

"Of course, cousin, but I haven't seen you since young William's funeral." He held out his free hand to her. "I've been remiss in keeping in touch. I didn't realize when we first met that we were related through my mother."

"I've never forgotten how kind you were to William when he was dying. Thank you for doing so much to stop the bombs."

"If only I could have done more at the time, but we didn't have the knowledge or the medical expertise. I know William's doctors did their best."

"We all hoped for a miracle." Sherry bit her lip as tears welled up in her eyes. She squeezed his hand, turned and blended back in with the crowd.

The grief of losing a child never ends. "If only I could have saved the children," Reese murmured as he thought of William and all the youngsters at the hospital in St. George. He recalled holding Liana's hand as she died in the hospital on Kwajalein—Liana and all the other native islanders from Rongelap. Because of his role in building the atom bomb, he'd always felt responsible for Rosa's death and Jimmy's cancer.

How could we? Were we so greedy for power? We were so young, so naïve, so eager to do the right thing—and look at the suffering we caused.

Chapter Forty-Two
The Atom's Eulogy

At the age of eighty-five, Reese Mayfield died peacefully at home with his wife Julie holding his hand. In a private graveside service, he was laid to rest at Forest Lawn Cemetery on a sunny Southern California day. A few days later, a gray marble tombstone was placed at the head of the grave, with his name on the left and a space for Julie's name on the right.

Nobody heard the atom as it sat on the tombstone looking down at Reese's grave.

* * *

Well, old buddy, here we are. I've won at last. You stopped the weapons testing here in America. I have to congratulate you on that. But you didn't reckon on power plant meltdowns. How about Chernobyl? It was just a bit of faulty design. That's all it takes for me to get a leg up. That and the fact that the Russians think they're invincible. They didn't even bother to install containment devices over the reactors to capture fallout in the event of accident or failure. Took 'em 600,000 people and 200 billion dollars to clean up the mess. That was one of my more spectacular meltdowns. Way beyond Three Mile Island. Radioactivity spewed for thousands of miles. A few people died. Oh well, that's the price they pay for fiddling around with my power.

But wait until you see the mess I create in Fukushima, when a tsunami generated by an earthquake strikes.

Oh, and how about that brash young leader in North Korea. He just can't stand not having a seat at the table with the big dogs. I know, he's just saber rattling, however it does give me opportunities to show what I can do. And who knows which way Iran will go?

Just thought I'd visit and let you know my future plans. I don't really want to see the planet without life, so I'll try to restrain myself. You never know, though—an accident here or there, a broken pipe leaking radioactive water. I'm watching the nuclear facility at Hanford. The nuclear waste storage tanks are leaking. Wonder if it will get into the Columbia River. Downwind was fun, I hadn't even considered downriver.

When I hear young men saying, "Nuke 'em" I know I still have my fans. As your friend Ward would say, toodle-oo and cheerio. It's been a blast.

The End

Or is it, said the atom.

Epilogue

The first atmospheric atom bomb test at the Nevada Test Site occurred on January 27, 1951.

Not until September 23, 1992 did atomic testing cease there after a total of 1021 tests, of which 921 were done underground.

For thirty-one years, Downwinders were exposed to radioactive fallout. It wasn't until 1980 that Congress admitted that bomb testing was causing cancer. Until then, the AEC and their contractors collaborated in a flagrant abuse of power, denial, and cover ups.

Since the Mormon people believed that their government was divinely inspired, they continued to be patriotic citizens. That is, until Divine Strake again threatened. A less naïve and compliant citizenry went to work to stop the renewed threat from radioactive fallout.

Seventy years after the Trinity test at White Sands, Downwinders in New Mexico fought for recognition and compensation under the Radiation Exposure Compensation Act (RECA) established in 1990. It pays Downwinders from $50,000 to $100,000, depending upon whether one was in the uranium industry or subject to radioactive fallout from bomb tests.

Bibliography

Hunner, Jon, *Inventing Los Alamos, The Growth of an Atomic Community,* University of Oklahoma Press 2004

Trinity Site Tour to Ground Zero

U. S. Army Public Affairs Booklet, *Trinity Site, July 16, 1945, Landmark Booklet on White Sands Missile Range.*

Tours of Albuquerque and Las Vegas Nuclear Museums

Tour of Los Alamos and Los Alamos Historical Society Museum

Conant, Jennet, *109 East Palace, J. Robert Oppenheimer and the Secret City of Los Alamos,* Simon and Schuster 2005

TV Mini Series, *Oppenheimer*

Hunner, Jon, *J. Robert Oppenheimer, The Cold War, and the Atomic West,* University of Oklahoma Press, 2004

Cook Steeper, Nancy, *Dorothy Scarritt McKibbin, Gatekeeper to Los Alamos,* Los Alamos Historical Society, 2003

Williams, Terry Tempest, *The Clan of the One Breasted Women,* Viking 1991

Fradkin, Philip L., *Fallout, An American Nuclear Tragedy,* University of Arizona Press, 2004

Ronald, Ann, *Friendly Fallout 1953,* University of Nevada 2010

Fuller, John G., *The Day We Bombed Utah* Signet 1984

Schweitzer, Albert, *A Declaration of Conscience,* April 24, 1957

Wikipedia – List of Atomic Bomb tests; Nuclear Weapons; United States Energy Commission

Timeline of Events 1951 to 1970, Department of Energy

Numerous archived files opened by the Department of Energy the Atomic Energy Commission 133 F. Supp. 885 (1955)

David C. BULLOCH, McRae N. Bulloch, and Kern Bulloch, Plaintiffs, v. UNITED STATES of America, Defendant. The sheep rancher's lawsuit against the Federal Government

Interviews with family members, other Downwinders, Bob Batley, who manned one of the gate houses at Los Alamos and personal experiences from living downwind of nuclear testing.

Other books and online research sources

About the Author

Roberta Summers is an award-winning author with a creative writing degree from San Juan College. A current resident of Farmington, New Mexico, Summers lived in Hawaii for twenty-five years, and on the slopes of Mauna Loa volcano in Hilo on the Big Island for five of those years. During that time, a friend of hers was murdered by the Hawaiian Mafia. Her novel *Pele's Realm* is titled after the Fire Goddess of the Volcanoes, Madam Pele, and is based upon that crime. She is also published in poetry and short stories and has served as an editor for the San Juan College Arts and Literary Magazine, *Perspectives*. She is a former co-owner the publishing house, Silverjack Publishing, which was housed at San Juan College's Enterprise Center.

Summers is a past president of Trois Rivieres Fiction Writers, a member of Pikes Peak Writers in Colorado Springs, where she served as a contest judge, and Women Writing the West. Currently active in several writers' groups, she has done numerous book signings and authors' panels around the Southwest. She has appeared in several newspaper and magazine articles, and on public radio where she was featured on the show, "Write on Four Corners."

A member of San Juan Writers, a critique group, Summers has two short stories in their anthology, *Into the West* coming out in summer of 2019.

About her writing, she says, "I write because I have something to say, and I want to be heard—it's a burning desire."

Raised in Southern Utah, Summers spent thirteen years researching and writing *Fatal Winds*.

Visit her website at www.robertasummers.com.

Author's Note

FATAL WINDS is a work of fiction although it is based on facts. Most events are actual happenings that have been fictionalized to develop the story. Some characters are real and some are fictitious, or their names have been changed. Most events are real, but conversations came from my imagination. In these fictitious portions any resemblance to actual events, locales, organizations, or persons, living or dead, is entirely coincidental and beyond my intent. As is common in Historical Fiction some characters are real and some are fiction. I've spent the past thirteen years researching and writing this story.

My personal experience with Downwinders include an uncle, two cousins, and my sister—all cancer victims. My two cousins died in their 50s. The latter three were all the same age and, as children, were told to get under their school desks when the bombs went off at the Nevada testing range. No awareness was exhibited about how fallout would affect, soil, plants, water, animals, and the humans exposed on a regular basis.

On August 5, 2019 I was diagnosed with Stage 4 lung cancer. I am a Downwinder.

Made in the USA
Middletown, DE
11 September 2019